WILLIAM B

THE

HOUSE

BY THE

MARSH

BEING WILLIAM BLYGHTON

William Blyghton is the name I have used to write this story. I have another name. It is the name by which I have been known throughout my life: a son, a husband, a father and a grandfather. It is the name I have used when, like everyone else, I have been trying to make things happen. I still use it. But in the writing of this book I have entered a world of imagination, a world of what might have been and what might be. To find this world, I have become William Blyghton.

Front cover photograph: Jonathan Wright

Published by Panacea Books, an imprint of The Write Factor

www.thewritefactor.co.uk

PANACEA
B O O K S
REIMAGINING THE WORLD

Contents

PART 1

A Small Madness

CHAPTER 1

LOSING CAROLINE

William Clarke was now a widower. For many years, he and his wife, Caroline, had lived in a village in northeast Essex, a part of England that hardly anyone knows about. It runs from the muddy estuaries of the Blackwater northwards and eastwards to the borders of Cambridgeshire and Suffolk. Undulating and somewhat tucked away. They lived in a large Victorian house in the middle of the village, its gardens running down towards a tributary of the Blackwater. The river was narrow and sometimes flooded.

Like many others, William and, in time, Caroline, commuted to London, leaving in the early morning and not getting back until supper time. Their children, Jane and Frederick, went at first to the local primary school and then to nearby boarding schools. In the early years, getting the children to school and making sure there was someone there to meet them at the end of their day, whilst at the same time, working in London, meant that life was quite frantic.

William had been an economist. Over the years, he had taken up a lot of different jobs, sometimes changing the direction of his career quite suddenly, disrupting the life of his wife and children. They would have just got used to being settled and comfortable when William would set off on a new venture and everyone would have to 'tighten their belts' whilst he recovered his income. Eventually, he discovered he could not work for anyone else and set up his own consultancy. Fortunately, this was a success and he built a reputation for helping companies come to terms with futures they did not understand and could not order. Oddly, as it was to turn out, futures that could not be understood or ordered were to become part of William's life. In later years, and especially after he had retired from his consultancy, he had also become interested in the poetry and writings of T S Eliot and in the realm of metaphysics, the study of how things are and how they have come to be what they are, the study of meaning and being, or rather 'Being.' He had been invited to be a Fellow of an Academy in London that taught the Perennial Philosophy and he had explored many spiritual traditions, including the teachings of the Buddha, the Vedas, especially the Bhagavad Gita, the legends of Arthur and the Grail Quest and the Celtic traditions of Britain. Some of his work was published in books and journals. His work and his being were now deeply entwined. It was who he had become.

To begin with, Caroline, who had been to art school and trained as a fabric designer, stayed at home to look after their children, but then she, too, started working in London. She had a talent for colour and pattern and worked for a company designing furnishing fabrics for a department store, Liberty in Great Marlborough Street, for some years travelling around the world to visit trade fairs and manufacturers in India and China. It was at this time that William and Caroline bought a small flat in an apartment block near Marylebone High Street, so that they did not have to commute. The village house in northeast Essex became their weekend retreat and, in the holidays, a refuge for the children, or at least somewhere they could come back to. And for many years, in the summer holidays, they rented a house overlooking the sea in Aldeburgh, a seaside town on the Suffolk coast, William and Caroline sharing time with the children to fit in with their work. Often, William would be there with them by himself, especially when Caroline's work took her abroad.

At the age of fifty, Caroline discovered that she had breast cancer. For many years it seemed to be in remission, until one day, just before Christmas, it returned in the form of a brain tumour. As if she had suffered a stroke, it turned her right foot inwards and took all the strength from her right hand so that she dropped cups and dishes onto the floor. She was treated with radiation and steroids, for a while losing her hair and wearing a variety of wigs as if all would one day be well. But it was not.

For a year, William cared for her, like many others who have had to do the same having to learn about district nurses and hospices, and eventually taking in a hospital bed, a commode and a wheelchair, trying as best he could, but not always with success, to make her comfortable and at ease. Towards the end, Caroline became more and more fragile, sleeping for long periods of time, until she was bedridden and had to be moved and washed with great care. A syringe of drugs was fitted and monitored.

One morning in December, she died. Earlier that morning the Marie Curie nurse who had been keeping the night vigil came into William's bedroom and said to him, "Something has happened." He called his daughter, Jane, who lived in Scotland but was fortunately staying with friends in London, and within two hours they were gathered around Caroline's bed. He also called his son, Frederick, who was working far away in São Paulo and who would now never see his mother again. Stricken with grief, neither he nor Frederick could speak.

Caroline's breathing became shallow until, just before one o'clock and in a sudden moment, it stopped. William passed his hand over her eyes to close them. She was no longer there. She had gone, slipped away. For a few moments, he felt a strange icy coldness and then a deep warmth as her soul left the body. The moment between being and not being is the shortest moment of a lifetime. In the snap of a finger, life has gone. William was left behind. He was seventy.

During the long time of caring for Caroline and in the many moments in which her distress was almost too much to bear, William had wondered what it was going to be like to be left behind, what it was going to be like to become a widower. But then it was just a thought, a worry, something that was going to happen one day, but not today. When it happened, when it was not something that might happen but something that had happened, he was utterly unprepared and the shock of the loss was deeper than he could have imagined. Bereft and alone, a small madness settled upon him. A deep wound was opened, a deep anxiety, and it rose up and then engulfed him.

At first, he withdrew into their house, keeping the window blinds pulled down. A raw and uncontrollable grief took hold and, day after day, he would suddenly find himself sobbing and even crying out loud. For about a month, his sorrow was because of the suffering and despair that he knew his wife had felt. He could not bear to think about how frightened she must have been. And then, as if somehow he knew that she was now at peace, his own loss bore down upon him, a dreadful, frightening chasm of loneliness. He walked about their house as if he were looking for her, expecting suddenly to find that it had been a mistake and that she was, after all, quite well and just about to go into her studio to work on one of her paintings. But, of course, he could not find her.

For the next few months, everything was left as it had always been, her clothes in her cupboards, her shoes upon the rack by the front door, her make-up on her dressing table and her paint brushes and sketch book lying in her studio. And, for William, fuelled by the pain of loss, his madness grew ever more intense until he felt that he could bear it no longer.

CHAPTER 2

LOSS AND

LONELINESS

It was a Sunday when he decided he could not stay at the house any more. He knew it at once and that evening, without waiting, he packed food, clothing, books and his laptop into cardboard boxes and suitcases. He rang the local taxi firm and asked if they could provide a driver to take him and his possessions to his flat in London. The next morning, when the car arrived, he packed it with the boxes and suitcases, locked the doors of the house and drove away. He would never return.

During the drive to London, William was silent. Sitting in the back of the car he took out a book that he had stuffed into his coat pocket and tried to read. He was unable to do so. He could only sit there and stare out of the windows of the car as they drove along the A12 and then the M25, eventually entering into the congested roads of East London and slowly making their way into the centre. It seemed as if, one by one, the traffic lights had deliberately been set on red to make his journey as difficult and uncomfortable as possible, as if he was being made to pass through some kind of barren landscape, some kind of 'place between.' Between what he had come to know and what was now unknown. Between being and not being. Distressed, his feeling of loss became exaggerated by the overbearing dullness of roads, shops, houses and traffic lights. Increasingly nauseated by the bottled fragrance of the car, he felt his energy falling away. He felt tired, alone and sick.

Then, at last, they were there, and the boxes and suitcases were taken up into the living room and the bedroom of his flat. William had paid for the taxi in advance, but now he folded a twenty pound note into a small square, transferring the tip into the hand of the driver as they shook hands. Then the driver was gone and he was alone.

The boxes and suitcases stood there, packaged memories of a time that would never come back. William sat on the edge of his bed and held his head in his hands. He did not cry, he was too tired to cry, but as the despair rose up from deep within his body, he was finding it difficult to breathe. He could not move, but just sat there, eventually lying back onto the bed and closing his eyes. Exhausted by the journey and by the shock of what he had done, he fell asleep.

He woke to hear his mobile phone ringing. It was his

daughter, Jane. He pressed the green 'Accept' button and they talked.

"Where on earth are you? I've been trying to ring you at home for the last two hours and you have not replied."

"Well, I am not at home. I have left home."

"What are you talking about? You can't possibly have left home. Where are you?"

"I'm in my flat in London."

"And when will you be going home?"

"I'm not going home. I have left home."

"Are you okay? You sound most odd."

"Well, since you ask, I'm not entirely okay, but I will probably be all right in a day or two. I have left home. I could not stay there any more. Too much loss. Too much no longer there. Sorry if this sounds a bit strange, but that is how it is. What is the weather like?"

"It's raining, as usual."

"It's dry here, but a bit overcast – but perhaps that's just me."

"Don't do that, Dad. You always do that. You always say things like that and I don't know what they mean. You always close yourself off as if I should take pity on you."

"Well, so you should. No, sorry. I don't really mean that. Call me again, here in London, in a day or two. I am fine. Bye for now. Love you."

"Love you, too. And I'll call you this afternoon."

"Okay, this afternoon then."

When Jane called him later, William was still surrounded by boxes, but now somewhat restored by black tea and Walkers shortbread and by the comfort of his flat, he was able to give some account of what he thought was happening to him. They talked about why he had come to London and then, because this was what they always did, they talked about Jane's children, Ben and Sally, about what was happening to them at school and what seemed to him to be the multitude of out-of-school activities they were engaged in. Cricket, swimming, fencing, riding, cycling, drama club. William could not understand how they ever had time to just be at home, and even when they were at home there was X-Box, texting, Snapchat, Facebook, YouTube, and What's Up or was it WhatsApp? He asked about her husband, Robert. Returning to the familiar helped William feel more grounded, and it helped Jane feel that he was not about to do something alarming. William did do alarming things, and because his sudden changes of plan had been part of her childhood, she was never surprised when it happened again.

"Give me a call when you have settled in, will you?" she asked.

"I will, I will," he replied and they said goodbye.

And over the next few days, they did speak, not of what was happening to William, because he couldn't talk about that, but again about his grandchildren and whether Jane had heard from Frederick. "Oh, he's fine apparently." Knowing Frederick was 'fine' was all that William needed to know. Fathers and sons.

For a while, the familiar stillness and emptiness of the flat acted like a balm upon William, and for some weeks he stayed there living the life of a hermit, trying by his withdrawal to heal the loss. Apart from going to the local Waitrose for provisions, he went nowhere. Each morning he would get up at about eight-thirty, shower and dress and then walk into his small kitchen, where he always made the same breakfast: porridge with almond milk and manuka honey, Ryvita biscuits with Bertolli olive oil spread and marmalade, and a cup of black tea. Then there were his supplements: fish oil capsules, Saw Palmetto Complex for his prostate, zinc capsules and vitamin D drops for his immune system and capsules for his digestion and bowel. Whether or not any of this did him any good didn't really matter, there was something comforting about the routine, something he could rely upon. Caring for himself. Breakfast finished and with the dishes put into the dishwasher, William sat at a table by the window in the living room, opened his laptop, and began to work. Order. Ever since he had been a small boy and once had felt abandoned, he'd learnt to manage fear through order. It was now a deeply ingrained habit.

In the days and months that followed, he lost himself in his work and stopped shaving. And as he did so, as he explored what had happened to him and what was happening to him now, it came to him as if by divine revelation, that the world, the cosmos, all that is, was governed, ordered and harmonious; that when Truth was present, Love was present, too; that Love was of the essence, was the shaping energy and force in all that is, its pulse, its very being. It was as if that last year of caring for Caroline and then her death, hard though it was, had opened him up. And now amidst the madness of grief, something else was happening. All that he had read and studied was now revealing itself to him: True Being was the manifestation of Love. And he could see that was always sorrow, too, a sorrow that could be at the same time both sour and sweet. Somewhere within, William felt the presence of this deep and profound sadness, not just the sadness of having lost Caroline, but something else.

In December, the first anniversary of Caroline's death came and went and William remained alone. Abandoned.

CHAPTER 3

SUSAN

One morning in January, William found himself standing in his pyjamas in his bathroom and looking into the mirror above the basin, his tousled hair and now beard still wispy with sleep. As they get older, some men say that when they look into the mirror they see their father. William saw a small and frightened boy doing his best to manage on his own. The story of this small boy was one of William's most important stories. It had made him.

Once upon a time, in the early years of the Second World War, there lived in the provincial East Anglian town of Colchester, a family called Clarke. The father of this family, Jonathan Clarke, was a gentleman's tailor with his own shop; a shop that had belonged to his father, Thomas Clarke, and to his grandfather, Richard Clarke.

Inside the shop there was shelf upon shelf of material, rolled into bolts. And when someone came to choose the material for their coat or suit, each bolt of cloth would be brought to the shop's counter and partly unwound so that the customer could not only see it, but also feel it. There was a fitting room at the back of the shop and, on the floor, a tiger skin rug, complete with its tiger head and teeth, something to which William, as a small boy was greatly attracted, for Jonathan Clarke was his father.

By the time William was born, his mother, Margaret, had already given birth to two other children, a boy who was named Peter and a girl who was named Emily. Peter was eight years older than William and Emily five years older. The family lived in a cottage called 'Brambles.' On the very edge of the town and overlooking farmland, it had a good-sized garden with vegetables, a lawn and some apple trees. The cottage was small but comfortable, with its own Andersen shelter to be used during the not infrequent air raids. William's family were third generation Quakers and his father, like many other Quakers who were pacifists, had registered as a conscientious objector at the outbreak of the war. This had caused some consternation amongst their neighbours, one of whom had taken Jonathan to the magistrate's court on a charge of sedition or 'giving comfort to the enemy.' Knowing of Jonathan's 'objection,' the neighbour had asked him what he would do if a German paratrooper had landed in his garden. Jonathan, gentle as he was, had replied that he would pick him up, see if he was okay and then bring him inside and give him a cup of tea. Shocked by such unpatriotic kindness, the neighbour had sought to bring Jonathan to justice. On the day of the trial, the magistrate threw the case out on the grounds that there was nothing to answer. Jonathan's views on the war were well-known and harmless, even if his willingness to give tea to a wounded German soldier would in fact have given comfort to the enemy.

Jonathan became an Air Raid Warden, with a black tin hat marked with a large white 'W'. He also carried a whistle to warn people of forthcoming bombing raids, his main task being to patrol the streets of his neighbourhood during the nightly blackout to ensure that no lights were visible, shouting out, if a light was spotted: "Cover that window." He also had to report on bomb damage and be ready to hand out gas masks and pre-fabricated air-raid shelters, like the one in William's parent's cottage, into which William could remember crawling with his mother. Mostly it was just the two of them as his father was out telling people to cover their windows, and his older brother and sister had been sent away to a Quaker boarding school in the countryside and only came home for holidays, at Christmas, Easter and in the summer. William could still remember that he had a Mickey Mouse gas mask, made of rubber with a red flappy nose and goggle eyes.

And so William's war went on, with American and Canadian soldiers from the local military hospital cycling along the lane by 'Brambles' and tossing sweets into the garden. Some of these soldiers were invited by his father to lunch on Sundays. In fact, Jonathan often invited strangers to Sunday lunch, surprising his wife, Margaret, who was never consulted and who simply had to make their meagre wartime rations spread a little further.

Towards the end of the war, however, a tragedy of quite a different kind came into their lives. During the spring and summer of 1944, when William was still only two years old, the first signs of a new birth began to appear in the roundness of his mother's belly. As the months went on, William in his childlike way began to sense the excitement of the preparations that were being made. A small bedroom in the cottage was being prepared as a nursery and there was talk of a new brother or sister for him.

On 14th September 1944, his mother gave birth to a baby girl, named Susan, and she took her place in the family, blonde and perfect. Except she was not perfect. Although William did not know that this was so, Susan had been damaged at birth and had been born with spastic cerebral palsy.

At first, William was unaware of the tragedy of Susan's birth, but soon he felt the anguish of his mother and father and, for him, as the months passed by, the loss of their attention, struggling as they were to cope and console each other. He felt abandoned. His life had changed forever, shocked as he was by all that was happening, unable to understand why it was so. And as the war came to an end and he began to grow into a small boy, going to school in his cap, grey sweater and short trousers, he learnt to take care of himself, turning for comfort to his own world of make believe, wanting above all else for Susan to be made better, so that the time of closeness with his mother could be recovered.

Of course that did not happen, and eventually Susan was sent away to the children's ward of a mental hospital many miles away. No one in the family talked about this. It just happened. He was never taken to visit her and she, the sister whom he had loved and thought to be beautiful, was gone. The small bedroom was empty.

In 1951, Susan died. Her death certificate reported that her cause of death was 'Broncho pneumonia spastic quadriplegia with idiocy.' Neither William, then almost ten years of age, nor his older brother and sister went to the funeral.

William carried his mother's distress and the loss of his sister with him for the rest of his life, always trying to make things better, so that ... so that many years later, when he was over sixty, he had written this story about an Old Man and a Small Boy: ◂

When the Old Man looked out of the window of his study on that early spring morning he saw the Small Boy standing by the pond in his garden. The Old Man had always known he would come, but now, just seeing the Small Boy there touched him, and for a moment he could not move. After a while he turned, took a deep breath and opening his door walked out into the garden.

The Small Boy was so taken with his thoughts that he did not know the Old Man was there, and for a while nothing happened – although, of course, everything was happening: the robin was feeding on the bird table, two crows were flying over the garden, the frogs in the pond were making frogspawn and the early morning mist was clearing as the sun rose into the sky.

But then the Small Boy looked up.

"I was just thinking of making some tea," said the Old Man, "and I wondered if you would like some?"

"With a biscuit?" said the Small Boy.

"Yes, of course, with a biscuit," replied the Old Man,

"and if I am not mistaken, it is shortbread that you like."

"How did you know that?" said the Small Boy.

"Ah," said the Old Man, "I know many things about you."

And so the Old Man and the Small Boy went into the Old Man's cottage, and whilst the Old Man filled the kettle and placed it upon his stove and took down a tin of tea and a tin of shortbread, the Small Boy looked at the Old Man's room. Strange as it might seem, he knew where he was; he had been here before. The large armchair, the even larger sofa, the table strewn with papers, the shelves of books, the many Kilim rugs on the floor, the pictures on the wall and even the cat curled up asleep on a cushion on the blanket box, all of these were familiar to him.

"I should have asked you," said the Old Man, "if you would prefer something other than tea, something like lemonade?"

"Could I just have a glass of water?"

"Just water?"

"Yes, just water," the Small Boy replied.

"Ah, of course, I had forgotten," said the Old Man.

So the Old Man brought in a tray with a mug of tea for himself, a glass of water for the Small Boy and a plate of shortbread for both of them. He cleared a space on the table and put the tray upon it. The Old Man sat in his armchair and the Small Boy sat on the sofa.

For a while they sat together and said nothing, sipping the tea and the water and eating the shortbread. But in a while the Old Man put down his mug and folding his hands upon his belly, he asked the Small Boy a question.

"So," he began, "now that we are sitting here together, I would like to know what is it that is making you so sad? And what is it that makes you feel so alone?"

The Small Boy did not reply, for he had thought that no one knew of his sadness and that no one knew of his loneliness. He thought these were just something he had to bear, something only he knew about. He had learnt to keep them to himself, learnt to put them aside and get on with things.

At that moment, as the sunlight had begun to move away from the blanket box, the cat stood up, stretched and walked over to the sofa, jumping up beside the Small Boy. Pausing for a moment, she looked at him. "If I were you," she said, "I would tell him what it is."

Somewhat startled by a talking cat, the Small Boy began his story.

"When I was very small," he said, "my mother gave birth to a baby girl. To me she seemed very beautiful with blonde curly hair. But something was wrong, because as soon as she was born, my mother wept and wept. Although I did not know it at the time, she was broken, damaged at birth.

A great shadow came upon our house. My sister had been born at night-time, but when we woke there was hushed, unspoken confusion and despair. Although our family doctor and someone called a midwife were there, no one knew what to do. For what seemed a long time, my mother was confined in bed and people came and went. I was taken away and my mother spent much of her time in her bedroom. I was frightened I would never see my mother again. Then, after some days, she was up and taking care of my sister. As a baby, my sister looked beautiful. And it was not until, after some months, when she could not sit up that I knew something was wrong. Even as a small child, I knew something was wrong.

No one talked about this. No one spoke to me about it. But quite soon Ada arrived. She was a young gypsy girl with dark hair, soft and comforting. From then on, until I was seven, Ada looked after me. She was my nanny and I loved her. For a while, my sister was looked after at home, but when she was five and it became more obvious that she was broken, she was sent away, and when she went Ada went too, and I was left alone. I went to school and did all the things a boy might do, but I played alone. My sister died in a hospital in Leytonstone when she was seven. I was ten, but no one talked about it, and I didn't go to her funeral or to her grave. And so, as you can see, I have never grown up. I am still that Small Boy who was left behind."

"Have another piece of shortbread," said the Old Man.

"Thank you," said the Boy. And he did.

Then the Old Man stood up and went to the bookcase, taking from it a rather tattered photo album with a blue cover.

"There is someone you must speak to," he said and began turning over the pages of the album.

"Here she is," he said, and he took from the album a faded photograph of a young woman. "This is your mother."

"It's no good having a photograph," said the cat.

"If you are going to talk to someone, they need to be here." And with a twirl of her tail and an arching of her back, she spun twice around and back again.

When the Small Boy had recovered from this rather unusual twirling, he turned towards the door of the cottage and saw … and saw his mother standing there, just as she had been when he was very small.

Slowly she walked towards him and sat down on the sofa beside him – much to the annoyance of the cat who, having lost her place, turned away and walked out and into the garden holding her tail high in indignation.

For quite a while the Small Boy looked at his mother, not knowing what to say or do. And she looked at him, also seemingly unsure of herself.

It was the Old Man who spoke. "I think," he said to the Small Boy, "I think you have something that you want to ask your mother."

To begin with the Small Boy could not speak, could not ask the question he had always wanted to ask. But then it came out of him almost as if it spoke itself.

"Why did you abandon me?" he said. "Why did you abandon me?"

His mother spoke very softly. "Can you imagine," she said, "what was happening? Do you have any idea how a mother feels to give birth to a broken child, to carry her for nine months, to look forward to her being born, to have prepared for the birth with joyful anticipation, and then, and then for her to be broken, damaged at birth? It was more than I could bear. I was broken, too. It was wartime and in the months and weeks before she was born, I had been set about by fear. I thought it was fear of the bombing, but perhaps it was a fear of what was to come."

"But what did I do that you left me?" said the Small Boy.

She replied, almost in a whisper, "You did nothing. Forgive me."

And then she was gone.

The Old Man put the photograph back into the album, closed it and put it back on his bookshelf. He walked slowly out into the garden, and stood there, with his hands behind his back staring into the pond where the frogs were sitting with their heads just out of the water.

After a while, the Small Boy followed the Old Man into the garden and stood beside him.

"It had to be this way," said the Boy. "And of course I forgive her. What else could she do? She was broken. They were both broken, and it was just that some of their sadness spilled over onto me. Why not? Sadness is a part of who we are. Being sad is part of being alive. I see now. It was not the loss of being loved, just having to be alone. Perhaps sadness has to be shared so that we can bear it?"

There was silence and then the Boy turned to the Old Man, "She was your mother too, wasn't she?"

"Yes," said the Old Man. "Yes, she was."

"And through my loneliness, you became strong," said the Boy.

"Yes I did," said the Old Man. "But there is something else, something that I did not remember until you came, something you have chosen not to recall."

"What was that?" said the Boy.

"Anger," said the Old Man. "Now that you are here, I can remember it, the raw anger of being abandoned by my mother, almost as if I had been torn from her. And also injustice. With the anger came a deep, spontaneous yet innocent sense of injustice. It just wasn't fair. I have carried these feelings with me for the whole of my life. Anger without reason. Anger that cannot be resolved, only acknowledged. Bloody, raging anger!"

"Yes, anger," said the Boy, "and fear, that is what I remember, the fear. I was very frightened."

The Old Man put his arm around the Boy and they stood together. And as they did so, the cat came and stood beside them.

And from that day on, the Old Man and the Boy lived together, each taking care of the other, and there was always shortbread in the biscuit tin. The Old Man looked after the Boy and the Boy looked after the Old Man. They were never far apart. And they took the photo of their mother out of the album, put it into a silver frame and stood it on the bookcase. It is there now.

Sitting alone in his flat, something of this story had stirred deep inside William. Driven by the memory of his sister, and of her abandonment, he was overcome with the need to find her grave. He had a memory of her having been buried in a Quaker burial ground in Colchester, the town in which he had grown up, and the town that his older sister, Emily, now lived in. And so one day he took the train from London to Colchester and met up with his sister who had managed to get hold of the key to the burial ground from the local Quakers. They unlocked the iron gates and entered the ground with its headstones in lines, each stone the same as all the others in true Quaker simplicity. The graves had been laid out in family areas and soon they came upon the headstone that marked their grandparents, Thomas and Matilda Clarke. From there they looked again and again, but could find no stone marked with Susan's name. Their parents, Jonathan and Margaret, perhaps too distressed or somehow ashamed of their disabled daughter, had left no sign of her.

William, who had brought flowers to lay upon the grave, was very upset. There was still no chance to make things right for Susan. And so they went away, William later taking the train back to London.

But the next morning, still unsettled, and with a fresh determination to solve the puzzle, William began to make enquiries. And it was not many days before, having spoken to one of the local Quakers, he discovered that the records of the local Quaker Meeting showed that Susan had, indeed, been buried in the burial ground, in the plot immediately in front of his grandparents, but without any headstone.

He now knew where she was and a great weight lifted from him. It was as if he could at last make her better. Perhaps his parents had not been able to cope with this death, had wanted it to be hidden away. That was okay for them. But it would not do for William, not now. At once he set in place plans for a headstone to be made and erected upon the grave. It would read:

SUSAN CLARKE

1944–1951

DAUGHTER OF

JONATHAN AND MARGARET

1907–1972 AND 1906–1972

SISTER TO

PETER, EMILY AND WILLIAM

It was to be made of Portland stone and carved in the simple lettering of the burial ground. And it would carry the dates of his father and mother because for reasons he could no longer remember they had chosen to be buried elsewhere.

Some weeks later, when the headstone had been erected, he again took the train and went to see it. At last he had made things right for Susan. Even if his wound remained, he had made things right for her.

CHAPTER 4

JENNIFER

Returning to his flat in London, William once more went back to work. He read and wrote, each day following the same reassuring pattern. But then, one morning, this solitary work, this withdrawal, was disturbed by an email invitation to join some friends for supper. Stephen and Sheila Crampton had known William and Caroline when they were all working in London. Sheila had worked with Caroline and the four of them had quite often met up for supper, sometimes in Stephen and Sheila's house in Notting Hill. Sheila had tried to keep in touch with William after Caroline's death and she knew he had taken refuge in his flat. After a while, she had become concerned about his life as a hermit and thought he should be brought out and 'cheered up.' How little those who have not been widowed understand that there is no recovery from loss; that it never gets better; that the one who is left behind is like a person who has been injured in the leg and now has to limp; they will always limp.

William was reluctant to go to supper, but felt that he would have to. And so when Friday evening came, he picked up a bottle of Beaujolais-Villages from Waitrose, hailed a taxi and headed west. He was fond of his friends and actually, as the taxi took him along the Marylebone Road and past Paddington Station towards Notting Hill, he looked forward to seeing them. He felt his spirits lifting. It was as if he was coming back to life, and by the time he arrived at their rather grand terraced house, he was in a somewhat heightened mood, looking forward to having supper with them.

He pressed the bell and Sheila greeted him, placing her hands on his shoulders and kissing him on both cheeks.

"How lovely to see you, William. I was quite worried about you; thought you might be turning into a hermit. I see you have the beard!"

William touched his bearded face, and feeling that perhaps he looked absurd, glanced at himself in the mirror that stood above the console table in the hallway. There he was, with rimless glasses, long hair and a beard, a crumpled linen jacket and collarless shirt, clutching a bottle of wine. Oh dear. At that moment Stephen appeared and greeted him and William gave him the bottle, relieved to be rid of it. Why had he come? What on earth made him decide that this was something he wanted to do?

"Come on in, William," said Sheila, "there are some really nice people here."

And she led him into her drawing room in which he could see a cluster of people, who had already met and were talking amongst themselves with loud voices and merriment. William had always been rather good at meeting people. In his work he'd had to be. Walking into a room of strangers and engaging them in conversation had been part of what he'd had to do. He had even thought it was one of his good qualities, being at ease with people he had never met before. But now he felt anything but at ease. Something tightened in his midriff, and a sudden nausea swept over him. Why had he come? Why, oh, why had he come?

He was introduced to a couple who lived "just around the corner." He was a lawyer (of course) and she worked for a small publishing house that specialised in books about food: cookbooks, books on diet and nutrition, food from France, food from Italy, quick food, slow food, food from all around the world. Fortunately for William, she spoke enthusiastically about her work and this gave him the chance to begin to fit himself into the evening. He listened and then asked her questions, pretending that travelling to all those countries and sampling their foods was something he would love to do as well.

"Oh, that must be wonderful."

Actually, and as he said it, he realised that travelling anywhere at all was the very last thing he wanted, let alone having to eat exotic food. What was happening to him?

The lawyer husband was much less forthcoming. He worked for one of the large international firms of lawyers in the City. Corporate law.

"Mergers and acquisitions, trading disputes, working our way round wretched regulations. You know, that sort of thing."

If the thought of world travel had made William feel

tired, mergers, acquisitions and trading disputes all but finished him off, and just as he sensed that the lawyer was about to ask him what it was that he did, he excused himself and went in search of a glass of water. He drank two large gulps, put down his glass and went back into the hallway to find the downstairs cloakroom, which he remembered was at the end of a passage at the back of the house. It was a small room without a window. Refuge.

William locked the door behind himself and, having emptied his now anxious bladder, turned to wash his hands in the little china basin, with taps in the shape of dolphins. As he did so, he looked up and saw looking back at him in the mirror an elderly and worried man. He took off his glasses and washed his face with cold water. That was good. He dried his face with the white linen hand towel hanging on a hook beside the basin and put his glasses back on. He examined his face. More of those blotches, than he had remembered. Liver spots, is that what they are called? The eyelid of his left eye seemed to be heavier than that of his right. His eyebrows needed trimming. And then what about this beard that Sheila had felt she had to mention? What was that all about? Why had he let it grow? Was it to mark his loss? "Stay away, I am a widower." Was it who he was coming to be, a man with a beard? Lots of men now wore beards: beards of all kinds, some large and full and some very small and neatly cut. And when he had last seen his son, he'd had a beard, quite a bushy one. William felt a pang of sadness. But who was this worried man? Had William met him before? Was he the kind of man William would like to meet?

William realised he was beginning to drift and so he

once more removed his glasses and splashed cold water onto his face, and dried it again. He put on his glasses, unlocked the door, walked along the passage into the hallway and went back into the drawing room. The couple he had been talking to were now in conversation with Stephen, talking and laughing at something funny the lawyer had said. William cast his eye across the room wondering who he might try and speak to.

And then he saw her. Standing somewhat apart was a dark-haired woman in a flowery frock belted at the waist and wearing around her shoulders a cardigan of yellow ochre. She held a glass of white wine in her right hand and with her left, took crisps from a bowl set on a low table in front of her. At that instant, something quite extraordinary happened to him. Happened without a thought.

Afterwards, William would not be able to say what it was, but it was as if, in that moment, the wound of his loss and his madness opened, and he was overcome by a deep-felt need to be loved, to be loved not just by anyone, but by this woman. It was, of course, absurd, but perhaps it was because she looked liked Caroline, slender, stylish, someone who knew that she looked good. Whatever it was, it was there and from somewhere deep within, from a place over which he had no control, he was filled with a certainty that this was the woman who could give him all he had lost. He needed her.

Just as William was about to approach her, Sheila announced that supper was ready and led her guests into the adjoining dining room. The table had been set formally with a white cloth and in front of each chair was a mat, knives and forks, glasses, a napkin, and a place name. As he was one of the last to enter the dining room, William had to wait for the others to find their places.

"William, you are over here. On my right,"

"The place of honour," thought William. Squeezing past some large and seemingly very tall men, William made his way around the table and stood behind his chair. And then, just as he was about to sit down, the woman in the cardigan came and stood beside him on his right.

"I'm William."

"And I'm Jennifer."

They took their seats, William waiting until Jennifer was seated, placing his hands on the back of her chair as if to assist her.

"Thank you, William."

William sat down and adjusted the knives and forks in front of him so that they were straight. Then he slightly repositioned the glasses and taking up his napkin lay it across his lap. He turned to talk to Sheila, but she had already begun to talk to the man on her right. He turned to Jennifer.

"How do you know Stephen and Sheila?" Feeble opening gambit number one, but there you are.

"Well, I've known them for about ten years, or perhaps a little more. All that time ago, my husband, John – well, actually he's now my ex-husband – played squash with Stephen, which meant we both got to know them. Got to know them quite well. John liked Stephen and I liked Sheila, and she and I became quite close. So when John and I divorced, she sort of 'gathered me in.' And that has remained. And you, how do you know them?"

"Similar story really. Well, sort of. My late wife worked with Sheila, and sometimes, not all that often, we came to supper here. So now, now that I am on my own, I think Sheila has taken pity on me, and is trying to 'cheer me up.' Perhaps she is gathering me in, too?"

"Maybe she is. But don't you think it rather odd, William, that we've never met before?"

"Well, I suppose it is. Perhaps Providence has other plans." As soon as he said this, he wished he hadn't, but fortunately Jennifer seemed not to have heard, or chose to ignore it. Either way she changed the subject.

"Did your wife die recently?"

"No, not that recently. It's about eighteen months now since Caroline died, but despite what everybody says, the measure of loss is not a matter of time."

"Well, my husband didn't die, although he might as well have done. We just lost touch. We had been married for almost twenty years, and both of us were very taken up with our work. I think we were just drifting apart. And then one day I discovered he was having an affair with a bright young thing who had just joined his design team. In my anger, I cut him adrift."

"Do you have children?"

How many times had Jennifer been asked this question? She took a deep breath.

"No, no children, just a dog. His name is Henry. He's a Labrador. So I now live in Putney with a dog called Henry. In fact he is Henry the Second. The first Henry died and I have only had this Henry for a couple of years. Do you like dogs?"

"Not really."

"Well, Henry is my almost constant companion. Do you live in London, William?"

"Yes, I do. I have a flat in Marylebone."

"Oh, I like Marylebone. Lots of lovely places to eat."

"Yes, I suppose there are."

My favourite is Galvin Bistrot de Luxe. Have you ever eaten there?

"I'm afraid not. Perhaps I should."

"Yes, you should."

There was something about the way Jennifer talked, a brightness, a directness that was drawing William towards her. There was something else about her too, an edge, that reminded him of Caroline. And then, at one moment, when she turned to talk to him, she touched his arm. She placed the fingers of her left hand lightly on the sleeve of his jacket. It had been a long time since anyone had done that and it felt good, very good. Connection.

"What sort of work do you do?" he asked.

"Well, when I was younger I worked as a journalist for a fashion magazine called *Patch*. You won't have heard of it, but for a few years it was quite trendy. Eventually it ran out of money. So then I had quite a number of freelance jobs in the fashion industry, marketing, writing copy, that sort of thing. And for a while, when I married, I stopped work. John had a very good job in one of the big advertising agencies, Brewin & Brewin, you know B&B I didn't need to work, and anyway we had just bought our house in Putney, and as it needed quite a lot of refurbishment, we agreed that I should take some time out to take care of it. Which I did. It took a lot longer than we thought it would, but eventually I went back to work freelance. Picking up with people I had worked with before. And that's what I still do. I am a fashion journalist and I love it. It's my passion really. Well, that and Henry the Second."

She sounded confident, a woman of the world, a woman of fashion. Brittle, pacey and of the moment. And yet he sensed she was wounded. That although she had been on her own for many years now, she still bore the wounds of loss. Saying that Henry was always with her; saying so little about her former husband. Seeing her as wounded made her even more alluring. Was she lonely, too? Might she understand what it was to be alone? Was she asking for comfort?

Of course, none of this was true. Jennifer wasn't asking for any such thing; but in his madness William thought she was. All at once, here was a beautiful woman, tall and dark-haired, her body angular and alive, her eyes a very pale green, who from time to time pulled back her hair with her right hand and tucked it behind her ear. Just as Caroline had done. It was irresistible. She was irresistible.

Although Jennifer felt no real interest in or curiosity about William's recent loss, she was drawn by his openness, and, of course, by his evident interest in her. He might have a beard and crumpled jacket, but he was listening to her, paying attention in a manner that was rather attractive. And even if he didn't like dogs, he did have a flat in Marylebone, close to one of her favourite restaurants.

As the meal proceeded, both William and Jennifer found this 'intimacy' enjoyable. As rocket leaves and parmesan led to a vegetable lasagne, then to a lemon mousse and a selection of cheeses, including a soft and pungent goat's cheese, and finally to teas and coffees, they turned more and more towards each other, listening and speaking in what had become a private space, almost as if the rest of the people in the room were not there. There was something about her restlessness that drew him in.

And when the supper came to an end and it was time to go, they scribbled down each other's phone numbers and email addresses. They agreed that it would be good to meet again, perhaps go to an exhibition or even have lunch together.

When William arrived back at his flat, he was aware that something unsettling was stirring within him, something that was at one and the same time both disturbing and wonderful. In that short time together, he had fallen in love with Jennifer and, alarming though this was, he could feel excitement rising in his body. It was intensely physical. The next day he sent an email to say how much he had enjoyed meeting her, suggesting that they meet for lunch at her favourite restaurant, Galvin Bistrot de Luxe in Baker Street to which he had never been before. She emailed back to say that that would be lovely.

And so they met. The restaurant was a short walk from William's flat, but as he was obsessed with not being late, he arrived early. He had learnt this from his father who used to say, and repeat, "Better to be half an hour early than five minutes late." And he would add, "You can always wait." So, of course, William arrived early and waited. As usual this gave him plenty of time to look at the menu by himself to make sure that there would be something he could eat that would not upset his stomach. This meant no meat, no fish, no onions, no spices (especially chilli, which seemed to be everywhere he went) and, especially no seafood or mushrooms.

He was shown to a table at the back of the restaurant and took a place that would enable him to see Jennifer when she arrived. Not knowing the restaurant, William was nervous. His somewhat bizarre preferences for food and his obsession about not eating the wrong thing was heightened by what he could see was a French restaurant of some distinction. He searched the menu and to his dismay found that it was not designed for him. He selected in his mind a salad of winter vegetables, goat's curd and mustard leaves to be followed by risotto of pumpkin, wild mushroom and comtè cheese, with a green salad (no onions). He liked neither risotto nor mushrooms, but there was little other choice that did not involve some kind of flesh. William prepared himself, pretending to study the menu and wine list. Jennifer was about twenty minutes late, so that by the time she came through the door, spotted him and waved, he was already beginning to feel anxious. He straightened the knives and forks.

Although William was beset by a deep anxiety, most people did not notice it, seeing him as self-contained and assured. His childhood trauma, the story of Susan, had left him fearful of being left out, of being abandoned or rejected. It wasn't about not being loved. Not at all. Indeed, as the youngest member of the family, his mother had rather doted on him. As a teenager, she would insist that he take her to the cinema in the school holidays, and this became something they always did, every holiday time. No, it wasn't about not being loved, it was about being abandoned. The imprint of that early tragedy had marked him, and however competent he might seem, it was there, catching him out in moments of disapproval or exclusion, friendships that went cold, not being included by others.

Indeed, uncomfortable about joining in, in case he would then be excluded, and for his own protection, he had developed an image of himself as someone who chose to be 'on the edge'. In a strange way, in his professional life, this had led to his success as a consultant. He had become someone who could look at a company's problems analytically 'from the outside,' unencumbered by conventions of established practice. It had freed him to question and to see things as they might be, not as they were. But it had also left him damaged, and now, now that he was indeed alone, now that Caroline had left him by himself, it was taking hold.

Jennifer walked towards him, brushing her hair off her face with her right hand and tucking it behind her right ear. What was it about this gesture that was so appealing? He had always found it so, and it reminded him of Caroline, too. He had no idea, but once again, as Jennifer walked towards him, it caught his attention. It pleased him. He stood up and they kissed each other on the cheek, both cheeks. He smelt her perfume, light but sweet. When he touched her arm, he felt her flesh soft upon the bone. It was, to him, a delight.

"You found it, then," he said.

"Yes, not that difficult. Even I can find Baker Street."

What was that? Almost a defence, almost as if she had meant to say, "Are you suggesting I would be too stupid to find a restaurant?" A statement of independence. "I don't need your help to find Baker Street."

Jennifer sat down and took off her jacket, letting it fall back onto her chair. Somewhat clumsily, William leant across as if to help her. She did that thing with her hair again.

"What would you like to drink?"

"I would adore a glass of red wine."

"Good idea. I'll have one, too. Any preferences?"

"Not really. Something to remind me of France."

William knew very little about wines, and so he waved his hand at a waiter and, when he came to the table, asked him if he would suggest, "something not too dry, something to remind us of France." The waiter looked as if he was pleased to have been asked and, without consulting the wine list, suggested that they might like to try the Galvin Côte du Rhône.

"I think you will like it. It should certainly remind you of France."

Before long they each had a glass of wine in their hand, clinking glasses, William saying, "Happy days!"

The lunch went well, Jennifer's choices being much braver than William's, not that that was difficult. She chose a French onion soup, with an Emmental and Gruyère crouton and then Navestock Estate Essex pheasant breast, white beans and smoked chorizo stew, with braised red cabbage. Neither wanted a pudding, but Jennifer ordered an espresso coffee whilst William just finished up his glass of water. They talked about holidays and business trips Jennifer had had in France and about her dog, Henry. They talked about the supper party in Notting Hill and about their mutual friends, Sheila and Stephen. Both liked Sheila, and both found Stephen difficult to get to know, as he was quite a closed man – something to do with working with banks and banking maybe. Neither of them was quite sure.

When the bill came, William took it and put it beside him, but Jennifer insisted that they should 'go Dutch'. And so they did. And that was that. Jennifer thanked William for being such a good listener and then they said goodbye, again kissing each other on both cheeks. The perfume, the touch upon the arm. Jennifer headed south towards Soho and William hailed a taxi and returned to his flat.

In the weeks that followed, they met again, sometimes for lunch and sometimes to see an exhibition. They even took a trip down the Thames in a ferryboat from Tate Modern to Docklands and back. They talked and talked, mostly about what was going on in Jennifer's life, her work, how wonderful Henry was and, since she had no children, how she loved being free. William should have heard that, but he didn't. Not then.

"I was thinking the other day how lucky I am to be free."

"Free from what?"

"From marriage, from having children, from having to please someone else."

"Except Henry. Henry the Second."

"Yes, except Henry, but he is easy to please: one walk a day, food, water, a comfortable blanket and basket to sleep in, and my company."

"Sounds a bit like a marriage."

"Very funny, but not funny at all. Anyway, how long were you married?"

"Forty-one years. Off and on."

"Off and on? What does that mean?"

"Oh, the usual. Minor infidelities or times when we chose to spend our lives apart. But then also times of wonderful closeness, everyday intimacy and tenderness."

"So were you unfaithful to Caroline?"

"Not really. Not very much."

"And was she unfaithful to you?"

"A bit. And once, more than a bit."

"So what happened?"

"Well, we more or less got over it. Some hurt. Some

damage. To us and, more importantly, to our children. But mostly we liked each other, a lot actually. Liked each other a lot."

"You don't think you're a bit odd, William?"

"What do you mean?"

"A bit odd in making so little of these infidelities. I would have been bloody furious."

"Well, I suppose it is a bit odd. But somehow or other that is how it was. You see, we had married very young. So perhaps it wasn't all that surprising. And we liked being together. We liked being us."

After a few weeks had passed, and most unwisely as he was later to learn, William rang his daughter to tell her that he had met a rather wonderful woman and that he thought he might be falling in love with her.

"Her name is Jennifer and she has a dog called Henry."

"No husband then, no children?"

"No, a long departed ex-husband, but no children. Just Henry."

"I suppose she is ludicrously young."

"No, not really. Younger than me, of course, but not ludicrously young. I don't really know how old she is. The dog is a Labrador."

"So do you go for walks with one of those disgusting poop bags?"

William heard the disapproval.

"No, we haven't done that. Not yet."

"Something to look forward to then."

"You sound cross. I thought you might be pleased for me."

"Oh, Dad, you are so naïve. What did you think I would say – 'How wonderful, do bring her to stay'?"

"How are the children?"

"They're fine, Dad, they're fine."

"And how is Robert?"

"He's fine, too."

And that was that. Unable to understand how Jane felt, he let it go.

Of course, William was naïve. More especially, he was captured by the fantasy he had come to believe in. The green eyes, the perfume and the touch upon his arm. He was enchanted. In fact, of course, he needed to believe in the fantasy, a fantasy that seemed to him to be a wonderful gift. It made him feel young and alive. But such was his wound, and such was his need, the need to love and be loved, that he failed to notice that he was the only one who believed it to be true. Jane did not believe it and nor did Jennifer. She liked being with William, enjoying his company and the chance to talk about all that was happening to her, and her work. But that was it.

At first, the excitement of falling in love and the delight that he felt as he imagined himself becoming close to Jennifer blinded William to the truth. He pursued the friendship and made plans for their being together. Perhaps they could go away somewhere, or perhaps she would like to come and stay overnight in his small flat, at least sometimes. But this did not happen, in part because it was not what Jennifer wanted and in part because of Henry. In truth, there was nothing really there to support William's sense of a greater togetherness. Jennifer had not introduced him to any of her friends or invited him to have supper with her in Putney. They would embrace whenever they met, and sometimes she would slip her hand through his arm as they walked through an exhibition or crossed the road to the cinema. And that was that. Nothing more than that. All these notions of becoming 'us' were figments of William's imagination. In his continuing sorrow, he needed to believe in the possibility of a special intimacy, not sexual passion, but something more tender, something closer to companionship, a 'being with.'

Weeks and months passed and, in time, although they remained friends, William became increasingly uneasy. Once more, he was beginning to feel that he was being left behind. One day, when they met for lunch at the French restaurant in Baker Street, William began to talk to Jennifer as if they were now becoming more than just friends, possibly becoming a couple.

"I wonder," he said, "how it might be if we were to let our friends know about our being together now, you know, being a couple?"

At first, Jennifer made no reply, but it was clear that he had overstepped some kind of boundary. He could see by the way in which her body stiffened and her eyes left his that she was withdrawing into herself. She looked up at him and then away again. Awkward. He was shocked by her response.

"Why would I want to be part of a couple? I tried that and it didn't work," she said at last. "And I have no intention of returning to it."

"What do you mean?" said William, now completely confused that his love for Jennifer should be seen as some kind of confinement.

"Well, being attached to someone is just what I want to make sure I never do again. I did try to love someone and to live with them, but it proved to be impossible. Company is great, but I like my freedom, free to be who I am."

"But are you saying that you never want to be with someone again?" said William, now beginning to feel from some deep place inside those recurrent feelings of loss and abandonment. "Surely you are not saying that, are you?"

But the damage had been done and the rest of the lunch was silent and uncomfortable. Jennifer finished her meal, leaving much of it on the plate and taking small sips of water from her glass. She did not order her normal espresso. William asked for the bill, giving an overly generous tip to try and make himself feel better. He did not. It was over. They parted and for some days there were no phone calls or text messages.

William was cast into gloom, but Jennifer was just feeling cross that William was asking her to do something she had long since decided never to do again, come close to someone. She rang her friend, Sarah, who lived in Brighton, and asked if she could come and stay. Packing her suitcase and Henry into her car, she fled. She was irked by William's neediness, his need to love and to be loved. And the more he came towards her, the more she withdrew.

William and Jennifer did not speak to each other for some weeks. Once or twice, William sent an email telling her about some exhibition he had been to and asking how she was, but her replies were short and without tenderness. The distance between them was widening, the connection between them weakening, being kept alive only by William's occasional emails. One day he decided that he would not send another one. Whatever it was that had brought William and Jennifer together had now gone away, and William was left with nothing but a painful emptiness. Another loss. The fantasy he had created for himself had evaporated, had slipped through his hands. Had there been something else there, something more solid, perhaps they would have found some comfort together, but, in truth, for both of them the attraction had been self-centred. William needed someone to care for and Jennifer wanted to be listened to. William had mistaken this for love. A deep weariness fell upon him as, again, he felt the depth of loss and loneliness return. He withdrew once more into his flat, closed the door, refused invitations to supper and gave himself to his work. He wrote a letter to Jennifer, sending it to her house in Putney:

My dear Jennifer

I doubt you will be surprised by this letter. I know you have begun to have some doubts about what I like to call 'us.' I know that this feels too overwhelming for you, something that asks too much of you. And maybe you are right. I do not deny I have a need for intimacy, a need to love and be loved. I am beginning to think that I am suffering a kind of madness, the small madness of grieving.

Perhaps we need to step back, take some time out, whatever the phrase is. Let's do that. I have very much enjoyed our times together. They came at just the right time for me. Thank you for all of that. I hope we remain friends and keep in touch.

Back to work!

With love, William x

When Jennifer returned from her visit to Brighton she found William's letter waiting for her. She replied:

Dear William

As you say, I was not surprised to receive your letter and, actually, I was a bit relieved. For a while I was becoming worried that you might be seeing more in our friendship than I had intended. We have had some lovely times together, William, especially our lunches at the Galvin Bistrot. That red wine is delicious! And I have grown fond of you. You are great to talk to, and have always been prepared to let me ramble on about my life.

I don't really know what 'us' means. But I do know that I want to enjoy my freedom and to explore the world without having to take responsibility for anyone else. I hope you can understand this.

Love from

Jennifer x

This is what Jennifer wrote to William, but in an email to her friend in Brighton she put it rather differently:

Hi Sarah!

Thank you for having me to stay. I have just said 'goodbye' to William, which is a relief. As you know I had come to find his neediness for comfort and tenderness a bit too 'sticky'. He had begun to talk about 'us,' which was worrying. Anyway, he wrote to me to suggest we take some time out. Phew!

As agreed, Henry and I look forward to having you to stay next weekend. Shall I invite some friends round for supper on Saturday?

Jenny x

It was true, William had wanted something more than just friendship, something more intimate and tender, something like the best of his times with Caroline, a memory, perhaps even a somewhat distorted memory, of what their lives had been. But there it was. He thought about ringing his daughter, but decided against it. He'd wait a few days and then call her and check up on the grandchildren. No news from Frederick.

The second anniversary of Caroline's death came and passed by. If anything the pain was more intense than before.

Days, weeks and months passed.

CHAPTER 5

THE HOUSE BY THE MARSH

O ver many years, as part of William's enquiry into metaphysics and the nature of Being – that which may lie beyond where we seem to be – he had received teachings from a religious community called the Brahma Kumaris, the daughters of Brahma, known as the BKs. They were established in the early part of the twentieth century by a retired jewellery merchant in India, now known as Brahma Baba, and their global organisation of nearly one million followers was run almost entirely by women. The most senior sister, Dadi Janki, now aged one hundred, was a wise and holy woman of great insight and clarity. The deep silence and simplicity of the sisters had affected William very much.

As chance would have it – although of course none of this is chance – some months before, William had been invited to take part in one of their retreats, 'Caring for the Earth,' and whilst he was there he had met a man called Roderick, who was visiting the BKs for the first time. William had told Roderick something of what was happening to him, and said that although he was presently living in London he wasn't planning to stay there. At the end of the retreat, they had swapped phone numbers. And then one morning as William sat in his kitchen with a cup of tea in his hands, his mobile rang.

"William, it's Roderick. Do you remember we met a month or two ago at one of those retreats organised by the BKs?"

"Oh, yes, I remember. I think it was your first visit, wasn't it?"

"Yes, it was. How are you?"

"I'm fine."

"William, I want to ask you something. I remember you said that although you were living in London, you might want to move back to the country."

"Well, yes, I suppose that's true. I have been living here for some while. You may recall I came here after my wife died? I had to get away from the house we had been living in."

"Yes, I remember that."

"The truth is, I am tiring of London, and I do miss the countryside. The trouble is, I can't go back to my old house. Too many memories …"

"Well, that's what I wanted to talk to you about."

"My memories?"

"No, not being able to go back."

"Oh that, yes …"

"The point is, William, I have a house in Suffolk. It's in a village called Frampton and it overlooks the marshes."

"Sounds wonderful."

"Yes, it is. I bought it some years ago and spent quite a bit of time making it how I wanted it. The odd thing is, now that it is finished, I have decided to go and live in Italy. Edward, who I don't think you have met …"

"No, I don't think I have."

"Well, Edward and I have decided that we want to live somewhere warm."

"Not on the coast of Suffolk then!"

"No, not on the Suffolk coast. Beautiful though it is, those northeasterly winds are not warm!"

"So, where are you going to?"

"We've bought a house in a small village in Umbria. It's called Tiberina. It is lovely there. Quite remote."

"And what about your house in Frampton?"

"Well, that's the point. I want to let it. I want to let it for three years, and I wondered if you would be interested in living there?"

"Well, how extraordinary. I suppose that might just suit me. I have been thinking of selling the house Caroline and I lived in, and I suppose I could do that and live in Frampton as your tenant."

"That's what I wondered. It would suit me to know who was living there, and it has a room overlooking the marshes and the sea that you could use as a study."

"Could I go and see it?"

"Yes, any time. The owner of the village shop, whose name is Mary, holds a key. I will let her know you are coming. But could you go quite soon? I would like to get things settled before we leave for Italy, which is in a month's time."

"Yes, of course, I'll go this week. Could you email me the address?"

"I will, although you can't miss it. There is only one street in Frampton and it leads to my house. It is the last house before the marsh."

Something shifting? Providence? ✦

Later that week, William took the morning train to the small Suffolk town of Saxmundham, having arranged for a taxi to meet him there and drive him to the nearby village of Frampton. The train left Liverpool Street station on time and made its way, slowly at first, past the Olympic stadium at Stratford and then through the inner suburbs of Maryland, Ilford and Romford until, crossing over the M25, it began to pass through the outer suburbs and into Essex. On to Chelmsford and then his childhood town of Colchester before entering Suffolk and arriving at Ipswich, with its elevated road bridge over the River Orwell. At the station, the train stopped and William disembarked and crossed the footbridge to Platform 1, where a small two-carriage Lowestoft train was waiting for the journey to Saxmundham. At each part of this journey, buildings and people were being replaced by fields and trees. And as the small train set off to Lowestoft, the countryside began to envelop him. And not only the countryside, because at Woodbridge the River Deben came into view, with boats and boatyards, marking the edge, the place where the land stopped and the water began. Somewhere beyond the river was the sea.

The train stopped at Saxmundham and William and

about six other passengers stepped onto the platform. Following them, he made his way across the level crossing to the other side of the track where his taxi was waiting.

"Are you William Clarke?"

"Yes, that's me. Are you taking me to Frampton?"

"Yes, I am. I'm David. Front or back?"

"Front."

William got into the passenger seat and David set off, driving out of Saxmundham and through open country towards the sea. William began to feel further and further away, not just away from where he had been, but 'away'. Eventually there was a signpost for Frampton, the road running between fields and woodland until it narrowed and ran into the village. William peered out of the window of the taxi.

"We're looking for the village shop, David. Do you know where it is?"

"Yes, everyone knows Mary's emporium."

The village of Frampton had only one street, which ran through it from beginning to end, Roderick's house being the last place it could go to before it ran into the marsh. The village had a church, St Peter's, with a square flint tower and the village shop had a tea room to one side, for in the warm weather and sometimes, when it was cold, visitors came to Frampton either for tea or to walk across the marshes, by the sea, and through the woodland, bird-spotting or just enjoying themselves. Some years ago the villagers had managed to retain the post office, which had now become part of the shop and the tea room. It had its own counter set behind a glass screen and Mary, whose shop it was, had to run round from her till to the post office counter whenever anyone came in with letters and parcels, or wanted to cash their old age pension or deposit money in their post office account. When she was sitting at her till, she was friendly and chatty. And when she was standing behind the glass panel of the post office counter, she was polite but formal. After all, she was then the Post Mistress.

Entering the village, there was one large house and garden, and the rest of the village was made up of cottages, some of which were holiday homes. The large house, High Winds, was occupied by an elderly widow whose husband, Sir Ronald Whitely, had, ironically, died in a great storm whilst crossing the Atlantic in a yacht, a voyage he had taken as "an adventure." His widow, Lady Melissa Whitely, was forever cross with her late husband for being so foolish and for leaving her to live by herself amongst what she regarded as the 'common people' of Frampton, forever having to open the local flower show and sit upright and alone in her pew each Sunday morning listening to a dull and modern vicar who seemed to have an irresistible desire to liken the world to some kind of inane television soap opera, from which he drew sermons of utter banality.

David drove down the street and pulled over and stopped before a wide-fronted shop with large windows and an open door. In front of the shop was a table upon which were boxes of vegetables, cabbages, cauliflowers, broccoli and red geraniums. William got out of the taxi and went in. There did not seem to be anyone there, but then a door at the back of the shop opened and a woman appeared holding a large box in both arms and walking uneasily towards him.

"Can I help?" said William moving towards her and holding out his arms to help with the box.

"No, I'm fine," came a voice from behind the box. "I'm just going to put it here." And with that, the woman bent her knees, spreading them wide under her black skirt, and lowered the box onto the ground.

"Good morning," said William, "I think you have the key for Roderick's house. I'm William, the person who is thinking of renting it."

"Oh yes," said the woman, "and I'm Mary. Roderick said you were coming. Wait here and I'll get the key."

And with that she disappeared through the door at the back of the shop, returning with a quite large brass key attached to a label saying 'Roderick's House'.

"Here it is. It is the key to the front door. Oh, you'll like Roderick's house. It's very … you know … very … very typical."

"What do you mean, typical?"

"Oh you know, typical. Typical of … you know … typical of people like Roderick."

"Oh, I see. Typical. Like Roderick?"

"Yes, that's it. Typical like Roderick. Are you like that, you know … like Roderick?"

"No, not really," said William, not being quite sure what Mary was saying. "No, not at all like Roderick really. Not that I know him that well."

"Oh, I see. Then you won't be like that then?"

"No, I suppose not. Anyway, I'd better get on."

"Yes, of course. You had better get on. And if you want to leave the key with me, I will keep it for you. Until you stay, that is. Until you decide to stay."

"Okay then."

And with that William left the shop and got back into the taxi. They drove a short way along the street until it came to an end at Roderick's house. Having paid David and confirmed that he would be returning to collect him later, William turned towards the house. He could not quite believe what he was looking at.

It was as if he were walking into a dream, a dream made especially for him. The house stood above the marsh on a platform set upon wooden piles, and with a veranda around three sides. Its outer walls were weatherboarded and painted the colour of the reeds in winter. The roof, which was sloped at the eaves to overhang the veranda, was tiled, and at one end there was a turret carrying a weather vane in the shape of a sailing boat. The windows and the front door were painted white and were triple-glazed to keep the house warm against the cold easterly and northeasterly winds from the sea. Behind the house, its garden ran into woodland, birch and pines, and beyond that, beyond its boundary, were open fields and pasture.

William walked up the steps and put the key into the lock, turning it clockwise. It opened with ease, as if it were a well-oiled lock made especially for turning. Leaving the door open, William stepped into the house. Inside, the rooms were painted in neutral greys and off-whites, 'Elephant's Breath' and 'Skimming Stone'. The floors were of oak boards and the living room-come-kitchen, which was open to the underside of the plastered slope of the roof, was large and comfortable, with two armchairs and a large sofa. It was kept warm by a wood stove that stood in the middle of the room, its shiny metal flue rising up and through the roof, and outside capped by a metal hat.

The house was all on one level and there were two bedrooms and two bathrooms at the back, one large with a bath and the other small and with a shower. At the front was the study Roderick had told him about. Its window overlooked the marsh, looking out towards a shingle beach and the sea, and the room was fitted with worktops and bookshelves. Along the rear wall was a campaign bed, cream in colour and painted with strands of leaves and flowers. The house was silent and still, and it welcomed him.

Slowly, William turned around and looked through the open front door. From the front porch of the veranda, there were wooden steps down to a gravel path between pots of lavender set on a shingle bed that led towards, and then through, the marsh on a boarded walkway, which in turn led to the beach and then the North Sea. On this day, the sea was no more than a faint unfolding of waves upon the beach. On other days it would be very different, often roaring as the cold easterly and northeasterly winds first whipped up the crest of the waves and sent them crashing onto the pebbles and then sucked them back, carrying the loose shingle of the beach with them as the tide rose and fell. But, today, everything was still and quiet.

William sat down in one of the armchairs and put his head into his hands, all his energy gone. For the past year he had been holding himself together, his body tense, his feelings held back, trying, trying hopelessly to love and be loved, for once to be at peace. Now the house, the marsh and the sea were welcoming him. Refuge. Quite suddenly, he began to weep. He could not stop. The sadness, the hurt and the loss poured out of him in gasping cries of anguish and grief. "Fuck, fuck, fuck," he cried. "Fuck, fuck, fuck."

William heard someone walking up the gravel path. He took off his glasses, rubbed his eyes, put his glasses back on and blew his nose on his handkerchief. It was Mary and she was walking up the steps to the front door, wobbling a bit and holding in her hands a tray covered with a white cloth upon which were a teapot, a jug, a cup and a plate. The jug was covered by a lace napkin.

"Are you alright, William?" she asked as she came to the front door. "I was just wondering if you were all right, or if there was anything you needed. And I've brought you some tea and an Eccles cake. Do you like Eccles cakes? I make them myself for my tea shop. It's my special thing. People come from the other side of Saxmundham to eat my Eccles cakes."

"I'm fine, Mary. Really, I'm fine," said William. "And a cup of tea is just what I want. Thank you. And I love Eccles cakes. No milk in the tea though, if you don't mind."

"No milk in your tea. Okay, I'll have to remember that … if you decide to stay that is. I'll remember that."

And setting down the tray on the kitchen worktop, Mary poured William his tea, without milk. Then, she brought to him the cup and the plate with the Eccles cake, placing them with care upon a low table in front of the sofa in the living room. Although she could see that he had been crying, she said nothing. She knew that people like Roderick did cry from time to time, and so she was not at all surprised. She left William, taking the jug of milk with her.

This short ceremony seemed to have marked William's arrival, and somehow he now knew that this was where he was going to live; that Mary and her Eccles cakes were going to be part of that life. As, indeed, they were. He finished his tea, stood up and walked onto the veranda to brush off the last crumbs of the cake, wiping his mouth and his beard with his handkerchief. Then he came back in and began to explore his new home.

Roderick had furnished the rooms. So there were beds, cupboards, chests of drawers and chairs, cushions and simple white pull-down window blinds, and wooden coat hangers in bedroom cupboards. And in the living room-come-kitchen, there was a fridge, a larder cupboard and even cutlery, white plates and cups, and a kettle and pots and pans for cooking on the cooker, which had a gas-fired hob and an electric oven. There was a small utility room with a dishwasher, a washing machine and a tumble drier. Roderick had left nothing out.

William walked once more into the study with its window overlooking the marsh. He sat in the desk chair, swivelling this way and that. Then he stood up, inspected the bookshelves and ran his hands over the smooth fitted worktop. Roderick had even thought to provide power sockets, with a BT broadband hub. Beside the hub, William found the password: Gu9efm4Ba7DF.

"I could work here."

William had asked David to return in an hour and a half, and there he was waiting for him as he locked the door and walked back towards the shop. He gave the key, the tray, the cup and the plate to Mary and assured her that he would return. "Oh, that's good," she said. "I like a man who likes an Eccles cake."

William set off back to Saxmundham station, texting Roderick to say, "It's wonderful. I would love to be your tenant, if you still want me to."

As soon as he had sent the text, William could see the word-bubble forming, and then, there was Roderick's reply.

"Great! I'll send you an email with a suggested rent and so on. Would you be happy with all of this being done by email?"

"Of course," replied William.

CHAPTER 6

FRAMPTON

A nd so it was that William went to live in Roderick's house in Frampton. One Sunday morning, having packed his clothes, his books and his laptop back into the boxes and suitcases that had brought them to London, he waited for the driver he had hired to come and take him to Suffolk.

This time the car journey felt altogether different from the one that had taken him to London more than a year before. Leaving the congestion of London behind him, within less than an hour William and his driver were moving easily around the M25 and heading for the A12. Each quarter of an hour took them further and further away from London and closer and closer to Suffolk. Past Chelmsford, then Colchester and the turning for Stratford St. Mary, they crossed the county boundary and, before long, they were travelling over the Orwell bridge on the outskirts of Ipswich. High above the river, with its sailing boats and marina, the cranes of Felixstowe on the horizon, William could feel his spirits rising. It was as if he were being liberated. He was moving towards the edge. Freedom. In a little over half an hour, they came into Saxmundham and were soon on the narrow road that led to Frampton, fields, hedgerows and woodland on either side as they drove towards the marshes and the sea.

Pulling up in front of Mary's shop, William got out of the car and walked in. Mary was at the other end of the shop, the part that was the tea room, each of the tables set with a white cloth, and a small spray of flowers in the centre. Mary was setting out tea and Eccles cakes for an elderly, white-haired couple. With care, she placed their cups and plates before them, assuring them of the provenance of the Eccles cakes and their fame beyond Saxmundham.

"Actually," said the man, "they are well-known much further afield than that. At the recommendation of my wife's friend from Pilates, we have come from St. Albans."

"Goodness me," said Mary. "St. Albans. And how far away is Pilates?"

For a moment, the man looked confused, but then his wife said, "No, dear, Pilates is not a place, it's a form of exercise, a form of deep stretching."

"Oh, I see," said Mary, bristling at being called 'dear.' "A form of deep stretching. That sounds nice." And she turned to go back to her kitchen, wondering as she often did about the things people got up to in places far away. "Deep stretching!" Then she spotted William.

"So you've come back then?"

"Yes, and I am going to stay. I simply could not keep away from your Eccles cakes for a day longer."

Mary beamed with delight. Such details were the breath of her life. A man who liked Eccles cakes and was now going to live in Roderick's house. A man with a sadness of which he could not speak. Well, not yet.

"I'll get you the key."

"Thank you."

She disappeared through the door at the back of the shop, returning quickly with the large brass key and its label.

"And how is Roderick?"

"I don't really know. I think he's gone to Italy with Edward."

"You're not that close then? Not close to Roderick?"

"No, not close. Not close at all. I only really met him once. At a retreat with the Brahma Kumaris."

"Oh, I see. A retreat. With the Brahma Kumaris?"

"Yes."

"That must have been nice."

"Yes, it was. It was very nice."

"So you've been at a retreat with him then?"

"Yes. It was near Oxford."

"Near Oxford, with the Brahma Kumaris?"

"Yes, just to the south of Oxford."

"Just to the south. That must have been nice."

"It was."

"And these Brahma Kumaris, are they like Roderick? You know, like Roderick?"

"No, not really. They are more like nuns. Brahma Kumaris means Sisters of Brahma. They come from India."

"So they're like nuns from India?"

"Well, a bit like that."

"Well, who would have thought that? Nuns from India, south of Oxford."

William took the key and asked his driver to follow him in the car as he walked to the end of the street – as he walked to Roderick's house.

Where the road came to an end, there was a pair of gates that led onto a short driveway and a set of steps up to the veranda. William opened the gates, and the car carrying his life in cardboard boxes and suitcases drove in. The driver turned off the engine and got out, looking across the garden to the marshes and the sea. Silence. Nothing could be heard. Well, almost nothing, for as his ears attuned themselves to the silence he could hear the faint sound of the wind moving through the reeds and the distant soft turning of the sea upon the beach. And then he thought he could hear, nearby, the thin piping sound of a bird, unseen amongst the reeds.

William walked onto the veranda and opened the front door, the key once more turning clockwise with ease. Unable to supress a broad smile, he stepped into the living room, now to be his living room. Quite suddenly, as if he had walked into another world, nothing seemed to matter very much.

William turned to see the driver standing by the front door, carrying two large suitcases.

"Where would you like these?"

"Oh, just put them in here or in one of the bedrooms at the back. I'll get to them later."

"Okay."

And so, one by one, the boxes and cases were brought from the car and left standing in the living room and the bedrooms.

"Do you fancy a cup of tea?" said William.

"Well, I do," said the driver, and so they walked back up the street to Mary's tea room and, of course, were served tea and Eccles cakes.

"I sometimes make shortbread," Mary said.

"Oh, that would be nice," said William. "I'm fond of shortbread. It reminds me of my childhood. I always think it's rather comforting."

"I'll see what I can do then," she said, as if she was already beginning to take care of him.

After their tea, William paid the driver and he set off back to London, the sound of his car disappearing along the street and then along the road to Saxmundham and beyond. William returned to the house. Silence. For a while he sat in an armchair looking out through the open doorway to his garden, his marsh, his beach and his sea.

"This is where I am."

Later, when he began to unpack, the first item to be taken out of the boxes was his laptop, and he walked into the study and placed it on the fitted worktop in front of the window overlooking the marsh.

"This is where I shall be."

And then he found his books, brought them into the study and put them on the bookshelves, placing the one he was reading by the bed.

"I will sleep here."

As the evening came upon the marsh and the house, the boxes and the suitcases were empty. Clothes were hanging in cupboards, socks and pants, handkerchiefs, T-shirts, shirts, sweaters and cardigans were in drawers, and Birkenstock shoes and a colourful pair of Pickett's Kilim slippers stood side by side on the floor of the smallest of the two bedrooms, which William had decided to use as a dressing room. Pyjamas were under a pillow on the campaign bed, which was now dressed in the sheets, pillowcases, duvet and white blanket that William had brought with him and his towels, toothbrush, toothpaste and deodorant were carefully set out in the smaller of the two bathrooms.

William had packed a small box of groceries, and these were now stacked in the fridge and larder cupboard of the kitchen. Enough for about a week if he ate only tinned soup, cereals, almond milk, rice cakes and peanut butter. Sorting this out was going to be top of the list, which he now began to write in a small yellow notebook – a list that included food, dishwasher tablets, and (most importantly), finding a housekeeper, someone to organise and manage his domestic life. He knew the very person who would be able to recommend someone, Mary.

It was quite late when William went to bed, placing his notebook by his computer, putting on his pyjamas and cleaning his teeth for the first time in his new bathroom. He switched off all the lights in the house and turned on the bedside lamp by the campaign bed. He climbed into the bed and, for a while sat, propped up by his pillow. He began to read a chapter from his book. It was *The Places That Scare You*, by the Buddhist nun Pema Chödrön, and it was marked with a bookmark. As if by chance – although of course nothing is by chance – it was titled, 'The In-between State,' and started with these words:

It takes some training to equate complete letting go with comfort. But in fact, 'nothing to hold on to' is the root of happiness. There's a sense of freedom when we accept we're not in control.

He read these words again, and quite suddenly he felt his eyes closing. He took off his glasses and set down his book. Placing both on the shelf at the head of the bed, he turned off the bedside lamp. Now it was very dark. A deep, deep darkness. He lay down, pulling his duvet around him. He had left open the window so that he could hear the sea.

"I am here. Lord have mercy."

There would come a time when those words "nothing to hold on to" as the root of happiness would need to be remembered.

The next day William woke early. The wind had risen, and the sound of the waves upon the shore was louder and more disturbing than the day before. There was a smell of salt water and earth, the smell of the marsh, and the alarming choking cry of herring gulls marking their ground. It was as if they were just making clear to William, and anyone else who might hear them, that they lived here, that this was their place.

For a moment, William could not remember where he was. Most unusually he had slept right through the night. A deep and dreamless sleep. He could remember nothing. But then it came to him. Here he was, waking up in another man's house; waking to new sounds and smells, but feeling at home. He lay there for some while, just letting all that was around him take him in; letting himself surrender to the bed, the study, the house, the marsh and the sea. And he felt a strange mix of delight and unease.

"Is this really happening to me? Am I blessed?" But then: "Might it suddenly be taken away or go badly wrong?"

Ever since the loss of his sister, Susan, such thoughts had always been with him. A deep and persistent anxiety settled somewhere far within him; a deep wound, as if something or someone might all of a sudden disrupt his ease, leaving him frightened and alone. And being in his seventies did not make any difference. In fact, in some ways it made it worse: a sudden heart attack, or a stroke, or the discovery of some terminal illness, were all things that were now happening to people no older than he was. After all, Caroline had become ill and had died in her mid-sixties. Within a year, she was gone, leaving him behind. And although he coped more than well, it was always there. It was what Mary had seen. That sadness. That place of sorrow.

Somewhere deep inside, William had always known that in order to cope he would have to protect himself. If no one else would take care of him, he would. At best, this enabled him to manage his life. At worst, it made him somewhat self-absorbed; his routines, his need for order, keeping himself to himself and never really giving himself to another. And this part of him had become reawakened by his loss. After Caroline's death, his natural reaction – natural to him – had been to turn inwards, to protect himself. Even letting his loneliness become something familiar, something he could rely on. And now here he was, living in another man's house, but making it his own. On his own.

William had a shower, dressed, made himself some breakfast and took his supplements. He set them back in their place on the worktop of the kitchen. Then he looked at his list. No time to lose. ⚘

Taking his old Waitrose shopping bag with him, he walked into Mary's shop to find her stacking tinned soup on one of her shelves.

"Good morning, Mary. Do you mind me calling you Mary?"

"No, that would be nice. If you're going to live here, that would be nice."

"Good. So that's it, and I would like you to call me William."

"All right then. You can call me Mary and I'll call you William."

"Good."

There was a pause, whilst Mary finished stacking the shelves and stood up. Watching her, William wondered whether she always wore black.

"I was wondering, Mary, whether you would know anyone who would be interested in helping me out."

"Helping you out?"

"Yes, helping with the house. You know, cleaning and shopping, that sort of thing."

"Cleaning and shopping?"

"Yes, that sort of thing. I suppose, well, I suppose I would say someone who would be my housekeeper."

"So you want a housekeeper then?"

"Yes, and I also want someone to help with the garden. I'm hopeless at gardening, and so I need someone to do that for me, too."

"Housekeeping and gardening then?"

"I could do that," said a voice from behind a rack of newspapers. "I could do that. I could do all of that."

And William turned to see a young woman dressed in dungarees and a purple cardigan, her black hair twisted up into a knot and wrapped with a pink ribbon. She had small gold rings in both ears and in her left eyebrow. She was wearing orange wellington boots.

"I'm Wendy," she said.

"Oh. And I'm William."

"William has come to live in Roderick's house," said Mary.

"And now you want someone to do housekeeping and gardening?" said Wendy.

"Yes, I do."

"Well, I could do both of those. And I'm looking for work."

"You could do both, could you?" said Mary, somewhat put out.

"Yes, I could."

"Well, could you come up to the house and talk it through with me?" said William.

"Okay, but not this morning. I'm dog-sitting this morning, for Lady Whitely. And I have just come in to pick up her newspaper. I could come this afternoon at about three."

"That would be fine."

Wendy paid for the newspaper, the *Daily Mail*, and left.

"She lives in a caravan," said Mary, folding her arms across her chest. "By herself. She lives in a caravan by herself. It's parked in one of Lady Whitely's fields. It's in return for dog-sitting."

"Oh. Is it a big dog?"

"Oh no. Not big. It's one of those horrid small dogs. Snappy. Some kind of terrier, I think. Horrid little thing. I don't allow dogs into my shop. They have to be left outside. I leave a bowl of water, but they have to be left outside. Don't want dogs in here."

"No, of course not. But it's nice that you leave them a bowl of water."

"You see, I'm not a dog person. I like cats."

"Me too."

"Oh, you like cats do you?"

"Yes, I do. One at a time."

"Just one at a time?"

"Yes."

"That's nice."

"Yes."

"Do you want a cat? You know, once you have your housekeeper and your gardener. Do you want a cat?"

"Well, I think I might. Being on my own, it might be company."

"Well, it would."

"I'll think about it."

"Yes, think about it. I could find you one."

"That would be nice. And now I have one or two things I need for my larder."

He bought his provisions: basmati rice, eggs, parmesan cheese, olive oil, Bertolli olive oil spread, Marmite and Ryvita. He was delighted to spot that Mary also stocked almond milk and his favourite organic crunchy peanut butter. "Not bad for a small shop in a remote Suffolk village," he thought.

And so having stocked up a bit and having probably found a housekeeper, a gardener and a cat, William walked back to the house, a bit overwhelmed, but at the same time excited at the way in which his new life was beginning to take shape. He put away his groceries, lining them up in the larder and in the fridge. Although he liked his new freedom, the freedom of those who live alone, he also liked order and regularity in his life: supplements on the kitchen worktop; his toothpaste and deodorant set out in the bathroom; books in order on the bookshelves; his pencil and notebook placed carefully beside his laptop. It was comforting. And he had noticed, although he never said anything about it to anyone else, that now he was on his own it was getting worse. He sometimes found himself straightening other people's pictures hanging on a wall or books laid out on a table. He sometimes wondered whether he was developing some kind of disorder, something like an obsessive-compulsive disorder. Still no one knew, so perhaps it didn't matter. Well, not yet, anyway.

"Was that what had put off Jennifer?" he wondered. "Or is there something equally disagreeable about me that I don't even know about? Unspoken, but there. Something about the ways in which I have learnt to survive. Turning within myself."

As soon as he began to think about this, and all that had happened with Jennifer, his mood dropped. He opened the door of his house and walked down towards the sea. The wind was cold but not strong, and he liked the sound of his Birkenstocks upon the boarded walkway, and then upon the shingle of the beach. He walked down to the edge of the sea. He would have to learn about the tide here, its pattern and rhythm. He could see that the waves had been higher than they were now and supposed that the tide was on the ebb. "I need a tide table and a moon chart." He marked the water's edge with a large stone.

That afternoon on the dot of three, Wendy walked up the steps from the garden and onto the veranda. Now the wellington boots had given way to a pair of yellow moccasins, which she slipped off her feet, and as the front door was wide open, she called out, "William! It's me, Wendy."

"I'm in the study, come in."

And as Wendy came in, William walked out of the study into the living room. They shook hands.

"Would you like some tea?"

"Yes please."

"I have mine black. Just ordinary tea, but black. And I only have almond or coconut milk."

"Almond milk is fine for me."

"Good. And a biscuit?"

"Yes, please."

And so William made the tea and set out the cups, the milk in a jug and a plate of biscuits on a tray, and brought them to a low table between the sofa and the armchairs of the living room.

"Take a seat."

"Thank you. I've often wondered what this house was like inside. It's lovely. And comfortable. Was this all here when you came?"

"Yes. Roderick did all of this. Did you know him?"

"No. No one did really. He came and went, but apart from Mary, no one really knew him. She held a key for him and sometimes he and his partner, Edward, had tea in her tea room. Apart from that, they were hardly ever here. Strange."

"Yes, it is. I didn't really know them. I just met Roderick once at a retreat run by the Brahma Kumaris in their country house near Oxford. We talked to each other quite a bit, and somehow he remembered that I had said I wanted to leave London and go back to live in the countryside. I was sort of hiding away in a little flat I own near Marylebone High Street. My wife died."

"Oh, I'm sorry about that. Was that recent or some while ago?"

"Some while ago now. About two and a half years ago. When she died I found I could no longer live in the house we had lived in, the house in which we had brought up our family – I have a son and a daughter – and so one day, quite suddenly, I fled to London. But that did not really work out. So, when Roderick asked me if I would like to rent this house, it was just right. And here I am. A refugee!"

"Nothing happens by chance though, does it?"

"No, that's right. And how did you get here? Mary told me that you live in a caravan."

"Yes, I do. Well, I do now. Until last year I lived for a while with someone I loved. Her name was Ruth and we lived together in her house in Totnes. But one day it came to an end. It was quite unexpected, but it just came to an end. And, like you, I had to get away. I had no house to go to, but an uncle of mine had a caravan and I asked him if I could borrow it for a while. I wanted to find a place a long way from Devon, but I needed to be by the sea, on the edge. I had been to the Suffolk coast before and so I decided I would go there, somewhere by the sea. My uncle brought the caravan here for me. A friend of his was a friend of Lady Whitely's, and as she needed someone to do dog-sitting, she agreed to let me park it in one of her fields in return for occasionally looking after her dog and doing errands, like picking up her paper from the shop. So I'm here. Another refugee!"

"And looking for work."

"Yes, I need to work."

"And you think you wouldn't mind being my housekeeper-come-gardener?"

"I think I could do that. What would you want?"

"Well, I'm not all that sure, but apart from the gardening, which is obvious, I would like someone to manage my domestic life. I hope that doesn't sound pathetic."

"No, not at all."

"Actually, after meeting you this morning, I made a list. It gives some idea of what would be needed. Shall I read it?"

"Yes, do. As it happens, I like lists. When I was living with Ruth I made all the lists. Perhaps that was the problem, too many lists!"

"There can never be too many lists for me," said William, and they both laughed. At that moment, just that moment, they felt at ease with each other – comfortable. They drank their tea and Wendy took a biscuit from the plate. So did William.

"So here is what I have on my list: 'Come in the morning at about nine.' Does that sound okay?"

"Yes."

"Prepare my breakfast."

"Fine."

"Check the larder to see if I'm getting short of anything and prepare a shopping list."

"I'd be good at that."

"Check the laundry basket and put clothes in the washing machine."

"I could do that, too."

"I could then put them in the tumble dryer or you could do that later."

"Yes. Fine."

"I may need some help with lunch, but I am not sure how that would work."

"We could talk about that."

"Good. Is this going okay so far?"

"Yes, it is."

"Do you think it would be possible for you to come back in the afternoon and make me tea. It is not that I couldn't make tea myself, but I really like the idea of someone coming in the afternoon. Does that make sense, Wendy? I write, you see, and writing can be quite solitary."

"What do you write about?"

"Love. I write about Love."

A pause. And then.

"Could we talk about that sometime, perhaps one afternoon when I come back to make your tea?"

"I should like that."

A silence came upon them, took them in, and each looked away. It was as if they both felt a door had been opened, but that they could not, at least for the moment, look at what lay beyond.

"Oh, by the way," said William, "I have another question for you. I am thinking of having a cat. I know you must like dogs, but do you like cats?"

"I don't like dogs."

"But you do dog-sitting."

"That doesn't mean I like dogs, does it?"

"Well, I suppose not, although you might think it would."

"Well, then you would be wrong. As it happens, I don't like dogs much, but I am fond of cats, or rather I like the company of a cat. Just one suits me."

"How odd, that is exactly how I feel, one at a time. So having a cat and feeding it could be part of our arrangement, could it?"

"Yes, I would like to care for a cat, although you will have to have a cat flap."

"There's a door out of the utility room at the side of the house. We could put one in there. I don't think Roderick would mind, but I will let him know and see if it is okay."

"That's good. Is there anything else?"

"No, I don't think so. But I was wondering about what I'll do for lunch. I haven't had a chance to explore Mary's shop yet. Do you think I would find something?"

"Yes, I think so. If you look in the freezer at the back of the shop, you'll find home-cooked ready-made meals. I often buy them. Not bad."

"Okay, I'll do that. Are some of them vegetarian?"

"I think so."

"You see, I don't eat meat or fish. It's the flesh. I don't eat flesh. Actually, I don't eat flesh, onions, mushrooms, spices or seafood."

She heard the anxiety in his voice, but said nothing.

"And now, Wendy, what would you charge me?"

"Does twelve pounds an hour sound about right?"

"It sounds fine. Do you want that in cash or shall I make a regular payment into your bank account?"

"A regular payment would be good. We'll work out the hours and then you can do it by standing order. It is a long time since I had a regular income."

"Well, now you have, and I like the idea of a standing order. It means we don't have to talk about it."

"Just so. By the way, there is just one thing."

"Yes?"

"Sometimes I might not be able to do everything, or I might go away for a few days. Is that all right?"

"Yes of course, that would be fine. I can look after myself for a few days."

But actually, it was not fine. Although William knew it was absurd, even this possible absence of someone he had only just met made him feel uneasy. He didn't really want to look after himself. He was still floundering. He didn't just want someone to take care of him, he needed someone to take care of him. He missed being cared for. He missed the easy tenderness of a long marriage and, in truth, was trying to find it again, not in a marriage, but in other ways, ways that he did not yet know. But he could not say this, of course. And, oddly, the conversation had touched something in Wendy, too. Unspoken, but there. Something about wanting to have someone to be with, but not being constrained by them.

After Wendy had gone, William again walked down to the sea to check the tide. As he had thought, the tide had fallen, the water having dropped below the stone mark he had set.

"I must get the hang of this," thought William.

And so it was that Wendy entered William's life, and soon Mary had found him a cat, a rescue cat, a neutered tabby she-cat, house-trained but abandoned. William took her in and named her Florence. She was soon familiar with the cat flap, going out at night to explore the woodlands behind the house, but always returning in time to be fed in the morning, and then sleeping in the sunniest spots in the house and garden, the chair in front of the radiator in William's study becoming a preferred place for her to be.

Rice with pesto, parmesan, olive oil and broad beans for lunch …

And so the days passed, and William returned to his writing.

William called his daughter, Jane. The phone rang a few times before she picked it up.

"Hello Jane, it's me."

"Hello Dad, how are you? Where are you?"

"Well, you know I mentioned that I was going to look at a house in Suffolk?"

"Yes."

"I've moved in. I've left London and moved into a house in the village of Frampton, near Saxmundham."

"That sounds good. Can you send some photos?"

"Yes, of course. I'll do that. And I have a cat and a housekeeper. The cat's name is Florence and the housekeeper is called Wendy. She has gold rings in her ears and in her left eyebrow. She wears orange wellington boots and lives in a caravan."

"Okay. I need to take all that in. How old is she?"

"Late twenties, early thirties, I think. I'm not sure."

"Dad, are you sure this is alright? She's rather young and people might wonder. You know, young woman, old man."

"Oh no, none of that. She's gay. She was in love with someone called Ruth who lived in Devon. But that went wrong and she fled to Suffolk."

"So, your housekeeper is a young gay woman who lives in a caravan and wears orange wellington boots."

"Yes, it's rather wonderful really."

"Well … It sounds a bit odd to me."

"She's a very good housekeeper. Very well organised. Very good with lists. And I like her company. How are my grandchildren?"

"They're fine, Dad. They're fine.

"And Robert. Is he okay?"

"Yes, he's okay too."

"Good."

There was a pause.

"Thought I would just let you know where I am and that all is well."

A day or two later his phone rang and it was Frederick on the line, calling from São Paulo.

"Hi Dad, what's all this I hear? You seem to have gone native. And Jane says you're living with a lesbian gypsy. All sounds a bit colourful!"

"Oh, hi Frederick. No, none of that is quite true. Living in Scotland seems to have narrowed your sister's grasp of reality. I am actually living in Suffolk in a beautiful house overlooking the marsh and the sea. And Wendy, my housekeeper, lives at the other end of the village in a caravan into which I have not stepped. She is delightful and I am old enough to be her grandfather. Why don't you come and see me?"

"I would do that if I were not living in São Paulo."

"Yes, of course. There is that. Are you planning a visit to London any time?"

"Well, not for a few months. But I will be back later in the year. And I will certainly come and see you. Do you have a spare room?"

"Yes, I do. I actually have two rooms, although I use one of them as a dressing room. You will be quite comfortable and you would be very welcome. I miss you. You know, I miss you."

"Yes, miss you too, Dad."

"Is everything okay in São Paulo?"

"Yes, everything is fine. Actually it is more than fine. I think I may have fallen in love."

"How wonderful. Who is she?"

"Her name is Ana. She is, of course, Brazilian, and is a school teacher. Small kids. You know, primary school kids. She works close to where I live, and we are thinking of moving in together."

"Excellent. She's not a lesbian gypsy then?"

"Very funny."

"Anyway, I'm glad you're fine. I like to know that. You know, fathers and sons."

"Fathers and sons."

CHAPTER 7

SETTLING IN

And so began the story of William's life in the house by the marsh in the village of Frampton. He and Wendy soon found a routine that suited them and they seemed to like each other's company. When necessary, she would drive him to the station when he was going to London, and because she had taken over all the responsibilities of shopping, he was content to limit his life to being close by, taking his time to explore Frampton and the marshes. Although there was a shower in her caravan, it was very small, and William agreed that Wendy could use his shower, and that she could launder her clothes in his washing machine and tumble dryer. It worked well and he liked having her coming in and out of the house.

Word had soon got round the village that a man,

living by himself, had moved into Roderick's house and had taken on Wendy as a housekeeper and a cat called Florence. Mary, was behind this, of course. As the days and weeks passed, William began to meet one or two more people. First, Richard, the postman, a former army sergeant who always arrived at eleven in the morning; and then Winny, who sometimes worked in Mary's shop and who lived further up the village street.

One morning, just after eleven, William found a small envelope with a second class stamp lying on the front door mat. Cutting it open with a table knife, William discovered inside a formal card:

Lady Whitely

requests the pleasure of the company of William Clarke

for tea on Thursday May 5th at 4.00 pm.

RSVP. Lady Whitely, High Winds, Frampton, Suffolk.

Thursday May 5th was a week away and so, intrigued by the invitation, William at once took one of his postcards from a drawer in the study and wrote upon it:

Dear Lady Whitely,

Thank you for your kind invitation for tea on 5th May. I am delighted to accept.

Yours sincerely,

William Clarke

Then he walked down to Mary's shop and stood in front of the post office counter. Mary who had been unpacking cereal packets and lining them up on her shelves, hurried round and adopted her Post Mistress stance.

"Good morning William, and what can I do for you today?"

"I need a stamp for this postcard, which I am sending to Lady Whitely. I have been invited to tea."

"First or second class post?"

"First, I think. I want it to arrive tomorrow."

"Right, one first class stamp. That will be sixty-four pence."

And she passed the stamp under the window towards William, whilst he passed a one pound coin in the other direction. He stuck the stamp on the card and passed that, too, under the glass panel to Mary.

"Thirty-six pence change."

"Thank you."

Mary put the card in an open sack of post behind her and walked round from the counter into the shop and sat by the till.

"So, you've been invited to High Winds then?"

"Yes, I've been invited for tea next Thursday."

"Next Thursday?"

"Yes, at four o'clock in the afternoon."

"Well, that will be nice. You won't need Wendy that afternoon then?"

"No, I suppose not. I must remember to tell her."

"Yes, or otherwise she will wonder where you've gone to."

"Yes."

"How are you getting on with Wendy, then? Is that all working out?"

"Yes, it is really. It feels comfortable. We get on very well. And she is very good with lists."

"I suppose that must be from living in a caravan. Keeping lists. Might be important if you live in a caravan."

"I suppose so."

"Has she told you how she got here? And her friend? You know, her friend in Devon?"

"Yes, that was sad, wasn't it? But then if she hadn't come here I wouldn't have been able to ask her to be my housekeeper."

"And gardener."

"Yes, and gardener."

"Strange really, her being, you know with her friend and Roderick being, you know with his friend. And now you."

"Yes, now me. And now Wendy and me."

Mary straightened her back and picked up a pencil as if she was about to write something down. But she didn't. Wendy being part of William's life continued to be something of an irritation to her.

"Florence? She's getting on okay, is she?"

"Yes, she seems fine. She is quite settled in."

"Well, that's nice."

"Yes, it is nice, and thank you, Mary, for helping me with that."

"You're welcome, William. I might be making some shortbread this afternoon. Would you like some?"

"I would love some. As I told you, I am very fond of shortbread."

"Good, I'll bring some over then."

"Thank you, that would be very nice."

"This afternoon then. I'll bring some."

"Good."

William walked back to his house, pausing to look at his garden. Now, in the springtime, some parts were beginning to flower. Some would come later. Everything that Roderick had done had been done thoughtfully and with great care. Apart from the lavender bushes and the tall grasses, there was aromatic rosemary, spiky sea holly, white flowered sea kale, pink and yellow verbascum and what would later be purple echinops. Planted in clumps, amidst the grasses and lavender, all were laid in a shingle bed either side of the gravel path. Already, bees were exploring the flower heads.

Later that afternoon, Mary brought to William the first of what would, over time, become many small teatime gifts. Again, the plate of shortbread was covered by a white linen napkin. She knocked on the open door and seeing the row of empty shoes, slipped off her sandals and came in, calling out his name and placing the shortbread on the kitchen worktop. William came from his study and asked if she would like a cup of tea.

"Well, that would be nice," said Mary.

And so William and Mary sat in the living room and this time William prepared the tea, bringing in a tray upon which was a teapot, two white mugs, a jug of almond milk and the shortbread. For some reason, William had felt it necessary to cover the milk with a white lace napkin. Mary was no longer wearing her usual black, but wore a flowered dress and a light blue cardigan. She looked rather lovely.

"I only have almond milk, Mary," said William.

"That's fine," said Mary, unsure what the taste would be like. "Wendy not here then this afternoon?"

"No, she's gone to Waitrose in Saxmundham. She'll call in later."

Once the tea had been poured, a silence fell upon them and, for a while, they sat looking out of the front door of the house towards the sea, its waves turning on the pebble beach. What was it about the movement of the sea upon the beach or the wind making its way through the reed beds? Ancient, ever present, timeless.

They sat there until, for some reason or for no reason at all, William felt rising within him the need to tell Mary why he had come to the house on the marsh. He was overcome with a need to share with someone, someone he hardly knew, his deep sadness. Did he sense that she understood? Perhaps so. And so he began to tell Mary about the death of his wife, Caroline, about his having to leave their house. He even told her about Susan and the burial ground.

"Do you have children, Mary?"

"I have a son, Nicholas."

"Does he live nearby?"

"No, he lives in Dublin. He works for Guinness.

He's a brewer. Like his father was. His father worked for Greene King in Bury St. Edmunds."

"And so Nicholas followed his father?"

"Yes, he did. And now he lives in Dublin."

"Is your son married?"

"Yes, he's married and has two daughters, Bryony and Iris. His wife, Chloe, is Irish."

"Do they come to visit?"

"Not very often. Chloe's parents live close to Dublin and so they spend quite a lot of time there. Her father is not very well. Some kind of heart condition. And Chloe does not like to leave her mother on her own too much."

Mary looked down at her hands, held together on her lap. She missed her son and her grandchildren more than she was saying. William felt a common but unexpressed bond. Loneliness. Separation. He told her of the comfort that was coming from him living in the house by the marsh and the sea, the comfort of the small community of Frampton that he was getting to know. And, of course Florence, who had now taken up a position on the sofa, curled asleep, her left ear twitching now and then as she caught the sound of a seagull.

Mary listened. It was as if being with William, in coming to the house by the marsh, not being in her shop or her tea room, not standing behind the counter of the post office, in being there, she had become another person, the private Mary. She sat quietly and listened to William. Reflecting on what he was saying. When he finished, or seemed to have finished, she said nothing. Silence.

Then after a while, she said, "When I lost Albert, I thought my life had come to an end. In a way, it had. My life with him had come to an end. As you know,

William, it does not get better, you just get used to it. Only those of us who are widowed know that. It does not get better. I was living in Bury St. Edmunds at the time, eleven years ago last March and, like you, I had to go away. A friend told me about the shop and the post office and I sold our house and came here. Then I added the tea room. I like Frampton. It is quiet enough for me to hear Albert when he comes by. Not always, but sometimes."

"You mean Albert speaks to you?"

"Sometimes."

No more was said. It had been said, and as the sound of Wendy's car was heard coming into the driveway, Mary stood up, put on her sandals and said goodbye, leaving the remaining shortbread behind. Wendy delivered the shopping and put it away in the fridge and the larder before setting off home, back to her caravan.

And so it was that William began to take care of himself. Living within the world he was creating for himself. His own world. He had long since stopped listening to the news or reading a newspaper. The news was no longer a part of his life, which had become centred on where he was and whom he was with. He found this to be most agreeable. He plugged in his earphones and listened to Brian Wilson singing 'Love and Mercy' – another man who needed to be loved. Then he checked the gas meter, went to his computer and submitted the latest information for his gas bill.

The next day, he put the remaining shortbread into a tin, and washed and dried the plate, folding the white napkin carefully upon it. As he did so, he had a memory of a monastery on Mount Athos, where he had watched the celebrant priest fold a linen napkin at the end of the Holy Eucharist.

Lady Whitely was in every way average. Neither very tall nor short, neither fat nor thin. Her face and hair quite ordinary. Her clothes were entirely as one would expect: blouse, skirt, cardigan, stockings and sensible shoes. It was as if any unusual or delightfully personal features that she might have had as a young woman had been worn away. And yet she seemed strangely out of place, as if she had been left behind, washed up by a higher than normal tide that had long since ebbed and left her, lost and now unsuited to her surroundings. Her husband had been a diplomat and they had served in places far away, places with embassies and chauffeur-driven cars, receptions and grand dinners. But now, left behind, left behind on her own, she was lost, bereft and perhaps deeply unhappy, but unable to say so.

Losing her husband had not helped. Once he had retired, they had sold their house in London and come to live in High Winds, a house that had belonged to his family for many years, a house that had been used as a holiday home, a house that had brought her husband here as a small boy during Easter and summer holidays, and which he had inherited on the death of his father. In turn, Lady Whitely had inherited the house on the death of her husband, and did not have the means to move away. Or so she thought.

At five minutes past four on that May afternoon, William walked up the gravel drive of High Winds and knocked on the door. He heard the barking of what he supposed must be the 'horrid little dog' of which Mary had spoken. The door opened and Lady Whitely, now holding the dog under one arm, welcomed William and took him through to a large sitting room at the rear of the house overlooking a garden of flower beds and a well-mown lawn. Along one side of the garden, an old and high brick wall supported an extensive wisteria, and at the far end there was a wooden fence with a gate that led into a large field, in the corner of which, behind an overgrown hedge, could be seen Wendy's caravan. They sat down and the dog, a small Jack Russell, was placed in a basket and commanded to stay there, which, to William's great amazement, it did.

Tea was poured, William as usual choosing to have his without milk or sugar. Sandwiches were offered. Their crusts had been removed. It was a very proper English tea. William took one sandwich of egg mayonnaise and one of cucumber in white bread, placing them on his plate, having set over his knees the small white napkin he had also been given.

"So, what brings you to Frampton, Mr Clarke?"

"It's a bit of a story really, Lady Whitely. And would you mind calling me William? I cannot remember when I was last called Mr Clarke, and when you say it I think you are talking about someone else."

"William it is then. And my name is Melissa. You should call me Melissa."

"Thank you, Melissa."

"And this is Toby, he is a rough-coated Jack Russell,

'*Canis lupus familiaris*'."

"Hello Toby."

At the sound of his name, Toby raised an ear, but remained in his basket.

"By the way, I have asked my friends, Neville and Virginia Cutler, to join us for tea. They live just down the road and will be here soon. They rang to say they had been delayed waiting for a parcel to be delivered. But they are on their way."

In a little while, William and Toby heard a car coming to a stop outside the front door. William remained seated, but Toby jumped out of his basket and made for the front door, barking in defence of his mistress, who had risen to meet her guests. A knock on the door and then the sound of voices in the hall, apologies for being late and assurances that this was quite alright. Toby returned to his basket, and then Lady Whitely reappeared leading in a man and a woman. He was tall and slightly stooped, dressed soberly in flannels, a sports jacket, a blue shirt and a tie with pheasants on it. She was large and more colourful. Long greying hair pulled back and fixed with decorative hair clips, not much make-up, but a flowery dress and pink cardigan. They were introduced, Lady Whitely explaining, as she had no doubt before, that William was now living in the house by the marsh, that he was a writer and that he had taken on Wendy as his housekeeper. Tea and sandwiches were served, Neville Cutler entering into an animated conversation with Lady Whitely about something that had happened at the last church meeting, leaving William to talk to his wife, Virginia.

"I hear that you are a painter."

"Yes, I'm a botanical painter. Well, I paint plants.

"My late wife, Caroline, was a botanical painter," said William. "She was rather good."

"Yes, I know."

"You knew Caroline?"

"No. I never met your wife, but I know her work. Well, some of it. Some years ago, a friend of mine took me to see an exhibition of botanical paintings at the Chelsea Physic Garden, and your wife's paintings were there. I remember because I thought they were exceptional. In fact, I bought one."

"You bought one of Caroline's paintings?"

"Yes. It's hanging in our drawing room just up the road."

For a moment, William was overcome by a feeling of both delight and loss. He looked away from Virginia and out into the garden with its wisteria.

"It's a small world, William," said Virginia.

"Isn't it?" he replied.

"Well, you must come and see the painting."

"Yes, I should like that."

"I expect you will know it. It is of red poppies."

"Oh, that one. How lovely."

There was a pause whilst they both drank their tea.

"By the way, William," said Virginia, trying one of the cucumber sandwiches in white bread, "do you read at all?"

"Yes, I read all the time."

"Good. So, would you consider joining our local book club? It's quite jolly, and we only meet every other month. Six times a year. There are nine of us, well, there were; one has just died and we want to find someone else to take his place. What do you think? There's Neville and me, Patty Witherington, who used to be a dancer, Stewart and Kathy Glossop who love music, Lady Whitely, John Baddington who is a dentist in Saxmundham and Gillian Fisher, who you will like. She is quite a well-known writer of cookbooks."

"Well, I think I would like that, if you think I would fit in."

"Oh, I'm sure you will. Let's write down telephone numbers and email addresses."

And so it was that William began to fit in, becoming part of a small but, for the most part, enjoyable community. The book club in particular proved to be more pleasing than he had expected. He had feared that the books selected might not be of much interest to him. But they were, and over the next six months, he found himself reading first a classic, Proust's *Swann's Way*, then Andrea Camilleri's *The Snack Thief*, a detective story based in Sicily, and then a shocking story written by Edna O'Brien, *The Little Red Chairs*. William had thought that having to read books he had not chosen might be a chore, but, on the contrary, it liberated him. By taking from him the burden of choice, he felt free to like or dislike each one. So far he had enjoyed all three, although it was probably not quite true to say he had 'enjoyed' *The Little Red Chairs*, as it was too harrowing. Well written though, and reading work that was well written was a joy.

Shortly after the tea party with Lady Whitely, William received a call from Virginia inviting him to come and have tea with her and look at Caroline's painting. And so he found himself in the sitting room of one of the village cottages eating one of Mary's famous Eccles cakes and looking at the painting of poppies.

"It is wonderful," he said.

"Yes, it is," she replied. And then Virginia talked about her love of plants and showed William some of her own work. She was a good painter, not really a botanical painter, but a painter of plants, painting in oils, with energy and vibrant composition. There was something in the work that suggested an unfulfilled passion.

"Tell me, William, what do you write about?"

"Well, it's a bit of a mixture. I have a couple of things going at the moment. One is an essay on T S Eliot's *The Wasteland*, and the other is about Love, it's for an organisation called The Forum. It's all rather chaotic, but they are trying to find ways of gathering people together to enable a shift in consciousness away from the conventions of a world driven by selfishness and competition and towards the nurturing of love and compassion in our lives."

"That sounds like hard work."

"In some ways it is, although you would be surprised how many people know this has to be done, and are struggling to make it happen. Somehow, it seems, people seem to know instinctively that things are not quite right, but don't have the words for it. I'm trying to help them find those words."

"Do you publish this work?"

"I have done a bit, and some of it is just work-in-progress. Anyway, it keeps me busy."

"So is that what you do at your new house, tucked away in the marshes, with Wendy looking after you?"

"I suppose I do," said William, "and Wendy is wonderful, and a great comfort to me."

"I suppose she cares for you."

"Yes, she does, and she is a good example of what that means, practical loving kindness."

"And when you go away is that in connection with your writing and The Forum?"

"Sometimes it is, and sometimes I just go up to London to keep an eye on my flat, or go to an exhibition or meet a friend. You know, that sort of thing."

After tea, William walked back to his house. It was cold and he pulled his overcoat tight around himself. Looking at Caroline's painting had, once more, touched that sorrow that lay within him, that loss. And, of course, he had again remembered those days when Caroline would go to her studio to paint, her music playing and the cups of tea he would take to her. Then the illness, and then the dying. That evening, he sat in his armchair looking out through the open front door at the marsh and the beach and the sea, with Florence curled up on the sofa. Once more, from deep within, the sadness rose into his throat.

Suddenly, Florence pricked up her ears and sat up peering through the doorway as if someone was there. William, too, thought he heard someone walking along the veranda. He sat forward.

"Anyone there?"

Just the sound of the reeds in the evening breeze.

"Anyone there?"

"It's only me, William."

"… Caroline?"

"Yes, William, it's me. And have you always been sad?"

He waited. And then he said, "Yes, I think I have."

"I wish I had known that while we were together. I knew you often felt anxious, but I didn't really know about the sadness."

William got out of his chair.

"No, William, stay where you are. You can hear me, but you cannot see me. Although I am here, you cannot see me."

"Are you okay, Caroline?"

"Yes, I'm just fine. Thank you for asking."

"That's good."

"I'm sorry I had to leave you, William."

"Yes, I'm sorry, too. And I miss you. I miss that simple intimacy we had. Nothing much said, but knowing you were there."

"But you seem to be settling down, here by the marsh. And I can find you now I know you are here. It was very difficult in London. Too much noise and too much activity. But now that you are here by the marshes I can find you."

"I'm very glad you have found me, Caroline. Nobody really knows how much I miss you. I don't show much of myself to other people."

"That was how we were brought up, William."

"Do you like the house?"

"Yes, William, I do. And I very much like your housekeeper. And Mary, too."

"You do?"

"Yes, just right. Mind how you go."

And then there was silence and, in a while, Florence settled back on the sofa.

It was three years since she had died.

CHAPTER 8

WENDY

All that happened next came about before the postcard arrived. For after that, everything might have changed, forever.

Once William had begun to feel at home in the house by the marsh, he was able to devote his time to his writing, with only occasional trips to London. Each morning, he would work, sitting in his study and looking out of his window towards the sea. This morning, the garden and the marsh were quiet and full of sunshine, but deep within his chest, there was that deep and profound sorrow that Caroline had spoken of. The sadness that Mary had seen in him.

During the day, the sadness remained, and later, with the coming of the evening, as the sun went below the woodland at the back of his house and it became cooler, it was still there. William rose from his chair and went to his dressing room to find a jumper, a particular jumper. It was a light sky-blue in colour, '75% silk, 20% cotton and 5% cashmere', a Banana Republic 'luxury blend' jumper made in China. It was a favourite jumper, and putting it on eased a small part of his suffering.

The following day, he again looked out of his study window towards the sea, the morning sunlight, the bees upon the lavender, the coal tit and then the blue tit feeding from the bird feeder, verbena, cosmos, sea thistle, hydrangea, white butterflies, a gentle breeze moving through the reeds of the marsh, everything moving, if only very slightly, moment by moment. Moment by moment, his life ebbed away.

The phone rang. It was Virginia Cutler.

"William, can you come to tea this afternoon?" she said. "We have someone visiting us who says that he would really like to meet you."

William thought that meeting someone you have never met before and who has said that they would really like to meet you would, of course, lead to great dis- appointment all round, but he said he would love to come and, at about four o'clock, set off up the village street.

It was a delicious tea, with raspberries, ice cream and lemon cake served in a round bowl with a small spoon. And the man who had really wanted to meet him was very agreeable and seemed to have the same intense energy that William himself had once had. The man wrote travel books and he and William had a discussion about writing, which they both did, and travelling, of which William now did very little.

Eventually, most of the tea party, including the agreeable and energetic man, went off for a walk across the marshes and along the beach, and William was left sitting in the garden talking to four women, only one of whom he had met before. Ellen was married to the travel writer; then there was Gillian from the book club, who was a nutritionist and wrote books on cooking; a woman called Lynne, who was recovering from being bitten on the arm by a large dog; and Matilda, who was staying with Virginia and Neville and who had been swimming in the sea. William liked being in their company and being part of the way they talked to each other: easy, personal and inclusive. He joined in until it was time to go and then he walked home and returned to his study to write it all down.

The next morning, William woke quite early, made himself some tea and went back to bed, where, as often happened, after reading for a while, he fell asleep until, at nine o'clock, Wendy knocked on his door to tell him that his breakfast was ready. Suddenly he felt the need for her company.

"I'll be through in a minute. Wait and have a cup of tea with me?"

"Okay."

When he came through, Wendy was sitting on the sofa with Florence, holding a cup of tea in her hands. William brought his tea with him and sat in one of the armchairs.

"Do you still sometimes feel the loss of Ruth?"

"All the time. And you, the loss of Caroline?"

"Yes, all the time."

"It never goes does it? I think love and sadness are kindred. They come together."

"I think so, too. If we choose to love, we will find sadness, too. If you want to love fully you have to allow a space for sorrow. By the way, I had a visit from Caroline the other evening."

"What do you mean a visit?"

"Well, I was sitting here and Florence was on the sofa when suddenly she pricked up her ears as if she had heard someone; and I thought I heard someone, too, someone on the veranda. The front door was open, so I called out and the voice of Caroline replied, telling me not to look for her but just to listen. For a short while, we talked through the open door. Just of this and that; how I was, how she was. You know that sort of thing. She liked the house, and she was pleased you were looking after me."

"Did it feel scary?"

"No, not really. Oddly enough it felt quite normal."

"That must have been rather wonderful. Perhaps it only works if the one you have loved is dead."

"Yes, I suppose that's so. Does Ruth ever get in touch with you?"

"No. She can't really. She doesn't know where I am."

"And you have never tried to get in touch with her?"

"No, I don't think I could do that."

"Perhaps only widows and widowers know what this is like."

"And those like me who have loved and lost. No wonder we mourn, William. Falling in love is just that, falling. And even if there is no return of love, you are where you are."

"Is it possible, Wendy, do you think it's possible to acknowledge one's love for someone, accept its loss, and then live at peace by oneself?"

Wendy did not reply, but looked out into the distance. William opened the door for Florence to go into the garden, but she declined.

"Sometimes I think I should wear black," he said.

"But not today, William, because today is too beautiful for black. And as you can see, I'm wearing my purple cardigan."

They sat and talked for a bit longer, but just about stuff that was going on in the village, and then Wendy washed her cup and left.

"See you later," she said.

"See you later," said William.

William sat for a while. He was okay living by himself in the house by the marsh, with Wendy looking after him and with Mary in the shop and the friends he had begun to get to know. But he needed something else, something more. He wanted to be at peace, at peace with himself, and with his life and where he lived. He wanted this very much, but he was not sure how it could be. Somewhere at the back of his head he remembered reading what the Buddha had said about peacefulness or equanimity. He had talked about 'the Divine Abidings,' which were loving kindness, compassion, joy in and for others and then equanimity. So perhaps that was it. Peace would only come through loving others, without grasping and craving, by being in harmonious relationship with all that is, being aligned with the whole. Right being. He wished he had asked Wendy what she thought about this.

William dreamt that she – he could not in his dream quite tell who she was – that she had held him in her arms, joyously and laughing as if it were a lovely thing to do.

"Stay with me tonight," she had said.

"Or you could stay with me," he had replied.

And, in the dream, this is what they planned to do. Stay together.

He woke and wrote it down. Then he looked at the book he had been reading before going to sleep to see if it was there, but it wasn't.

He wondered whether somewhere out there she, whoever she was, had dreamt it too. But he could, of course, never ask her.

Starting the day with Wendy was becoming a big part of William's life. She was very easy to talk to and she seemed at home in his company. Now, they often sat at breakfast time and had tea together.

"Wendy, do you ever think like this: 'I must do this, and then I can do that'? And then do you find that you do this, but you never get to do that, because once you've done this, there is another 'this' to do, and then another? So you are always doing this and never that."

"It's a bit early in the day to answer conundrums,

William. Isn't there anything else we could talk about?"

William had a sense that everything might be otherwise. Somehow he knew that nothing was as it was said to be. Every explanation was at best provisional, a pointing towards; fingers pointing at the moon. No sooner was it said to be so than it was found not to be. There are no straight lines and no linear progressions, however much we might suppose there might be. So he asked Wendy about it.

"Have you ever thought, Wendy, that nothing goes from worse to better or from better to worse in a straight line; all that is, is just as it is. And nothing can be described completely. At best, there is a glimpse, a catching of a breath of wind, a water drop in a stream. No more than that. And what is, is infinitely more wonderful than anyone can imagine. No beginning and no end – or rather no beginning no end; no centre no perimeter; everything intermingled, interfused in ways we cannot see."

"You're very philosophical this morning."

"Well, it seems to me that this must be how it is, otherwise none of it makes sense. Do you think that can be how it is? The unknowable mystery and the simple everyday and nothing in between. That's how it seems to me, and the rest is mere speculation. All we can do is eat our breakfast and wash our bowl, wash and go to bed. There is nothing other than this. Sadness, sorrow and love. I have been having another look at the poetry of T S Eliot. I studied his work quite closely some years ago, and I am coming back to it again. He said a lot about being and time. 'In my beginning is my end.' Do you think that's how it is?"

Wendy did not respond, but stood up and took her cup

to the kitchen. As she passed behind William's chair, she bent down and kissed him gently on the head. She washed her cup and began to dry it with a plain white tea towel.

"Have you ever wondered, Wendy, whether there can be anything other than all that is, whether there can be nothingness? No-thingness?"

"Stop, William. Couldn't you just ask me about my new dungarees?"

"Well, they are lovely, but what do you think about the possibility of no-thingness?"

Wendy sighed, and came to sit in the chair beside William.

"Well," she said, "the men in white coats say there cannot be such a thing. They say there must always be something, and their latest idea is that nothingness is some kind of energy or dark matter. In fact, they say that this dark matter, which sounds sinister but apparently isn't, is said to make up most of the observable universe. But we don't know what it is, or at least the men in white coats don't know because, it seems, we cannot measure it."

"I read something about that the other day" said William. "Apparently, they now think, well, scientists now think, that instead of slowing down – which is what everyone thought before – the expansion rate of space is increasing over time. It's all a bit of a mystery. What they call 'dark energy' accounts for more than seventy percent of the mass of the universe."

"That is very mysterious."

"Yes, but here's another thing, Wendy. When the Buddha spoke of nothingness, or emptiness, he put it in a different way. He said there is no thing that is not contingent upon some other thing. There is no absolute, solitary thing-ness. Everything is in relationship, part of what he called dependent origination. Everything is coming to be, coming to be, ceasing to be, ceasing to be. Causing to be, caused to be."

"I think I like that idea of nothingness better," said Wendy. "Give me your cup."

"Thank you. And thank you for letting me waffle on like this. Shall I see you this afternoon?"

"Yes, in fact I might do some work in the garden and then come and have tea with you."

"That sounds like a plan, a good plan."

"See you later."

"Yes. See you later."

William's colleagues in the Academy in London had asked him to present a paper on Eliot's poetry and what it said to us now. So he was sitting in his study, staring at his computer screen, hoping he could find the words he needed. He wanted to combine Eliot's notions of time and being with his own ideas about Love being of the essence. He wanted to place all of this within the present crises of environmental, social and economic disorder and possible catastrophe. It seemed to William that wherever he went people were always asking the wrong questions. "What shall we do about this … ?" "Isn't it that terrible … ?" Trapped by the frenzy of the news, no one stopped to wonder why things were as they were; why it was that this or that happened; why it was that one calamity seemed to follow the next. It seemed that whilst the questions that everyone was asking were often important, they ignored the need, first, to be sure about the causal questions: how are we and how might we be? "Surely," he thought to himself, "being must precede doing, otherwise there is no foundation for what we do; no ground on which to stand. Everything has its cause. Nothing comes from nothing – nothing ever could." Was that Parmenides or Julie Andrews? He couldn't quite remember. Unless, of course, everything comes from nothing, the primal darkness within the universe and within each one of us. "That," he thought, "might well be so."

Apparently, those Existentialists (where are they now?), when they were not smoking Gauloises and drinking Pernod, or perhaps while they were, suggested that we all suffer from the fear of meaninglessness, powerlessness, isolation, and freedom. These, they said, are not to be denied, but to be acknowledged, because this is what it is to be alive. Each one of us does what we can, forever bearing the imprint or shadow of our childhood. William certainly knew about that, and now thought that this shadow arose from our capacity to fear. He thought he should ask Wendy about it. Perhaps all species have some kind of fearfulness, but for us, as in so much else, the capacity is so developed that we can do great damage when we are afraid. He began to write.

Some days later, Wendy and William were, as usual, having their morning tea together.

"So, William, tell me what you're writing about at the moment."

"It's still Love."

"So tell me something about it. Speak to me of Love." And she laughed.

William was silent for a moment, unsure whether he could speak of Love to this young woman who had entered into his life. He knew so little about her, and yet, oddly, he felt strangely at peace with her.

"Well, my dear Wendy," he began, and she smiled at his patronising, but gentle, endearment. "Let me read you a bit of what I was writing yesterday. It's about Love and Fear." And he got up and went into his study, returning with a few pages of text.

"Are you sitting comfortably?" She smiled again. "Well, I'll begin. This is what I was writing yesterday. 'Once upon a time, a time which was then and now and forever will be, Love dwelt amongst us, in the corners and shadows of our lives, emerging now and then in the arms of a mother, or in a father teaching his son to ride a bicycle. Love was there all the time, the pulse of all that is, but we felt unable to speak of her openly. Living as we did, and as we do, and perhaps as we shall do, we dared not speak of Love, lest we should be thought to be foolish. Instead, we nourished her sibling, Fear. It was Fear that set us apart, Fear that encouraged us to always want more than we had, lest we should not have enough, Fear that lay beneath our hatred and our greed. And for a while this seemed to serve us well. But most recently, we have had more and more, seeking identity in 'stuff,' and we have been able to vent our Fear on people far away without much harm to ourselves.'"

William paused and looked towards Wendy who was now curled up in her chair, her head to one side, resting on a cushion.

"Shall I go on?"

"Yes, please."

"Where was I? Yes, here we are: 'Most recently, we have had more and more, seeking identity in 'stuff,' and we have been able to vent our Fear on people far away without much harm to ourselves.' So I finish up by saying, 'However, perhaps this is about to change and the true consequences of our fearful actions are about to be felt. Perhaps this will arise in the greater disturbance of our weather, with at the same time both drought and inundations of storm, rain and flooding, and with the migration of peoples from the most damaged and fearful places to those that seem to be safe. Those who do not have enough to eat or drink or who are in the midst of violent conflict will become a multitude of migration. And, in part, they will be fleeing from what we have brought upon them.'"

William put down his papers, and drank some of his tea.

"Not much fun, then," said Wendy uncurling herself and sitting forward with her head in her hands, her elbows resting upon her knees.

"I suppose not."

"Unless we choose Love."

"Yes, unless we choose Love."

As often happened when they were having tea together, they fell into silence, each letting thoughts come and go.

"Did I ever tell you about Jennifer?"

"Jennifer? No, I don't think so."

"I fell in love with her, or I thought I did."

"When was this?"

"Shortly after my wife died, when I had escaped to London. I was invited to supper with friends and there she was. Beautiful. Vulnerable. Or so I thought. She had been divorced for some years and now lived with her dog, Henry."

"And you were captured, I suppose?"

"Yes, I was. Entirely. We spent quite a bit of time together and I thought – remember I was hopelessly vulnerable too, mad, quite mad – I thought we were in love."

"Oh dear."

"Yes, as you say, 'Oh dear.' And, of course, it all went wrong. We weren't in love. I wasn't in love with Jennifer, I was in love with the idea of being in love. In the end, we just went our separate ways. And then I came here."

"What are we like, William?"

"What are we like, Wendy?"

The next day, when William woke, it was raining, raining hard, the wind sweeping the rain across the marsh and the sound of the rain on the roof. He had woken, lost and alone, but felt better once Wendy had come to the house and was making breakfast. Later the rain passed away and the day became clear and sunny.

It is the rhythm and punctuation of the everyday that opens up the possibility of our transformation and transcendence. "Eat your breakfast. Wash your bowl," as the Master said to the Buddhist monk. "It is necessary," said William to himself. True 'being' can only be in the moment. We have our supper; we go to bed; we wake up; we wash; we have our breakfast; we wash our bowl. We dwell moment by moment, not in the future or the past – no plans, no regrets, no expectations. "And, at the end of the day, wash your face and go to bed." And so the sadness remains.

What else is there to say?

As the days passed, William came to rely more and more upon Wendy being with him. It wasn't just the work she did for him, it was her presence, too. It was good to know she would be there in the morning, that they would talk and that she would come again in the afternoon. Without noticing it, he was growing very fond of her, the differences between them seeming to make their relationship more open, generous and comfortable. There was an ease in just being with this young woman, something he had not before experienced. It was a kind of love, but without the complication of any sexual entanglement, it seemed especially tender and nourishing. It was true that when she came to the house and used his shower he enjoyed the sensation of her newly washed body as she walked back into the living room and sat down for tea, her smell and the flush of her skin, but for reasons he could not understand, it was simply that, a thing of beauty, a thing to be enjoyed, not a thing to be possessed. She was just there. And it was clear from her behaviour and the easy way she moved about the house that Wendy also felt at home. Something about William attracted her to him. Perhaps it was that he liked to talk to her, that she could be so direct with him and that he opened himself up to her without wanting anything from her except that she should be there.

One day William asked her about Ruth. He wanted to know how they had met and what had attracted Wendy to her; whether it had happened at once or whether they had known each other for a while and had grown to love one another.

"I tell you what," said Wendy, "why don't you come and have supper with me in my caravan this evening and then I will tell you. Would that work?"

"I'd like that very much. Would six-thirty be too early for you? You know what I'm like, not liking to eat too much or too late in the evening."

"That would be perfect and it will be very light. Probably scrambled eggs on toast."

"Excellent."

And so that evening William walked to the other end of the village and knocked on the door of Wendy's caravan. There was nothing special about it, it looked like all the other caravans he had ever seen, white and humped. But when Wendy opened the door and invited him in, he entered another world, her world. The interior of the caravan had been decorated with drapes of coloured material, red and orange and yellow and gold. It was like the inside of some kind of exotic tent, lit by oil lamps, with cushions large and small and then the smallest kitchen you could possibly imagine. A table had been set with napkins and a white cloth and William slid into his place on the bench seat feeling an odd excitement, as if he was setting off on an adventure, sitting in a tent in some wonderland far away. Wendy had put a bottle of red wine on the table and asked William to pour them both a glass, which he did. Glasses in hand they toasted 'friendship' and laughed as if they were in some way misbehaving, as if the grown-ups would not be told about it. Then Wendy cooked the scrambled eggs, which came to the table with two bowls of green salad.

"No onions, William."

"Thank you, Wendy."

For a while, they ate their supper and talked about what each one had been doing that day, William writing his paper for the Academy, and Wendy dog-sitting for Lady Whitely and running errands for her. But both knew that there was a story to be told. And so as they sat together Wendy began to tell William the story of how she had first met Ruth at a party in London and how they had quickly become close friends before, at Ruth's suggestion, Wendy had moved into her flat so that they could live together.

"You know, William, I'd had friends before that, close friends, lovers. But I'd never lived with anyone before. Just slept over sometimes. And, at first, it was strange. You know getting used to sharing someone's life up close, toothbrushes in the same glass, knickers and T-shirts in the same wash. But I really liked it. I'd been on my own for a while and I liked being part of Ruth's life, buying food together, curling up on the sofa and watching TV, laughing at gossip and work stuff. I liked being loved and cared for, having someone hold me in their arms. And I was riding high, loving and caring for Ruth. I loved that. For a while, it seemed like a small part of heaven. We were really happy."

William leant across and filled Wendy's half-empty glass with wine, pouring the last few drops into his own. Wendy continued her story, telling it with an intensity that made clear that the telling was important to her. She wanted the story to be heard. She wanted to hear it.

"And so, after about a year, we decided we wanted to get away from London and we went to live in Totnes, in Devon, where Ruth used to live. Her dad had a house there, which he'd been letting out, and, as if by chance, the tenant had moved away and it was empty. He asked Ruth if she would like it. We jumped at it. We had this idea that we would be starting a new life together. You know, a grown-up life. Ruth is an occupational therapist and, again, as if by chance, there was a job vacancy in the local hospital. It seemed too good to be true.

"We loved the house; a small terraced house with a long garden at the back. Ruth was busy in her new job, and sometimes she had to work during evenings and at weekends. I didn't mind, I'd taken up an interest in gardening, and I soon found jobs gardening for other people. And I loved our garden. We had vegetables and herbs and flowers. We even had an apple tree, cooking apples. And I took on the domestic chores, laundry, shopping, cleaning. I suppose I was the housekeeper and gardener,"

They laughed.

"For a while it all seemed to work well and our

relationship, our living together, seemed to be deepening. But, looking back, I can see something was missing. It was almost as if we were playing 'happy families.' In a funny way, I think we both wanted to be a family and we convinced ourselves that we were.

"Anyway, one day, quite unexpectedly, we had a row. Ruth had taken exception to something I'd said about the possibility of her taking a few days off so that we could explore the countryside around Totnes together, you know just bed and breakfast and a few visits, nothing very special. For some reason, she thought I was saying that she was always at work and never had time for fun. She said something about being the one who always paid for everything. And I said it wasn't that. And she said, well, what was it then? You know how that happens. You are cross with each other, but don't know why.

"We let it go and nothing more was said. But the next day I realised that something had been broken. I felt I'd been told off. As if I was just a silly little girl made to feel small by her mother. It was probably a misunderstanding, but, for whatever reason, there seemed no way of putting it together again. Well, not then. And when the end came, it was sudden.

"I woke up one morning and it felt as if I had been sleeping in a bed with a stranger. Ruth went to work. I rang my uncle about his caravan. I packed a bag and left on the lunchtime train to London. I stayed with a friend for a few days, and then I came here. It's a bit odd, isn't it?"

"Yes, it is a bit odd. But sometimes the rows we have with people we love have nothing to do with what seems to be the cause. They're about something else, something we haven't been able to say."

"Perhaps I got it all jumbled up. Anyway, I know she didn't like the rings in my eyebrows."

"I quite like them."

"Yes, but you are not my lover."

"No, that's true."

Silence. The telling of the story had drawn them closer together. Caring for each other.

"Thank you for listening, William. You are good to me and I am very fond of you."

"And you are good to me, Wendy, and I am very fond of you, too."

"I will always tell you if I have to run away again. Tell you before I go."

"Thank you. Yes, that would be helpful. But not for a bit, I hope."

"Nothing planned for the moment."

"Good. By the way, if you ever need to be in London for a while, you can always borrow my flat. Just ask."

"Thank you, William. I will."

"Good."

Wendy made some camomile tea, which they drank without talking, just sitting together. Quiet and at ease. After a while, William said he should be off to bed, and giving Wendy a hug, he opened the door of the caravan and walked out into the night, leaving behind the exotic tent. He walked through the village, which was now silent. No lights nor any sound from High Winds and just one or two lights in the houses along the street. He walked past Mary's shop and on towards the marsh. As he came to his house he could hear the sound of the sea moving the shingle up and down the beach, the moon now high in the sky, its beam touching the reeds of the marsh. He unlocked his door and went inside, returning once more to his own rooms, the familiar sound of his feet upon the oak floor and the sight of Florence curled up on her cushion on the seat in his study. He undressed, washed his face and beard, cleaned his teeth and went to bed, pulling his duvet around him without putting on the bedside lamp or reading his book. The light of the moon was enough. For a while, he lay there, quite still, letting all that had happened to him and all that Wendy had told him come to rest. And then he slept.

CHAPTER 9

THE POSTCARD

It was morning. Another day was beginning. It was a quarter to nine and he was still in bed. He had woken earlier and had sat up to read his book, but as usual, he had fallen back to sleep, his book lying on his chest. Now he was awake again and could hear Wendy moving around in the kitchen, preparing his breakfast and, as it turned out, dusting and polishing the bookshelves. For a moment he thought he would go back to sleep, but then he got out of bed and went to have his morning shower.

He washed and cleaned his teeth. Then he dressed: pants, T-shirt, brown cords, blue top, socks and Kilim slippers. He brushed his hair, put on his glasses, picked up his notebook and his water glass and walked through to have his breakfast. Another day had begun.

"Morning, Wendy, thank you for supper."

"My pleasure."

"And I loved your caravan. It was like entering into a world of make-believe."

Wendy smiled and brought William his tea.

As he sat there, he made a list of things to buy: soap, shampoo and toothpaste. Something to do, something to encourage him to walk down to the High Street. He looked out of the window and saw that it was grey and still, with a light rain. Not so very encouraging.

So the weeks and the months passed, summer giving way to autumn. The days became colder and William now kept the front door closed during the day, and in the evening lit the wood stove for warmth. The light was ebbing and the dark part of the year was in flood. Florence found warm places to sit, when in doubt always favouring the cushion on the chair in William's study with the radiator close by.

And so on, and so on. His life seemed to proceed on its own, and he was happy to drift. Mostly. It was the moments of waking that were difficult. Either a dream or something he had read would mean that he would often wake, anxious, or with a dull sense of gloom. In those waking moments of half sleep, he would lie on his back, not moving, but with his eyes open, trying to reconstruct his world, putting it back together with memories and regrets from yesterday and fears for tomorrow, eventually clothing it with a sufficient cover of competence to get out of bed and start again. On these mornings – and it was not every morning – on these mornings, he felt as if he was waiting. Yes, that was it, it was like sitting in a waiting room, fearful of what he was about to be told, just as he had done many times during those years of remission when he and Caroline had gone up to Harley Street for her annual check-up. Sitting there almost unable to move. Unable to speak. Until one day they had said, "There's a lump." And later there was the brain tumour. Sudden. Unexpected.

But then one morning towards the end of November he had to go to London for a meeting with a colleague from the Academy. Wendy drove him to Saxmundham to catch the train. Saxmundham to Ipswich. Change trains. Ipswich to London. He took a taxi from Liverpool Street station, and as it made its way westwards towards his flat, he was soon beginning to wish he had stayed at home. It seemed so difficult to move in London, so many people he did not know, the traffic congested by endless roadworks or by building sites that took up half of the street. Anyway, eventually he was there, and now, full of grumpiness, he opened the front door and found the usual pile of post on the doormat. Most of it went straight into the recycling bin: flyers, letters from estate agents to 'The Owner,' charity envelopes with pens inside and so on. Then there were a few envelopes to be ripped open, bills mostly. But, unexpectedly, this time there was a postcard. It was a picture of a beach with parasols and palm trees and a sky-blue sea. He turned it over. It was from Jennifer: 'Taking a holiday, but will be back soon. How are you?' And under her signature she had written her mobile phone number. It was dated ten days earlier. William put the postcard into his pocket.

It was still in his pocket the next day when, at lunchtime, he took the trains from Liverpool Street to Ipswich and then from Ipswich to Saxmundham, where Wendy was waiting to take him home.

"How was your trip?"

"Fine, I suppose."

"That sounds a bit …"

"Well, I find London so tiring, all those busy people and all the traffic, sitting in taxis, hardly moving, not going anywhere."

"Anything exciting?"

"No, nothing really."

As they came to the village, William took the postcard from his pocket.

"This was lying on my doormat at the flat."

"What is it?"

"It's a postcard from Jennifer. It had been lying there for several days. Just lying there waiting for me."

"Jennifer, the one with the dog?"

"Yes. And she has written her mobile number under her signature."

"That must mean, 'Please call me.'"

"Yes, I think it must."

They had now arrived at the house, and William got out of the car and stood looking across the marsh and the beach towards the sea. They went inside and Wendy made some tea and brought it to the table between the sofas and the chairs. They sat for a while until William got up and lit the wood stove, leaving the postcard on the table.

"So, are you going to call her?"

"I don't know. When I first saw her signature and the number underneath, I thought I would. But then I didn't."

"And now?"

"And now I don't know. What do you think?"

"It's hardly up to me, William," said Wendy, somewhat

surprised by a sudden feeling of jealousy. Ridiculous.

Later William took the postcard into his study and propped it up on one of the bookshelves. And Wendy said goodnight and drove back to her caravan.

Left alone, and now back beside the marsh, with the sound of the sea and the wind, William, tired by his journey, wanted to be at ease, but something was in the way. He picked up some papers from his study and sat down in his armchair. It was a text he had been preparing for a meeting of The Forum, drawing together earlier work on the nature of the sacred. He had been working on it before he had been to London, before the postcard. He looked at the words, but could not pay attention.

Two days later, William received news that Neville Cutler had died. A heart attack. Apparently, he'd had a weak heart for some years, and one morning when he didn't come down for breakfast, Virginia had found him collapsed in the bathroom. He was wet all over and had a towel wrapped round his body. He must have been getting out of the bath. She had called for an ambulance, but when it came, he was already dead. It was very shocking. Sudden. Virginia would never recover from it.

William wrote a letter of condolence and posted it through her letterbox, unable to meet her in her grief. Too difficult for him. But he did attend the funeral the following week. Someone had made up two large flower arrangements, each one placed on a pedestal either side of the coffin, and all of the people of the village William had come to know were there, sitting in rows on the old wooden pews, dressed in black, with overcoats and scarves. Mary sat with Winny and the postman, Richard. Wendy was there with Lady Whitely. William sat by himself. The church was quite full with Virginia's children and grandchildren, people who had known Neville in the past, colleagues who had worked with him, the book club. The inside of the church was very plain, white plastered walls, with ancient roof trusses and some decoration where the timbers crossed or came together. One of their sons spoke kindly of his father, remembering things from childhood, and even the vicar managed to restrain his talent for banality and took care with the prayers and the committal.

After the service, a reception was held at their house, where the painting of the poppies still hung, but William did not stay for long. Too many memories. He walked home and sat in his study looking out towards the sea. He had not been there long when he saw Mary coming along the veranda. She knocked on his door and he went through to the living room and let her in. She was carrying a plate covered in a white napkin.

"I thought you might like some shortbread. Cheer you up."

"Cheer me up?"

"Yes, you know, after the funeral. Cheer you up a bit."

"That is very kind of you, Mary."

"Well, I don't like funerals very much either."

"Would you like some tea?"

"Alright then."

And so William and Mary had tea and shortbread together, each one bringing comfort to the other, as widows and widowers do. Who else?

"I don't quite understand how the pain lasts for as long as it does," said Mary.

"No. It just stays there, doesn't it?"

"Yes, it does."

"What do you think Virginia will do now, now that Neville has gone?"

"I don't think she will stay here."

"No, perhaps not. Nothing stays still for very long, does it? Thank you for coming to be with me. It was very thoughtful of you."

"You are welcome, William. Most welcome."

The next day William returned the plate and the napkin to Mary, storing the remaining shortbread in a tin. The plate had been washed and dried and the napkin folded neatly upon it. The monastery on Mount Athos.

Three months after Neville Cutler's funeral, a 'For Sale' board was erected outside Virginia's cottage. Left on her own, she had decided to leave Frampton and go to live in a village in Kent, close to where her oldest son lived with his family. And, within a few weeks, a removal van was parked outside and Caroline's painting of the poppies and what now remained of Virginia's possessions were carried out and taken away, Virginia following in her car.

A few days before, William had been invited for a

'Goodbye' drink with the now familiar company, Lady Whitely, the book clubbers, Winny and Mary, and, of course, Wendy. There were also two women William had not met before, and they were soon introduced to him as the new owners of the cottage. Their names were Brenda Rankin and Penelope Brown. They were sisters, the first being a spinster and the second having been widowed some years before, after which they had decided to live together. And now they were to come to Frampton, because it was where they had been brought for holidays as children. Both full of bubbling energy, they now set about discovering who William was. Holding his glass of elderflower cordial, William did his best to explain how it was he had come to the house by the marsh. And talking over each other in a continuous burble of comment and question, the two sisters soon made it clear that they hoped he would be amongst the first to come and have tea with them, "or even supper!"

The day after Virginia departed, another removal van arrived led by Brenda and Penelope in a small, but quite new car from which they bounced clutching armfuls of cushions and pillows, and giving a stream of orders to the removal men about what was to go where, and to take care not to break anything or bang the furniture against the walls. And when William went down to Mary's shop to buy some Sellotape, there they were, with baskets and bags, buying not only provisions for their larder but also bottles of Fairy Liquid, shampoo and Flash window cleaner. They had already put together such a pile of goods beside Mary's till that she had to take William to the post office counter to let him pay for the Sellotape.

Brenda and Penelope greeted William and he asked them if they had settled in.

"You've met Mary, of course. Have you tried her Eccles cakes?"

"No, not yet," said Brenda.

"Well, you must. They're legendary. And she also makes the most wonderful shortbread."

"Well, Mary," said Penelope, not wanting to be left out of the conversation, "we must try some. We are beginning to feel quite at home. You know our parents brought us here as children, and now we live together, so we have come back. We have such happy memories."

"That's nice."

Mary was clearly reserving judgement.

"We shall soon be asking you to supper, William," said Brenda.

"Oh, that would be lovely."

And with that William walked back to his house with his Sellotape, leaving Mary to cope with her new customers.

In the weeks that followed, William did have supper with Brenda and Penelope.

"And would you like to bring a friend?"

Obviously they were not sure what 'a friend' might mean for William, but he said yes and asked Wendy if she would like to come with him.

"Well, actually I would like that" Wendy said. "I

wonder what they are like?"

"You are about to find out."

The supper was very good. Brenda and Penelope had clearly sought guidance from Mary about what William liked to eat, which as it turned out, suited Penelope's own vegetarian preferences. They provided an egg and tomato quiche with potatoes and green salad, followed by an apple crumble and ice cream, just the kind of food that William liked. A glass or two of red wine. Brenda and Penelope were delightful company, irreverent, sardonic and witty, with a charming and deliberate over-the-top-ness of opinion that had everyone laughing.

"So, Wendy, however did you come to be living in a caravan and looking after a frightful old man?" To which Wendy gave a shortened story of her life, including her flight from Devon.

"Oh, I know all about that," said Brenda taking a large gulp of her wine. "That's just what happened to me. Many years ago, but just the same sort of thing. My love was called Veronica and she was a headmistress. Totally taken up with her work and, as I later discovered, with the French language teacher. Left me high and dry and I bolted, just like you. Went to live in Portugal for a few years. Then I came back and got on with the rest of my life. Loss is such a pain."

"I don't know what you ever saw in her," said Penelope with a touch of indignation in her voice. "When I met her, I thought she was a dreadful woman, bossy and dull as dishwater. But then I didn't know she was your lover."

"Well, you were very naïve, my dear Penelope. It must have been living in Bedford all that time. And anyway, I thought your Reggie was utterly dull. Those awful baggy cords and that pipe."

"Well, at least he didn't run off with a French language teacher."

"He wouldn't have had the imagination."

This skirmish brought conversation to a standstill for a moment or two. William took the last spoonful of his crumble and placed his spoon and fork together on his plate.

"Isn't it odd," he said, "the people we fall in love with? Love. Odd really."

"What do you mean?"

"Well, until my wife died, I thought I understood love. We had met and married when we were very young and so we knew nothing about love really. We just made it up as we went along. Some of that was good and some was not. Looking back, I don't think either of us ever really grew up. We managed our lives dutifully, but we never asked questions about it. So, when Caroline died, I was left with a gaping hole. Not only was I grieving for my loss of her, I was grieving for what had happened to me, inside me. And I still am."

Again, they were silent, and Brenda went into the kitchen and put the kettle on the stove.

"Coffee or tea?"

"Coffee," said Wendy.

"Could I have a mint tea?" said William.

They left the table and went to sit in the sitting room at the back of the cottage where a fire had been lit. Brenda brought in the teas and coffees with a box of chocolates. Perhaps it was the red wine, but in such a short time they had opened themselves up to each other, and now it was as if they felt they had said too much. The conversation slipped back into village gossip, with Brenda and Penelope asking questions about Lady Whitely, the vicar and their neighbours. At about ten-thirty, William and Wendy left and William walked Wendy to her caravan. As they walked up the village street, she slipped her arm through his. Being 'a couple' at a supper party had somehow made a difference.

When William got home he found a queen bumblebee on the windowsill of his study. She had been trying to find a way out and was now exhausted. He lifted her up on a bookmark he found lying by his computer and carried her to the front door. Opening the door, he placed her carefully on one of the lavender bushes in his garden.

William woke early the next morning, unable to sleep. He got up, put on his dressing gown and sat at his computer looking out over the marsh, the beach and the sea. After a while, he stood up, wrapped a scarf around his neck, put on some shoes and, opening the front door, walked down the steps of the veranda and onto the walkway through the marsh. The bumblebee had gone.

He walked onto the beach and went down to the sea. It was cold, but there was no wind and the sea was calm, lapping onto the shingle. The sun was still below the horizon. For a few minutes he stood there, taking in the silence broken only by the first of the seagulls calling out to each other. William turned and walked back to the house, closed the door behind him and, still wrapped in his scarf, took off his shoes and walked back into his study. He picked up his phone and rang his daughter's telephone number.

"Hello Jane. It's me."

"Dad?"

"Yes."

"Are you alright? It's a bit early, isn't it?"

"Well, I couldn't sleep and I have just walked down to the sea and back."

"You sound a bit odd."

"I was just wondering whether you had felt loved as a child. You know, whether your mum and I made you feel loved."

"I think so. Most of the time anyway."

"And do you make sure Ben and Sally feel loved?"

"Yes, I think so. Dad, what's this all about?"

"Just sadness, darling. Don't take any notice."

"It's a bit difficult not to take notice at seven o'clock in the morning."

"Yes, sorry. I had better go and have a shower and get dressed. Let's speak later. Bye."

"Okay. Bye. But ring me later."

"Okay. Bye."

William put down the phone, showered, cleaned his teeth and dressed – pants, T-shirt, linen trousers and a black zip-up cardigan. He tied a favourite dull green cotton scarf around his neck and put on bright green socks and Kilim slippers.

When Wendy arrived at nine o'clock, she found him in his study, searching through some papers.

"Morning, William."

"Good morning, Wendy."

"Well, that was a bit unexpected."

"What was?"

"Supper. Brenda's story. All of that."

"Yes, it was a bit."

Wendy stopped and looked at William as he lifted one heap of papers and then another, sorting through each pile as if something had been lost.

"Are you alright, William?"

"Well, not quite."

"Anything special or just the general gloom of being?"

William laughed.

"Were you happy as a child, Wendy? Did your parents love you, make you feel loved?"

"Yes, I was loved. Why?"

"I was just wondering."

"My father was very easygoing. And my mother took charge of our lives. Everything. She really mothered us, and Daddy was just there, always there. He encouraged us and praised us and made us feel special, whereas Mum did all the things mothers do, all the everyday management of our lives, clothes, packed lunches, teatime, dentist appointments, swimming lessons. All that sort of stuff."

"Are they still alive? I realise I've never asked you if they are still alive."

"Yes, they are. They live in Wales, which is why I don't get to see them very much. But we talk on the phone a lot."

"Do you have a phone in the caravan?"

"Mobile phone, William. You know, those slim shiny things we carry with us everywhere we go."

"Yes, of course. Sorry. Stupid."

"You seem a bit uneasy this morning," Wendy said,

sensing his anxiety. "Did something happen?"

"Well, I didn't sleep very well. Probably the wine and eating later than I like. And when I got home I had to rescue a bumblebee. Then this morning I went out early and walked down to the sea. The bumblebee had gone. Something unsettling. I don't know."

"I'll make breakfast."

"Good. That's good."

All that day, the unease remained with William. Just there, a few paces off, but there. His deep wound making itself felt. He sat in his study most of the day, answering emails, working on his papers for The Forum. But when Wendy came back in the afternoon to make his tea and feed Florence, he came through into the living room.

"Would you mind staying with me for a while, Wendy?"

She turned towards him and, for a moment, and for the first time, she saw an elderly man, a man coming towards the last span of his life. She poured two mugs of tea and came and sat down. For a while, they just sat there, William on the sofa and she in one of the armchairs.

"Is there something worrying you, William?" she asked.

William drank some of his tea and then put the mug on the table in front of him.

"It's not just loss, Wendy. There is something else, something much more difficult to see. The loss is evident, but this 'something else' is felt much more deeply and is much more difficult to name. Somehow or other, on days like this, I am ill at ease. I know that in my innermost being I am nothing but a tiny part of something all around me and far beyond. It's alright, but it is a bit scary. We spend so much of our lives trying to take control, but in the end we have to surrender to what is. 'Coming to be, coming to be, ceasing to be, ceasing to be.' A dot in the universe, or rather a dot upon a dot."

Wendy made no reply, but she stood up and came to William, sitting beside him on the sofa. Without a thought, she put her arms around him and held him.

"We may be dots upon a dot," she said, "but, for the time being, we care for each other."

"Yes, let's do that, Wendy. Let's care for each other." He put his arm around her and she rested her head on his shoulder. For some time they stayed there, and soon Florence joined them until, after a while, they separated and drank some more of their tea.

"Wendy, did I ever tell you about the Buddhist sage, Nagarjuna?"

"No."

"Let me read you something."

And standing up from the sofa, William went into his study and came back holding a book.

"I thought you might like this. It is from Stephen Batchelor's *Verses from the Centre.*"

And opening the book, and once again sitting beside her, he began to read:

"In seeing things
To be or not to be,
Fools fail to see
A world at ease."

"It's rather wonderful, isn't it? 'A world at ease.' Wonderful. And so ancient. It's the being in control and holding on, that causes our suffering."

"And are you 'holding on,' William?"

"Just a bit."

More than four years had passed.

One Monday morning in April, as Wendy was preparing breakfast, she said, "William, can you look after yourself for two or three days? I am going to London to see some friends."

"Yes, I'll be fine. Anyone special?"

"Just friends. I'll be back on Thursday morning."

"Okay. Have a good time. See you on Thursday."

"I'm going to set off this afternoon. Is that okay?"

"Yes, of course. By the way, do you want to use my flat?"

"Well, that would be great. Are you sure?"

"Yes, of course."

And he went into his study to fetch the key and gave it to Wendy, telling her where the flat was and how it worked, hot water, heating, that sort of thing.

"This is really kind of you, William."

"My pleasure. If there is any post for me, perhaps you could bring it back with you?"

"Yes, of course. Especially postcards!"

Wendy finished clearing away the breakfast things, put a white load into the washing machine, and left, leaving William a note reminding him to feed Florence and transfer the washing to the tumble drier. Then she was off.

William went into his study and began to look at his list of things to do. For some reason, he felt unsettled, as if aware of something that might have gone wrong, but unable to tell what it was. And that afternoon, he walked down to Mary's shop.

"Hello, William."

"Hello, Mary. I've come for tea."

"Good. Where would you like to sit? By the window?"

"Yes, that's fine."

"Just tea, William?"

"And could I have some of your shortbread?"

"Tea and shortbread."

"Thank you."

Mary disappeared and came back a few minutes later carrying a tray with a cup and saucer, a plate, a napkin, a pot of tea and a plate of shortbread. She set them down on William's table and then, as there was no one else in the shop, sat down opposite him. She was wearing black again.

"Everything all right with you, William?"

"Yes, mostly so. Wendy and I had supper with our new neighbours, Brenda and Penelope."

"Oh," said Mary sitting back in her chair and folding her arms, "so you went with Wendy? That must have been nice."

"Have you got to know them at all?"

"Not really, but I thought they might be inviting you because they came in the other day and asked what sort of food you liked. I felt like saying Eccles cakes and shortbread, but I told them what you usually chose from the freezer. I hope that was okay."

"Yes, it was fine. Thank you. Nothing worse than going out to supper and finding you are being asked to eat something you can't bear."

"They could have asked you."

"Yes, they could. But they asked you and that was fine."

"They seem very jolly."

"They are very entertaining."

William poured his tea and took the first bite of his shortbread.

"Very good shortbread, Mary."

"Well, I know you like shortbread."

"I do. Something very comforting about shortbread."

"Childhood memories? Just like you said."

"I suppose so."

At that moment, the vicar came into the shop and began to fill a basket with boxes of cereal and cartons of milk. Mary went to help him.

"Good afternoon, Mary. We are always running out of cereals."

"Well, this should stock you up for a while."

Mary rang up the till. The vicar paid and putting his provisions in a large hessian bag, left with a wave that seemed to be half farewell and half benediction. Mary came back to sit with William who was brushing the crumbs of shortbread off his jacket. Mary sat quietly for a while, but then, turning her chair at an angle to the table, she crossed her legs, clasping her knees with her hands, her eyes cast towards her foot as if she were examining her shoe, her body very slightly rocking forward and back.

"I've been meaning to ask you something, William."

"Ask away."

Mary looked up and towards William. She uncrossed her legs and turned her chair back to the table leaning forward as if she wanted what she had to say to be just between the two of them. He noticed the colour of her eyes, which were dark brown.

"You know how it feels to be lonely, knowing not just that you feel a bit lonely today, but that this loneliness is going on forever? You know that feeling?"

"Yes, I do."

"Do you think you can ever get rid of it or do you think you're just stuck with it?"

"I don't know, Mary. Before Caroline died, I would say that I sometimes felt a bit on my own, sometimes when she was away for a few days or sometimes for a week or two, but I knew she would be back and, anyway, I was still at work then so I had things to do, people to be with. The kind of loneliness I now feel is quite different and, as you say, it seems to be ever present, even when I am with other people. It is as if some part of me has been cut away. And I miss coming home to someone being there."

"Yes," said Mary, "I know that feeling, going home to emptiness, silence."

The door of the shop opened again and in came Richard, the postman, back from his rounds.

"Hi, Mary. Oh, hi William."

"Everything okay?"

"Yes, everything is fine. Letters and parcels delivered. All tasks completed."

"Good. I'll be through in a moment."

Richard disappeared into the rooms at the back of the shop to sort out the post he had collected from the two village post boxes, putting the letters into bags for the mail van to collect.

"I'd better go and help him," said Mary.

"I suppose so," said William.

William stood up, paid for his tea and walked home. For reasons he could not identify, he still felt unsettled, as if he had caught a glimpse of something out of the corner of his eye, but could not for the moment see what it was. This uneasy discomfort was something he was becoming more familiar with. It was happening more often. Something at the edge of vision, at the edge of feeling. And there was something about Wendy's visit to London that troubled him, some premonition of unwanted change. Some possible disruption.

The next day it was raining. It had begun in the early hours of the morning and he had heard it falling onto his roof. "Rain before seven, fine before eleven," he had said to himself as he turned over and went back to sleep. But it rained all day, and although it was summertime there was a cold northeasterly wind. He put on a cardigan and went to his study. It was very quiet.

Was it the rain? Was it that Wendy was not going to be there? He couldn't tell. But that day he stayed in his pyjamas and a cardigan. And now, in the afternoon, he had wrapped the blanket from his bed around himself and was sitting on the sofa, propped up by cushions, with Florence coming to sit beside him in one of the armchairs. The unease of yesterday had remained and had got worse. He was reading a book. It was a novel by John Banville called *The Sea* and its themes spoke to William's condition: the loss of a wife, and an escape to be by the sea, memories of childhood. It disturbed him and deepened his discomfort. Something was going on inside, something he could feel but not quite know. He rang Jane.

"Hi, Jane – it's me."

"Hi, Dad. All well?"

"Just about."

"Only 'just about?' Anything wrong?"

"Not really."

"'Just about' and 'not really' are hardly convincing, Dad."

"Well, I think it's just where I am. Being a widower. Getting older."

"Frederick phoned this morning. He is going to call you. He is coming to London for some meetings and hopes to visit. He is bringing Ana with him."

"Excellent. Has he said whether he can come and see me in Suffolk?"

"I think that's his plan. He'll tell you when he calls."

"Excellent."

"And maybe I could get down to your hermit hideaway, too. Maybe we could all meet up by the marsh and the sea."

"Would you be able to do that? I would love that."

"Let's see what Frederick is thinking of. Call me when he has spoken to you."

"Will do."

"And try and be a bit more cheerful."

"Will do. Bye, Jane."

"Bye, Dad."

Not long after he had finished talking to Jane, William's phone rang and it was Frederick

"Hi, Frederick. Very good to hear you. I've just been

talking to Jane and she said you might be making a visit."

"Yes, that's the plan. I have to come to London for some meetings and I have agreed to take some holiday so that I can extend my trip and come and see you. I shall be bringing Ana with me. We got married."

"You got married? Just like that; you got married?"

"Yes, we did. We are having a baby. So we got married."

"Congratulations. Congratulations on having a baby and congratulations on being married. In that order, I guess."

"Yes, in that order."

"And is Ana okay for travelling?"

"Oh, yes – the baby isn't due until November."

"Well, it will be lovely to see you both – well, all three. And Jane says she might try and meet up with us."

"Good, that would be lovely. I'll ring you soon to give you the details. You're not going away or anything like that are you?"

"No, not going away just yet, Frederick."

There was a pause.

"Are you okay, Dad? You know, okay?"

"Yes, I am fine. And very much looking forward to seeing you and Ana. Is there anything special I need to prepare for you or things you don't eat?"

"Unlike you, Dad, Ana and I eat almost everything, even flesh, spices, seafood, mushrooms and onions! I am sure we will find something to eat."

"There is a very good village shop that sells food of all sorts and our nearest town, Saxmundham, has a Waitrose. I am sure that Wendy will find something for you."

"And how is Wendy? Is that all working well?"

"Wendy is fine, although at the moment she has gone

to London to meet some friends. Incidentally, would you and Ana like to use my flat while you are in London?"

"Actually Dad, that would be a good idea. I've stayed there before, remember? You gave me a key just in case I ever needed it. I still have it."

"Excellent. Just let me know when you have settled your flights and so on."

"Will do."

"See you soon then."

"See you soon."

William put the phone down and then rang Jane.

"It's all fixed. Frederick is going to let me know the details in a day or two, and they can use my flat while they are in London."

"Good."

"Had Frederick told you about the baby and the marriage?"

"Yes."

"You didn't say anything."

"Of course not, I wanted Frederick to tell you himself."

"Of course. Yes, of course. Well, it's all very exciting."

"It will be good to be together for a few days, even if we missed the wedding."

"Did they have one, or did they just get married?"

"Apparently they had a wedding with a riotous party afterwards, South American style."

That night William went to bed with a fresh sense of possibility. His children were going to visit him. He would meet Ana, his son's new wife, and a new grandchild was on the way. "Caroline would have liked to have been part of this," he thought to himself. "To have seen her son's child."

The next morning, William woke with an unexpected sense of purpose. He made his breakfast, ate it, and then walked down to the sea. The sun had risen above the eastern horizon and now shed its light like a pathway to the shore. William breathed deeply, tasting the salt and the wetness. This was a good morning. He strode back to the house and walked into his study, where he took down from his bookshelf the postcard from Jennifer. He turned it over and looked at the telephone number written beneath her signature.

When he rang, he thought at first that she was not going to answer, but then suddenly she was there.

"Hello, Jennifer. It's William."

"William! How good to hear from you. I wondered whether you would call me, but had rather given up. How are you? Where are you?"

"I'm fine. I'm in Suffolk."

"Suffolk? What on earth has taken you to Suffolk? I thought you might still be in your flat."

"No, I'm renting a house in a village called Frampton. It's a long way from anywhere and looks over the marshes, the beach and the sea. The North Sea. And today the sun is bright and warm."

"Not cold and wet, then?"

"No. Today it is sunny, warm and beautiful with a light breeze, and I have just walked down to the sea and back, without having to go through an airport."

"Is that what you do there, walk down to the sea

and back? Don't you miss London?"

"Well, I do what I usually do. Reading, writing, that sort of thing. And I go to London sometimes. When I have to."

William felt a distance between them.

"Anyway, where have you been?" he asked.

"I've been travelling. I spent some time in France with an old girlfriend of mine, but this meant leaving Henry in kennels which neither he nor I was happy with. So then I came back to Brighton. You may remember I have a friend who lives there. So I went back and rented a flat with a garden close to the town centre. Which is where I have been since then. Last year, I took a course in English Literature at Brighton College, which was really good, and then I took my holiday. Hence the postcard."

"Yes. Thank you for the postcard. You were obviously somewhere far from Brighton when you sent it."

"It was Bali. I went with a group of friends from the college. I hardly knew them, but they were going and asked if I would like to come too. So I did. It was beautiful and fortunately we all got along well. Lots of late nights, I'm afraid. You should try it."

William thought he probably wouldn't.

"What happened to Henry?"

"He stayed with my girlfriend in Brighton."

Once again, William felt the distance. How odd it was. Here he was speaking to the person he thought he had fallen in love with and now he felt nothing at all. Or if he did, it was discomfort. He had nothing to say.

"It would be good to meet," said Jennifer. "I often go to London for an exhibition or a concert. The trains from Brighton are good. Will you be in London at some point?"

"Nothing planned at the moment, but if I do I will call you."

"Okay, make sure you do that, then we could meet up. Perhaps we could have lunch in Baker Street."

"Okay."

"So just call if you're coming to London."

"I will."

But he never did.

When Wendy came through the front door on Thursday morning, William was up and dressed.

"Morning, Wendy. How was your trip?"

"It was fine. And staying at your flat worked out really well. It's a lovely flat, William."

"And you met up with your friends okay?"

"Yes, it was all fine. And you managed to remember to feed Florence?"

"Yes. Florence fed. Washing tumble-dried. Pots and pans washed. Everything in order."

"Good. Shall we have tea?"

"Yes, let's do that. The weather has been a bit mixed. One or two quite cold days and then yesterday was warm and sunny. Like today. What was it like in London?"

"Same sort of thing. Cold and then warm and sunny."

"Good. Was there any post?"

"Nothing but fliers and letters from estate agents. I put them in the recycling bin. I hope that was right?"

"Yes, of course. Oh, by the way, my son called. He's

coming to visit me. He and Ana are having a baby. And they got married. In that order. Apparently, they had quite a wedding party, South American style. Anyway, they're coming to London and are going to stay with me for a few days too. Jane is also hoping to come over. She's staying with some friends in London."

"That sounds good. When will that be?"

"I'm waiting to hear from Frederick, but soon."

"When you know, tell me so that I can prepare the bedrooms for them."

"Okay, as soon as I know."

"Now, tell me about your trip."

"Not much to tell you. I caught up with friends I have not seen for a long time. Supper, drinks in the pub, that sort of thing. It was good to be in touch again. I have been invited to a party at the end of the month. I think I'll go."

"You must stay at the flat again, if that works for you."

"Thank you, William." Then a pause. "Thank you for caring about me and looking after me. It means a lot to me. Your kindness and generosity. They mean a lot."

"Well, I should tell you that I missed you, especially at first. I was quite grumpy."

"But then you heard from Frederick and I bet that cheered you up."

"It did. It definitely did. We are quite independent, my children and me. Quite independent. But it will be very good to have them gathered here for a day or two. I hope you will like them."

"I'm sure I will. Unless of course they come when I'm in London."

"Oh, yes. I hadn't thought of that. I suppose you might miss them. We will have to think about that. I have offered them my flat whilst they are here."

"Yes, of course. I can always stay with a friend."

Wendy cleared the table and William walked into the kitchen with her to put away the Ryvita and the marmalade.

"And I rang Jennifer."

Wendy turned and, for a moment, looked as if she had not understood what William had said.

"Yes, I found her postcard again and just thought I should ring her."

"And how did that go?"

"Well, it was fine. She told me all that she had been doing, travelling, living in Brighton, taking a course in English Literature. Living with Henry."

"And did you tell her all about your life here in Frampton?"

"Not much really. She seemed surprised I had left London. Obviously thought Suffolk was a dead end. But she didn't ask me much about it. She suggested we should meet in London when I was next there."

"And will you?"

William said nothing for a moment; he had opened the front door and walked out onto the veranda, standing there as if he were listening, or hoping to hear something. He walked back into the house leaving the door open.

"No, I don't think I will. I might write to her though."

"Really. Not see her at all?"

"No, I don't think so. Too much distance. Nothing there now. Odd that, isn't it? You think you love someone and then you find there is nothing there."

"Yes, that is odd."

"Is that how you feel about Ruth?"

"I don't know, William," Wendy replied. "I haven't

seen her or heard from her since I left Devon."

"Nothing at all?"

"No, nothing at all. I needed to cut myself off. I even changed by mobile number and email address, and I've never used Facebook or Twitter. I wanted to find another place to be. To be myself."

"I understand."

"Actually, something did happen in London. One of my friends who knows Ruth and is in touch with her told me that she had been trying to find out where I was. I have no doubt she will be told now. She might come to the party later this month."

"Wow, that's something to think about."

"Or not."

"Yes, or not."

In that moment, William felt a nip of anxiety. The possibility of abandonment. Was this what had unsettled him a few days before? Had he somehow known this would happen? And if it did, what would that mean for him? Not a noble thought. Entirely selfish. But there it was. Sensing his unease, Wendy slipped her arm though his.

"I know what you are thinking, William."

"You do?"

"Yes. And remember I promised that I would always tell you if I was going away. Promised to tell you in good time. These are very early days and nothing might happen at all."

"No, but I would want you to find love again, Wendy, to find someone to be with. You are too young to choose loneliness."

"Let's walk down to the sea." And, taking his arm, she walked with him through his garden, across the marsh and the beach until they came to the sea. The waves were gentle, unfolding onto the shingle and then drawing back. "Do you mind if we sit here for a while, William?" They sat together on a slope of shingle.

"Sometimes, William, you catch me out. You know, one minute I think you're okay, but then, suddenly, you're not. I only said I might meet up with Ruth again. I didn't say we were eloping to Marrakesh."

"No, I know."

"But something about that has made you sad, hasn't it? It's the possibility of someone going away. It seems to touch something inside you, some old wound, and *pow!* Your vitality slips away."

"I know. I'm just being silly."

"You're not being silly. It's just that most people never see this part of you. They only see you as self-assured and generous. They like being with you. You make them feel comfortable. You're their favourite uncle."

"God, I hope not."

"Well, you know what I mean. But I've come to know you close up, and I see this other part of you, childlike and uneasy, as if at any moment you might be left behind. And then I don't know what to do for you. It's as if you are carrying a deep sadness. And no one can reach it."

William looked out over the waves, running his fingers through the shingle, hesitant, unsure what to say. "This is the problem of letting people come too close," he thought. He had long decided that once people came close, really close, they would see behind the covering of competence in which, from an early time, he had clad himself. And, in truth, it was more than a covering, because the more he had practised it the more he had been able to manifest it.

"Wendy, did I ever tell you about my younger sister, Susan?"

"No, I don't think so. I didn't know you had a sister."

"Well, actually I have two. The one who is a bit older than me lives in Colchester, but my younger sister died when I was ten."

And William told Wendy the story of Susan and all that it had meant to him, all that he had carried from earliest childhood. What it had done to him and how it had left its mark, a deep imprint. He ended by telling her about the gravestone.

"So in the end she found her way back to Colchester," said Wendy, taking William's hand into hers. "Would you take me there one day? I would like to see the gravestone. I think that was a lovely thing to do, William. Tying up loose ends. Making things as good as they can be."

"Yes, let's do that, Wendy. Good thought."

They stood up and looked out to sea. Then they turned and made their way back across the pebbled beach and through the marsh and garden, back into the house.

"Are you going to be alright this evening, William?"

"Yes, I shall be fine."

"Okay. See you tomorrow morning then."

"Tomorrow morning."

Wendy left, walking back along the village street towards her caravan. And William walked into his study and began to write. The melancholy of the day had left him thoughtful. There was loss, but there was also something else, something like an opening. Something was happening to him. He did not quite know what it was, but, at one and the same time, it had to do with both the loss of some of his physical, sexual, energies, and the matching arising of something else; something to do with tenderness, opening, surrender and, perhaps, even the prospect of peacefulness. He now knew he could not make it happen, only wait without resistance for it to come into being. He put a potato on a tray and placed it in the oven to bake. "One and a half hours," he said to himself. He went to the fridge and took out a small goat's cheese and put it on a plate. Baked potato and goat's cheese for supper. He opened the front door and walked onto the veranda. Everything was still; almost no movement. Waiting.

"I really wonder if I can do this," he said to himself. "But suppose I could?"

Waiting was not something that was easy for him. Being patient, holding back, checking his natural enthusiasm and pace, these were all things that he put in the 'difficult to do' box. But suppose he could?

"I suppose I could start by imagining what this waiting would be like."

And so he did. With a slow and deep breath, he closed his eyes, imagining a restfulness, a stillness. And he began to let go of intention and wait upon a space filled with love. He came back into the house and again walked into his study. There was a book open on his desk, a book called *Practicing Peace* by the American writer, Catherine Whitmire. There it was, on page 43, a verse by an early Quaker, Isaac Pennington.

There is a river, a sweet flowing river,
the streams whereof will make glad thy heart.

And learn but in quietness and stillness to retire to God,
and wait upon the Spirit;
in whom thou shalt feel peace and joy,
in the midst of thy troubles from the cruel and vexatious spirit of this world.

The next morning, before breakfast and still dressed in his pyjamas and dressing gown, William sat at his computer and began to write his letter to Jennifer. When he had finished it and printed it, he topped-and-tailed the typed text with his own handwriting:

My Dear Jennifer

It was good to speak to you on the phone and to catch up. I am glad that you are finding a new life in Brighton and hope Henry does not miss Putney. Perhaps he gets walks along the beach!

It is difficult to believe that our time together in London was more than two years ago, but it was. Of course, I now realise that in my madness I thought we were in love when we were just getting to know each other and enjoying each other's company. But then I needed to believe it. And I fear that my neediness may have scared you off.

It's not that my madness is entirely cured. Perhaps it will never be. Grief is such a raw thing. It marks us, I think, forever. But I have found some peace here in Suffolk, some acceptance, and friendship, too. Good friendship. You would be surprised what Providence can provide even in a small and somewhat remote place overlooking the marsh and the sea.

And what I thought I was looking for, what I thought I needed turned out to be not so. I have discovered that no one else can heal my wounds of loss but me. Odd that, isn't it? We think someone else can do this for us, but they can't.

So now here I am, living a bit like a hermit, living within a quite small space, but one that I am getting to know and feel at home with. Part of this means that I do not expect to be in London much. So I cannot promise to be in touch, but only hope that you will continue to find that freedom you often spoke of. You seem to be doing that.

Thank you for being in touch and thank you for the time we had together. It may have been madness on my part, but it helped me survive, helped me to get through. Thank you.

Thine

William

William read through the letter, put it into an

envelope, and addressed it to Jennifer's house in Brighton. Then he walked down to the post office. Mary was in her shop and seeing William come in and go to the counter she came round past the newspapers and stood behind the glass panel.

"Good morning, William."

"Good morning, Mary. Could I have a first class stamp please?"

"That will be sixty-four pence."

William passed a pound coin under the glass and Mary passed him the stamp and thirty-six pence change. Having stuck the stamp on the envelope, William passed it back to Mary who put into an open sack beside her, ready for the midday collection. He left Mary's shop and walked home.

So that was that.

An ending.

CHAPTER 10

Arrivals

Late in July, on a warm and sunny morning, with a breeze coming off the sea and the lavender in flower, Wendy set off for London in her car. She had made arrangements to stay with a friend and go to the party together. Later that same day, Frederick, Ana and Jane came to Frampton. They had arranged to travel together on the train from Liverpool Street and William had asked the taxi man, David, to meet them, and when they arrived William was waiting for them, standing on the veranda and then coming to help them with their cases, before hugging his children and shaking Ana's hand, welcoming them all.

Frederick's hair had been cropped and so had his beard. Ana, who was dark haired and taller than William had imagined, was beginning to show a roundness in her belly, and Jane was as she had always been, her fair hair pulled back and held in a hair grip, her usual blouse, cardigan and dark blue trousers. When William put his arms round her he felt her body stiffen as if she was holding back from him.

"Well, here it is," said William. "The house by the marsh. And there is the beach and the sea. The North Sea. I have put you two in the larger bedroom, Frederick. And Jane, I have put you in my dressing room. I hope that's okay? The beds are quite comfortable. You settle in and I'll make some tea. Or would you prefer coffee? I thought you might be coffee drinkers so I have bought coffee and a coffee filter from Waitrose. It's standing on the side in the kitchen. But you will have to make it for yourselves. I have no idea how it works. I use almond milk, but I bought you some ordinary milk. It's in the fridge."

Frederick made himself coffee and Jane made tea for the rest of them. They sat in the living room with the front door open. Florence walked in, tail held high and inspected each of the guests before turning around and going out again to sit on the veranda.

"This is some place, Dad," said Frederick. "And is that your study?"

"Yes, have a look if you like."

Frederick stood up and walked into the study, looking out of the window towards the sea and then prodding the bed to see how soft or hard it was, running his hands over the painted bedhead.

"So you write and sleep in the same room? That is something. I can see why that would work."

"This is a beautiful house, William," said Ana.

William looked at her and smiled. He liked the woman

Frederick had chosen as his wife. There was a stillness to her.

"I am so pleased you have come to see me, Ana," he said.

"Well, Freddy told me a bit about your coming here but, of course, we did not know how beautiful it was. São Paulo is so busy and noisy. And here it is quiet and still. I like it here."

"You are welcome to stay here any time you like."

Frederick and Jane had walked out into the garden, talking together, heads bowed down, serious faces.

That evening they made a supper of rice and pesto and Parmesan, with beans and peas. And afterwards they sat together talking about Frederick's work and his and Ana's life in Brazil, her family. Jane was very quiet. Preoccupied.

At about a quarter to ten, Ana decided she needed to go to bed and both she and Frederick stood up and stretched, leaving Jane and William still sitting there. Once they had gone, Jane sat forward in her chair.

"Here we go," thought William.

"Dad, there's something I have to tell you."

"I thought there might be."

"It's not good, I'm afraid. You see Robert and I are getting a divorce."

"Oh, my dear Jane, I am so sorry. Whatever has happened?"

"It's not much really, Dad. No drama. No fights. It's just that we no longer love each other. And because we are unable to talk about it, we find being with each other very difficult. The ill feeling and tension between us is suffocating. He's not a bad man, Dad, I just don't love him any more. And he doesn't love me. It's been happening for quite a while, and it's not good for us. And it's not good for the children who, of course, sense that something is wrong. Something that nobody is talking about."

"I am so sorry, darling. I am so sorry." William leaned across and took his daughter's hands in his.

"And I miss Mum. I miss her badly. If she were here she would know what to do." Jane began to cry and then to sob.

"Have you spoken to Frederick about this?"

"Yes, I told him on the way down here this morning."

"Well, you are always welcome here, and I would like to get to know Ben and Sally more."

"Thank you, Dad."

"And when is all of this likely to happen?"

"Quite soon."

Jane stood up and said goodnight to her father, holding him close this time and kissing him on his bearded cheek. She made her way to bed, settling into her father's dressing room, comforted by the smell of his dressing gown hooked to the back of the bedroom door, and by his Kilim slippers lined up beside his Birkenstocks.

When Jane had gone, William opened the front door and sat on the veranda. Silence and stillness. But then there was a slight movement in the reeds.

"I thought you might be nearby," said William.

"Yes, I could hardly be far off with the family gathering together like this," said Caroline.

"Ana is lovely, isn't she?"

"She is, and Frederick seems very happy at the prospect of being a father."

"Yes he does, doesn't he?"

"Poor Jane. Of course she pulled me close when she said she missed me. Actually I would have no better idea about what to say than you. But she doesn't know that."

William smiled.

"Well, we had our moments apart," he said.

"Yes, we did. But I don't think we ever got bored, did we? And, of course, we liked each other so much."

"We did. We liked each other a lot."

"Keep an eye on them."

"Yes, of course."

The reeds moved again and there was silence. William sat there for quite a while, listening. And then he got up, walked back into the house and closed the door behind him. He went into his study and put on the bedside lamp. Taking off his clothes and putting on his pyjamas, he lifted the duvet, stepped into his bed and turned off the light.

The next morning both Frederick and Jane were up early and went out for a walk along the beach. Ana was slower and so when William emerged from his study in his pyjamas, she was making coffee, still in her dressing gown.

"Good morning, Ana, did you sleep well?"

"I did. Very well, thank you. Frederick and Jane have gone for a walk."

"Okay. I'll just take a shower then and get dressed."

"Shall I make some tea?"

"Lovely. I take mine without milk."

"Okay. And no sugar?"

"Yes, no sugar. Thank you."

William went into his dressing room and took a shower, washed his hair and cleaned his teeth. By the time he reappeared, Frederick and Jane were walking back up the boarded walk between the reeds.

"Morning, you two.

"We're going to catch the lunchtime train, Dad, the 12.55 from Saxmundham, and I have arranged for David to pick us up at about 12.25 if that's okay. Sorry this is such a short visit, but I have more meetings tomorrow in London."

"Yes, of course."

And that was that. After they had all gone, William walked down to the sea and stood watching the waves as an easterly wind began to freshen on a rising tide. Alone once more, but content to be so. Loneliness in old age is quite unlike being lonely as a young person. Then it seems wrong, something that should not be. But, in old age, it is somehow expected. Its cause might vary, but it is just what happens to people who become separated from the pack, left behind. There may be family who come to visit, there may be book clubs and there may be friends who become part of your life. But the loneliness remains, eventually becoming familiar and – is this possible – even a comfort?

And then there was Wendy.

The following Monday morning, Wendy arrived as usual at nine o'clock. William had already been up for a while and was in his study going through some papers. Coming into the house, she called for him.

"Hi, William. You up and about?"

"Yes, Wendy, I am here in my study."

"How did you get on with your family?"

"Well, it was mixed really. Frederick was fine, and Ana is delightful. Pregnant and delightful. But Jane is getting divorced."

"Oh no, poor Jane. What has happened?"

"Nothing very dramatic. Just an ending, I think."

"Poor Jane."

"And you, Wendy, how did it all go at the party?"

"Do you mind if I get breakfast ready before we talk?"

"No, of course. Let's do that."

William knew what was to come.

Breakfast set and ready, Wendy and William sat at the kitchen table and William began to drink his tea. Then he took two pieces of Ryvita out of the tin, spreading them first with the Bertolli olive oil spread and then with marmalade. Wendy held her mug of tea in both hands, elbows resting on the table.

"So then, how did it all go?"

For a moment, Wendy looked straight into William's eyes, looking at the comfort that had grown between them, but knowing she was about to break it.

"It was good really, William. I met up with a lot of my friends, some of whom I hadn't seen for some while."

She paused and drank from her mug.

"And then Ruth arrived."

"You said she might be there."

"Well, she was."

"And how was she?"

"She was friendly, interested in what had been happening to me. Not quite believing I was living in a caravan in a field in Suffolk. 'No wonder I couldn't find you,' she said. And she said she had missed me."

"And is she still living in Totnes?"

"No, she has left that job and come back to London. She's working in a hospital in Croydon. Not as lovely as Totnes, but she said that she had felt a bit cut off there."

"And how was it to see her again?"

Wendy paused before replying.

"It was good, William. It was good. We talked a lot about what we had both been doing and she said that she hoped we might 'get to know each other again.' Learn a bit more about each other this time."

"That sounds encouraging Wendy," said William. "Really encouraging."

"Well, we will see."

Another pause.

"But it does mean I will want to be in London a bit more Especially at weekends. Is that okay with you? Maybe we could rearrange our times a bit so that I could go to London on a Friday afternoon and get back after lunch on Monday. That sort of thing. Would that work?"

"Of course, Wendy. That sounds good. Very good. I am sure that would work."

He had always known this would happen. And now it was. Wendy's departure. It had begun. It might take some time, perhaps some months, but it had started. She had promised to let him know with plenty of time, and she was doing that. But it was happening.

They talked more, their words together gentle and open. Wendy wanted William to feel the love she had for him and William wanted Wendy to feel free to let her life unfold. Old life watching new life unfold. And then Wendy stood up and began to clear away the breakfast things and William left the table and went back into his study. He couldn't quite make out how he was feeling. Pleased for Wendy, that love might be returning; that there was a chance that something good could come to her; but aware that this would be a loss for him. Another departure. He felt an ache in his chest. A closing off. A withdrawing into himself, lest he be hurt.

In the first week of September, William received an email from Ana.

Dear William

We are now back in São Paulo. Thank you for having us to stay. We had a lovely time with you. And I have news. Your grandson – yes, our baby is going to be a boy – will be named Jonathan William, after his great grandfather and his grandfather. Just as Freddy wanted. I hope you approve. And how shall we address you? Would you be happy with 'Papa'?

With love,

Ana x

William replied:

My Dear Ana

*That is great news. I like 'Jonathan William' very much.
And I am happy to be called 'Papa'.*

*You will always be welcome here overlooking
the marsh.*

Thine with love

William

William called his daughter on Skype.

"Have you heard about Jonathan William?"

"Yes, Ana sent me an email. It's wonderful news."

"And are Ben and Sally there? I just wanted to say hello."

The children said their hellos, Ben asking his grandfather about the house by the marsh.

"It must be great living by the sea, Grandpa."

"Well, any chance of you coming to see me?"

"That would be excellent," he said, turning to his mother as if she might arrange it there and then.

"Have you time before you go back to school or will we have to wait until Christmas?"

Jane reappeared behind her children. "I think it will have to be Christmas."

"Let's try and arrange something."

"Okay, I will see what we can do."

William talked for a while with his grandchildren,

asking them about what they had been doing over the summer. Although, in truth, they had never spent much time together, Ben, in particular, was very much at ease with him. There was something that seemed to draw them together, and William now looked forward to having the chance to get to know him better, to share the house by the marsh with him. Sally was much quieter, and more reserved. She seemed studious and serious. She talked about the subjects she liked at school, mathematics and physics. She had already decided she wanted to study medicine. And she would. William asked to speak to their mother again. And once they had disappeared, he asked Jane how the divorce was going and what her plans might be.

"You know we could have Christmas together here. I can fit you all in. The bed in the spare room splits into two singles and you could have my dressing room again."

"I like your dressing room."

"Well, let's see if we can make that happen."

"Sounds like a plan!"

"Yes, it does. Go carefully Jane. And ring me whenever you want to. I thought Ben and Sally sounded okay."

"It's a bit up and down."

William had not been in touch with Roderick for some while but now he remembered that his three-year agreement would soon be coming to an end. He sent an email:

Roderick

I hope you and Edward are well and enjoying Umbria.

Everything is fine here by the marsh, although I am aware that our agreement runs out soon and I was wondering whether you have given any thought about what you want to do with the house. Are you coming back? It's up to you, of course, but I would be happy to continue here for a while. It has become quite my favourite place to be. Even when the wind is coming from the northeast!

Could you let me know what you would like to do?

Thine

William

There was no reply for a few days, and William was beginning to think that this meant that his time by the marshes was coming to an end. No doubt Roderick and Edward had grown tired of Italy and would want to come back to London, and take up their country retreat again. He walked down to Mary's shop to buy some copier paper for his printer, and found her sitting quietly behind the till, her eyes cast down and her thoughts some way away. Perhaps she was thinking of her son in Ireland.

"Morning, Mary. You look a bit thoughtful."

"Nothing special. Just taking a rest."

William paid for the copier paper and put it into his shopping bag.

"I've sent an email to Roderick."

"Oh, yes?"

"Yes, I wanted to know whether he and Edward were thinking of coming back to England next year. They have been away for nearly three years."

"Is it three years?"

"Nearly."

"I suppose they might come back, although I was never really sure that they were Suffolk people. I was never really sure they took to the marsh and the sea. Not the way you have, William."

"Well, we will soon know."

"I can't think of you not being here now, William. Whatever would you do? You won't find Eccles cakes like mine in London."

"I don't know what I would do, Mary. At the moment I don't want to think about it."

But William was thinking about it. And he didn't like what he was thinking about. Would he go back to London? Not for long. Could he find another part of Suffolk to live in? Perhaps.

Perhaps he would buy a caravan and travel? He didn't mind the thought of a caravan, but the travelling bit was most unsettling.

And so William waited.

Two days later, whilst he was working at his computer, sorting out emails, including one from Ana with a photo of their new house, an email from Roderick appeared:

Hi William

I am glad everything is going well in Frampton. Good to hear from you.

Edward and I have become quite absurdly Italian and do not want to come back to England for the time being. Would you be interested in extending our agreement, perhaps by another three years for now? I know you will be looking after the house really well and so I am content to leave the rent as it is for this next period.

What do you think?

Warmest

Roderick

Although autumn was now well advanced, the day was fine and the garden, the marsh, the beach and the sea were in sunlight. Just that morning William had sat on his veranda and taken in the stillness, wondering how many more such mornings he would have. And now here it was. An extension. And possibly for three years. Three years 'for now.' It felt like forever.

He could not resist telling Mary about it. And so he walked to the shop where Mary was serving tea to a table of four young people with rucksacks. They had never heard of Eccles cakes and were now covered in pastry flakes, their mouths full of the soft, sweet and sticky currants.

"Hello, William. I hope you haven't used all that copier paper?"

"No, not yet. But I want some of your shortbread. To celebrate."

"Is it your birthday?"

"No, I am celebrating staying here."

"Staying here?"

"Yes, you remember I was telling you about whether Roderick and Edward might want their house back? Well, they don't. At least not for now. In fact, not for at least three years. Three more years from next year. So I can stay."

Mary was evidently pleased and smiled at William.

"That is very good news, William. Very good. We have all become very fond of you and cannot imagine what it would be like without you in Roderick's house."

"Nor can I Mary. Nor can I."

"Have you told Wendy?"

"Not yet. But I will when she comes in this afternoon. I wanted to tell you though."

Mary was pleased.

"Thank you, William. It's very good news. And take the shortbread as a present. To celebrate."

They both laughed and William picked up the shortbread and walked home.

As usual, Wendy came to William's house at about three-thirty. She had been to Waitrose and was carrying two bags of shopping, including olive oil, some cheddar and roasted tomato tartlets and a piece of fresh Parmesan. As usual, she slipped off her moccasins and called out for William.

"Hi, Wendy. I'm in my study. I'll be through in a minute."

Wendy put away the shopping and then made up the tea tray and brought it into the living room, setting it down on the low table between the sofa and the armchairs.

"I've been to Waitrose to stock up on a few things."

"Thank you. And did you see I have some of Mary's shortbread?"

"I did. Would you like some with your tea?"

"Yes, please."

And so they sat together having their tea. As usual. Only today with the shortbread.

"The shortbread is to celebrate."

"What are you celebrating? It's too early for your birthday."

"Yes, but not too early to celebrate my extension."

"Your what?" She laughed and raised her eyebrows.

"My extension. I heard today from Roderick. He is prepared to extend the present agreement I have with him for the house. It ends next year, but he wants to extend it for a further three years. And he said, 'three years for now,' which I think means that it might be longer than three years. At my age that sounds like forever!"

"Oh, yes. You're clearly going to die tomorrow."

But Wendy was delighted and she came across to William and gave him a big hug. He could not help but enjoy her smell and the feeling of her body pressed against him.

"Thank you, Wendy. Glad you're pleased."

"I am. And since we are celebrating your 'extension,' I have something to talk to you about. You see Ruth is coming to stay with me this weekend, and as I have told her quite a lot about you, she would like to meet you."

"Ruth coming to stay. That is something to celebrate. Although I am not sure she will find me very interesting."

"Rubbish, William. You're just fishing for compliments, which I shall not give you!"

They laughed at each other and ate the shortbread. Something was shifting. Patterns adjusting to the Dance of Providence.

On the 12th November, Ana Clarke gave birth to a boy, Jonathan William. The phone rang. It was Frederick.

"Good morning, Papa. Wonderful news. Jonathan William was born this morning. Seven pounds and six ounces. Mother and baby well."

"That is wonderful, Frederick. Well done to Ana and welcome to Jonathan William. How was the birth?"

"Not too bad, I think. I was there and it all sounded horrendous. But apparently that is what it always sounds like. A lot of yelling and swearing and gasping. I'm not sure I was ready for it. But I managed not to faint. Which is better than you did, I seem to remember."

"I'm afraid that's true. I did faint when Jane was born. The nurse asked me if I wanted to see her 'popping out into the world' and rather stupidly I said 'yes.' And so

I looked. And then I fainted. Well, stumbled about a bit rather than fainted. I know, pathetic. And then I was on my way to the hospital when you were born and did not get there in time. Probably Providence was taking care of me. Anyway, I remember, as I arrived, your mother was being wheeled back to the ward, red-eyed and shouting, 'It's a boy!'"

"Well, I didn't faint and am now fully engaged in the endless duties of the modern father. Ana has already given me instructions about what I have to get in order that my son – I like that! – in order that my son can come home."

"So, now my son has a son. That is very good, Frederick. I think I might not have been an entirely successful father, but I always loved you. And do now."

"I know, Dad."

Fathers and sons.

Wendy was excited about the possibility of Ruth coming to stay with her, and she made the caravan extra-specially beautiful, with an arrangement of wild flowers. On the Friday morning, she came to the house earlier than usual. She got William's breakfast and put some laundry into the washing machine, leaving him a reminder to take the washing from the machine and put it into the drier later that day. But there was something else, too. When William came through for breakfast, he found amongst his tubs of supplements an envelope with a card inside. He opened it. It said:

Wendy and Ruth invite

William Clarke

To Supper

On Saturday November 14th

At the caravan, 6.30 pm (your favourite time)

No need to reply. Just be there.

Dress as you like and think we would like.

William smiled as he read the card. He thought it was wonderful. Funny, beautiful, generous and just what he would like. He liked it so much that he felt cheerful for the rest of the day, that night and the following morning.

In the evening, just before half past six, he set off. He wore one of his favourite linen jackets and trousers. Dark blue, the jacket with a mandarin collar and the trousers baggy. Underneath the jacket was a David Beckham T-shirt. On his feet were his Birkenstocks, but he carried with him his Kilim slippers. He also carried a bottle of red wine and some salted almonds.

As he walked through the field he could see the lights of the caravan, and an awning over the front door hung with candles in jam jars. At any moment the whole thing could of course go up in flames. William could not resist a chuckle. In fact, he laughed out loud at the sheer pleasure of it. And Lady Whitely's terrier, Toby, ever alert for danger and strange noises, started barking.

Coming to the awning, and ducking between the hanging lights, William knocked on the door of the caravan. Wendy opened it.

"Welcome to the caravan of delight!"

William climbed in and gave Wendy the bottle and the almonds. He placed his Birkenstocks by the door and put on his slippers. Wendy thanked him and kissed him on both cheeks. And there was Ruth. Somehow or other he had imagined that she would be taller than Wendy and, well, more sturdy. But she wasn't. She was slight and blonde, her hair cut short. Both Wendy and Ruth had dressed like gypsies in colourful blouses and long sparkly skirts, their shoulders swathed in patterned cotton scarves. Wendy had found a pair of large earrings, long and golden, but Ruth had simple pearl studs. They were barefoot.

"William, this is Ruth. Ruth, this is William."

"Hello, Ruth. I am so pleased to meet you."

"Likewise, William. It is good to meet you. Wendy has said some rather nice things about you."

"All of which are true," said Wendy drawing the cork from the bottle of wine and pouring it into glasses.

"I hope some of it is true," said William. "But the real truth is that Wendy and I have come to like each other very much. We have found a way of taking care of each other. Of course, I am old enough to be her grandfather. That probably helps."

They laughed together and before long were sitting at the table.

"I've told Ruth about your bizarre taste in food, William. All the things that cannot be included in any meal that you eat: flesh, seafood, spices and onions. Not even wild mushrooms. And as a special treat – to celebrate your 'extension' – I have prepared your signature dish, poached eggs on Marmite toast."

"Hurrah!" cried William. And they laughed again. It was the kind of laughter that mocks and loves at the same time.

Somehow or other their conversation was flowing, soon becoming deep and intimate. Perhaps it was because Wendy and William had long since come to be open with each other, or because Wendy was so evidently happy. Perhaps it was because, although somewhat reserved and serious in her words, Ruth was gentle and thoughtful. Perhaps it was because of all of these things. Or perhaps it was because Providence intended that it should be so.

They shared stories from their lives. Stories about the times before they had known each other. Stories of things they had done together. They spoke of their frailties and their wonders, of loving and being loved. And they spoke of loss and sorrow, too. It was as if being inside the caravan had become a small place of shelter into which they each had drifted and found each other and fallen in love. It was rather extraordinary and no doubt no one else would believe it to be true, but there it was. And frankly, no one else need ever know about it.

They had found their own delightful and private place.

"Oh, by the way, Ana gave birth to Jonathan William on Thursday. Apparently, it all went well. Frederick was there and did not faint. Unlike me for my first born. I know, pathetic. And anyway, it was more of a stumble than a proper faint."

They laughed and toasted the health of Ana and her baby.

Wendy had, of course, made a rhubarb crumble and custard and William's bottle of red wine was followed by a delicious desert wine, a Rustenberg Straw Wine that Ruth had brought with her from Waitrose in Croydon. Then Ruth made coffee in a filter for Wendy and herself, and Wendy made a mint tea for William.

At ten o'clock, William took his leave, receiving a hug first from Wendy and then from Ruth. He wished them "sweet dreams" and putting on his Birkenstocks and carrying his slippers made his way home.

It was dark, but there was enough moonlight for him to find his way across the field to the street and then home. He was happy. And so was Wendy. And now Ruth, too.

The next day, Sunday, William rang Jane to see how she was. The phone rang and then Jane answered.

"Jane here. Who is it?"

"It's me, Jane."

"Oh, hello Dad. Sorry. Not a very good morning."

"Are you okay?"

"No. Not really. I've just been talking to Ben and Sally about all that is going on here and about the arrangements that are being made for them to spend time with their father. They are not happy about any of it. And somehow they seem to think it is my fault."

"That is neither helpful nor fair. But they are children and I expect it is all very distressing for them."

"Yes, of course it is, but at least they are settled here with me. They are in their own house and with their own friends. Their friends seem to be their entire world."

"And do you have your own friends, Jane?"

"I do and one or two of them, my best girlfriends, are being really thoughtful. Coming round to see me. Going out for a coffee and a chat. A couple of them are in the same boat, as it happens. Odd, isn't it? That there are so many of us. So many singletons. Divorced, widowed. Like you, Dad."

"Yes, like me. There you are, we have something in common."

They laughed and, for a few moments, said nothing.

"And what do you think about Jonathan William?"

"Yes, that is lovely news. Frederick called me just after he had the fainting conversation with you."

"Yes. I'm sorry. Pathetic. Didn't stop me loving you though. You were just what I hoped for. A beautiful daughter. I felt very close to you when you were a child. Still do."

"You are pathetic, Dad. You have always been a soft touch and far too emotional for your own good. Too much unrestrained enthusiasm."

"Do you think so?"

"A bit. But I forgive you."

"Well, let's assume that we are going to be together for Christmas. It's only a few weeks away. See if you can organise the train tickets and I will ask David to meet you at Saxmundham station."

"Okay, I will. You've cheered me up a bit. Thank you. Of course, I shall have to check this with Robert. Custody and so on. But he might have plans to go and stay with his parents in Perth. He has friends up there."

"Good. And I will sort out things here. Wendy will help me get it all together. Oh, by the way, I met her friend Ruth, yesterday. She's very nice. Serious and reserved with blonde hair. Cut short. And she wears pearl stud earrings. More modest than Wendy. But delightful. I liked her."

"So they're back together then?"

"Yes, very much so and I am pleased for Wendy. Of course, I suppose she might now go and live in London with Ruth. But we will see."

"Yes, I suppose so."

And so it was that whilst Wendy was in London with Ruth and their friends, William, Jane, Ben and Sally had Christmas together in Frampton. William had ordered a local, organic turkey, plus chipolata sausages from a butcher in Saxmundham, and Wendy had put them in the fridge before she left for London. All the vegetables had been bought from Mary, who had also been able to provide homemade bread sauce, a

Christmas pudding, brandy butter and mince pies.

"Happy Christmas, everyone!"

They lifted their glasses. Clink, clink.

After lunch, William and his grandson, Ben, went for a walk along the beach. And, at teatime, they made a Skype call to Brazil and wished a very happy Christmas to Frederick, Ana and baby Jonathan.

Five years had now passed and something quite unexpected was about to happen.

CHAPTER 11

THE GREAT STORM

Jane, William Ben and Sally saw in the New Year, standing in a line on the beach by the water's edge, each one throwing a pebble into the waves and making a wish. Ben, who felt at home by the sea, wished that he might soon come and stay with his grandfather again.

As they walked back to the house, William thought for a moment he could hear someone on the shingle behind them. But when he turned to look, there was no one there. He didn't say anything to Jane. And on the 3rd January, she and her children took the train back to London, staying in William's flat for the night so that they could take the early morning train to Edinburgh the next day.

On that day, Wendy returned and it felt as if his life was back to normal. Well, that is what it felt like then.

William was pleased to have his house back. He walked barefoot through the rooms, attending to the wood stove, sometimes sitting at his computer and sometimes with a blanket round him reading on his sofa. He returned to his routine. Waking and going to bed alone. Almost for the first time, he felt no loneliness. Something else was rising in him. Not loneliness to be feared, but something else. Although he did not know what it was, it was something that was a comfort to him. Some kind of contentment.

He worried about Jane and kept in touch with her as she settled back into the life of her children and her friends. The parenting schedule was apparently a bit difficult to get used to at first, but, after a while, Ben and Sally seemed okay with it. In fact, they began to look forward to their weekends with their father because he took them ice-skating or to films, eating out afterwards and always letting them order whatever they wanted. He bought them new clothes and even, as a late Christmas present, an iPhone each. Sometimes they would be taken to Perth to visit their other grandparents. When this happened, Jane was not sure what she felt. She was now the one being left out.

In São Paulo, Frederick and Ana were busy with Jonathan. And Frederick was enjoying his work.

In the dark months of January and February, Ruth became a more and more frequent visitor to Frampton, and although they did not repeat their supper party,

William, Ruth and Wendy would sometimes go for tea in Mary's tea room. A threesome coming together to sit around Mary's table, white tablecloth and cups and plates placed with care before them.

"Now this is a bit complicated, Mary, but we want one pot of tea for two, ordinary tea, and one pot of your Rooibos tea. That's for Ruth. No milk for me, of course, but Wendy would like some almond milk if you have it."

"You may think me a bit simple, William, but since Wendy and Ruth have been visiting more often, I have kept a stock of Ruth's special tea and Wendy's milk. Actually, they come to tea more often than you do."

"Yes, of course. Sorry. And can we have two Eccles cakes and a plate of your shortbread?"

"What did you think I was going to bring? Jammy Dodgers!"

Over the years, Mary had grown fond of Wendy, accepting her special relationship with William, and she was now pleased that her friend, Ruth, came to stay. Mary and Ruth shared a secret. They both liked the crime stories of Margery Allingham, which they had discovered one day, when Ruth had come to buy her Saturday *Guardian* and she had put her copy of *The Return of Mr Campion* by the till whilst she was looking for change in her purse.

"Oh, I see you're reading Margery Allingham."

"Yes, I'm a fan."

"Me too."

As there was no one else there, Mary came and sat with them. Now the threesome was a foursome. The conversation ripened and Mary began to fill in some of the details of village life that Ruth, in particular, liked.

"Have you met Brenda and Penelope, Ruth?"

"No, not yet – tell me about them."

"Well. They are sisters and they came to live here about a year ago. They live in the cottage that used to belong to Neville and Virginia Cutler. He died you see, and Virginia went to live with her son in Sevenoaks. They were a nice couple. Neville and Virginia. Very nice."

"So then Brenda and Penelope came?"

"Yes, they moved in when Virginia moved out. Quite different. Very … what shall I say? What would you say, William? Brenda and Penelope. Very. You know, very …"

"Very entertaining," said William.

"Yes, very entertaining. And a bit odd."

"What do mean by odd?" asked Ruth, now wanting more details.

"Well, Penelope lost her husband some years ago. So she's a widow and Brenda isn't."

"Isn't what?"

"Isn't a widow. You know, isn't a widow. Until Penelope came to live with her she lived by herself."

"You mean she's divorced?"

"No. Not divorced. She has never been married, and until her sister came to live with her she had always lived by herself. You know, never been married."

"You mean she's gay?"

"Well, if you say so."

"I didn't say so. You did."

"No, I didn't."

"Well, you sort of did, didn't you?"

"I might have done." And they looked at each other and burst into laughter.

Mary felt a kind of kinship with Ruth. There was

something about her that Mary was drawn to, a gentle thoughtfulness. Ruth was straightforward. No rings in her eyebrows.

And Ruth liked Mary.

"By the way," said Mary, "Did you hear the news this morning? Apparently, a great storm is on its way, with very high winds and rain. I hope you'll be okay in your caravan."

"We'll be fine," said Ruth.

But they weren't.

That night, on the 17th February, a great storm, which had begun in the Atlantic, came spiralling across the UK. It hit the east coast in the early evening. Gale force winds from the northeast and a turbulent sea, the waves breaking heavily on the pebble beach, and the strong wind disturbing the marsh. By midnight, the rain was driving hard against William's house. Florence had taken shelter on her chair in the study, her ears catching the sounds of the storm. At three o'clock in the morning, the phone rang. It was Wendy.

"William?"

"Yes ..."

"I know it's the middle of the night, but we have a bit of a crisis. Part of the roof of the caravan has been ripped open by the storm and we are being rained on. Not just a bit, a lot. Could you give us shelter?"

"Yes, of course, come at once. I may have to be in

my dressing gown, if that's okay."

"Compared to being drowned in the rain, you being in your dressing gown is not a problem."

"Okay, come at once."

A few minutes later, Wendy's car pulled into the drive and she and Ruth ran from the car to the veranda. Hearing the car, William had opened the front door, and he ushered them in. They were bedraggled and wet.

"I can make you some tea, but looking at you I think you might need to go and dry off. Take the spare room and use the bathroom. Wendy knows where the towels are. There are a couple of dressing gowns and various jumpers, T-shirts and cardigans in my dressing room. Help yourself."

"Thank you, William."

They disappeared into the back of the house. Not knowing quite what he should do, William filled the kettle and put it on the hob to boil.

After a while, Ruth and Wendy appeared, towels around their heads and clad in a mixture of William's clothes. Wendy had found a grey T-shirt, a green sweater and pair of black cord trousers, which she had tied with a belt. Ruth was wearing a pair of thick cotton pyjamas, one of William's dressing gowns and a pair of his socks. Frampton was living up to its reputation as a place for refugees.

"Do you want a warm drink? Would you like hot water bottles?"

"I'll do it," said Wendy.

William was rekindling the embers of the wood stove, placing small pieces of wood criss-cross. Before long, it was alight and William fed it with small dry logs.

Ruth and Wendy brought their drinks and their hot water bottles to sit beside the stove and William found some blankets for them.

"Thank you, William. Thank you for rescuing us," said Ruth,

"Have I?" he said.

"I think you may have."

They sat for a while, the warmth of the fire making them comfortable.

"I think I'll go back to bed," said William. "Help yourself to anything you need. Anything at all. See you in the morning." And he left them and went back into his study, climbing into his bed and pulling the duvet close about him. The storm was still up, but he fell asleep, a deep sleep without a dream.

When William woke, the storm had gone and a wet but calm stillness had settled on the marsh. He opened the window of his study and smelt the damp air. The sea was quiet. Putting a coat over his pyjamas and finding his wellington boots and woolly hat, he walked out onto the veranda, through his garden and across the boardwalk towards the sea. On the beach were remnants of the storm, the bric-a-brac it had tossed onto the shingle. But apart from that, and apart from a freshness in the air, it was but a memory.

William walked down the beach and then stood for a while marvelling at the capacity of the sea to rise in temper and then subside without so much as a 'by your leave'. The sea was at ease with herself and with her moods, and whatever we might think about her mattered not at all.

William walked back to the house, looking to see if there had been any damage to the roof tiles, but all seemed to be intact. Some small branches from the trees had been broken and now lay upon the ground. That was all.

When he went back into the house, Wendy was up, clad in one of his dressing gowns and making coffee for Ruth.

"Morning, William. Thank you for last night. I dare not think what has happened to the caravan."

"Perhaps you should go and have a look."

"Yes okay. Would you mind coming with us?"

"No, of course not."

Ruth appeared wrapped in a blanket.

"Good morning, Ruth."

"Morning, William. What a night. And now everything seems so calm and still."

"Yes, it does. The storm seems to have blown through and left us behind. I have just been down to the sea. The fury has passed. It is as if the storm is no more than a distant memory."

"There is something really special about this place, William. It's odd. It seems to draw you in. I know I haven't been here many times, but I feel it."

"Yes, it feels odd at first, but that is how it is. And I'm glad you feel it. Not everybody gets it. I'm glad you do. I think it is a kind of surrender. We give way. Somehow or other we become part of the sea and the marsh. But what a night!"

After getting dressed and having breakfast together, William, Ruth and Wendy drove down the street to see what had happened to the caravan. The grass across the field was wet, and their passage was marked by Toby's barking.

Then they saw the caravan. The wind had forced its way under one of the panels of the roof, ripping it and lifting it up, so that it now stood at a jagged angle. The hole through which the rain had poured was dreadfully apparent. The water that had poured into the caravan had escaped through ventilation holes at the bottom of the door, and a large puddle had formed in front of it, a large muddy puddle. Stepping round it, Wendy opened the door and climbed in. Ruth and William followed. Wendy put her hands to her mouth. Ruth and William were silent. Everything within sight was wet. The cushions and bedding that had been on the bench seats had been swept onto the floor. Water had run down the sides of cupboards, one of which had sprung open, buckled and broken. Ruth moved forwards and put her arms round Wendy. William stood still. Nothing could be said. After a few moments, he turned and stepped outside. He inspected the outer fabric of the caravan. Its main shell was intact, but the damage to the roof was more than he had expected. The wind, of course.

Inside, Wendy and Ruth had begun to recover clothing and Wendy's laptop, which fortunately had been left on a shelf that had not been damaged. They had taken their iPhones with them when they had fled. Everything they collected went into plastic bags from the kitchen. Ruth had not brought much with her that weekend. There was just her cardigan that had been draped over one of the benches. It was now wet through. Two pairs of their shoes, which had been on the floor were sodden. They would dry out though. They gathered up what they could and drove back to William's house, where Wendy and Ruth huddled together on the sofa, whilst William put the bags in the laundry room. Having set the wood stove alight, he came to sit beside them in one of the armchairs.

"I am so sorry, Wendy," said William. "There was more damage than I expected."

"Yes, it was much worse," said Wendy.

They were shocked by what they had seen. And now, as they sat together, each one was trying to figure out what might happen next. William was the first to speak.

"If you'd like to stay here for a while that would be fine by me. You know, until you decide what it is you want to do."

"Thank you, William," said Ruth. "That would be such a help. Would you mind me coming and going?"

"No, of course I wouldn't mind. I meant it to be for both of you."

"Two lesbian gypsies and one old man living in a house by the marsh. What will the village say?"

They laughed and William stood up and went into his study. He felt that Ruth and Wendy needed time to be with each other, alone.

A few days later, Wendy spoke to her uncle and discovered that he had no insurance for the caravan and no inclination to spend more money on having it repaired, even if it could be. Sorry though he was for Wendy, as far as he was concerned it was a write-off. The broken and bedraggled caravan would have to be towed away for some kind of 'burial'.

So, for the next several weeks, Wendy lived with William and Ruth visited at weekends. Then one Tuesday morning, whilst she was putting sheets and pillowcases in the washing machine, Wendy's mobile rang. It was Ruth.

"Hi, sweetheart, it's me. I have some news for you."

"I hope it's good news. I am feeling a little down and vulnerable at the moment."

"Yes, it is. You know I applied for that job Ipswich?"

"Yes."

"Well, they want me to go and see them. Apparently, I have been shortlisted."

"That's great, darling."

"Yes. I've arranged to see them this Thursday so that I can come up to Frampton that evening and we can have a long weekend."

"Good, I'll let William know. Actually, I think he may be going to London so we might have the house to ourselves."

"Sounds good. I'll let you know later today. Must go. Patients waiting to see me."

"Lucky them! Bye."

William was delighted with the news and confirmed that he had to go to London on Friday morning to check on some things at his flat and that he would not be back until lunchtime on Monday. Wendy made a note of the times of his trains so that she could take him to the station and then meet him on Monday

Ruth arrived on the Thursday evening. She had driven from London to Ipswich for her interview, so there were now two cars parked in William's drive. She and Wendy decided to take themselves out to supper in nearby Aldeburgh, and William had gone to bed before they returned. On the Friday morning, Wendy took William to Saxmundham station. Wendy and Ruth now had the house by the marsh to themselves. The day was fine. A fresh wind from the southwest promised the possibility of a shower or two. But no more than that. It was wonderful to feel the liberation of being by themselves.

Ruth had been offered the job at Ipswich hospital. It was three days a week with the occasional weekend. But this was perfect for her as she had also been asked to do some lecturing on occupational therapy for children at City University in London and needed time to prepare the work and teach it. Now she was thinking about selling her house in Croydon and moving to Suffolk. She had talked about the possibility of finding a house in Ipswich itself, but then Wendy had said that she would like to be earning a living, too.

"I just feel that it would be good if, this time, I was able to share costs with you, so that we worked out things together."

"You're right, that would feel good."

The more they talked about it, and the more Wendy spoke of how much she liked taking care of William, the more this seemed to become important to their plans.

Wendy liked living by the marsh and the sea.

"Why don't we live close to Frampton," she said, "so that I can continue to look after William? You would be able to drive to Ipswich on the days you are there. It's less than an hour to the hospital. And although it takes two hours to get to London by train from Saxmundham, you would not be going there all the time, and you have plenty of friends in London who would have you for the odd night."

"I do love it here," said Ruth. "But where would we live? We can hardly stay here with William."

But they did.

That is the strange and unexplainable way of things. Although they thought that living together would be impossible, the truth was that, as the weeks passed and Wendy and Ruth found they could not find a place to live in as easily as they had hoped, an odd alchemy began to work. Somehow or other their lives began to entangle. William, Wendy and Ruth. Although not one of them had thought this would happen, it did. Sometimes Providence decides these things for herself.

When William returned from London that Monday morning he was met by Wendy who told him all about Ruth's job interview and her decision to move from Croydon in time to take up her new post in the autumn. She also explained that they had agreed that they should both be working and that she hoped that he would still want her to be his housekeeper and gardener, at least for the time being. He was delighted and said that that was, of course, what he would want.

"Well, that is the way it shall be, then," he said. "Incidentally, isn't it about time we looked at your hourly rate again? I don't think we have ever changed it. Let's agree a new number."

And they did.

The following weekend, Wendy made supper for the three of them and William opened a bottle of red wine.

"I think this must be a celebration," he said as they sat down and raised their glasses. Clink, clink.

"Well done, Ruth. Congratulations on your new job. And the teaching work."

"I was looking at the websites of local estate agents," said Wendy, "and I have printed out some properties for us to look at. There's nothing actually in Frampton at the moment, but there are one or two in Saxmundham."

"We'll have a drive around tomorrow," said Ruth. "I spoke to the agent I bought my house from in Croydon and he says he could sell my house within days, which is encouraging. And I have spoken to my bosses who've told me that apparently I have rather a lot of accumulated holiday time that I have not taken. They are prepared to let me go in six weeks' time. Do you think you could bear having us both around while we sort all this out, William?"

"Why not? Let's see if it works."

After supper, Wendy and Ruth went for a walk and William sat in his armchair and read.

The next day, William rang his children. First Jane.

"Hi, Dad. Haven't heard from you for a while. Are you okay?"

"Yes, pretty much. What about you?"

"Well, things have settled down a bit. Ben and Sally are happy at school and even the shared weekends are working quite well. Gives me some time to go out with my friends, or just have quiet time for myself. They're with Robert today, actually. Strange how time by yourself comes to be important."

"Yes, it does. Very important. Talking of which, I have to tell you that I have Wendy and her friend Ruth living with me at the moment."

"What on earth is that all about? I thought Wendy lived in a caravan."

"She did, but we had a dreadful storm about a month ago and it ripped off a large part of the roof of her caravan, which unfortunately was not insured. It belonged to her uncle and he hadn't bothered. Nor was he prepared to pay for the repairs, which would have been extensive."

"So you took them in. Waifs and strays."

"Well, I could hardly pass by on the other side."

"No, I suppose you couldn't. Very noble, Dad. I bet it has caused a bit of a stir in Frampton. Now you're living with not one, but two lesbians."

"Jane, provincial Scotland may be shocked at such things, but here on the east coast of Suffolk we pay them no attention."

That was not quite true. No one had said anything to William, but the *ménage à trois* was of great interest in Frampton. Lady Whitely and the vicar had discussed it over tea and Mary had been asked about it several times by people coming into her shop, coming in for that very purpose and thus, having to buy items for which they had no need. Mary, who thought that it was delightful that William, Ruth and Wendy should be helping each other out, had enjoyed feeding the imaginations of her more puritanical customers, sharing their comments with Wendy.

"Did you know, Wendy, Mrs Brinkley asked what the sleeping arrangements were in the house? I told them I didn't know, but that there was only one bedroom which, fortunately, had a very large bed in it. She nearly dropped her jar of pickled onions!"

"You are dreadful, Mary."

"And Brenda and Penelope cried 'Hurrah!' and asked if they should send a food parcel. They, of course, would have you live there forever."

"Which I don't think we can."

CHAPTER 12

CHOSEN FAMILY

It was now April and, as the time came near for Ruth to leave her job in Croydon, she and Wendy began to look more urgently for somewhere to live. Ruth's agent had been right, and her house was sold within a couple of weeks of being put on the market, making not only its asking price but a bit more. She had the funds and the only constraint on finding a new house was just that – finding it. They were planning to use the following weekend to do some serious house-hunting.

William was thinking about something else. He had decided to buy a caravan. For many years, he had nurtured a fantasy of travelling across America in a classic Airstream trailer. Of course, it was a fantasy, for William had always disliked travel of almost any kind. In fact, his nightmares were often about trying to find his way to railway stations and then being unable to find the right platform or train. So finding his way across America in a caravan was never likely to happen. Which is why it had always been a fantasy. And it still was. Ever since the demise of Wendy's caravan though, he had been searching on the internet. And now he had discovered it, an Airstream trailer which was 'built for long-term adventures'. William noticed with approval that it said long-term adventures, not long-distance travel.

There were different Airstream models, but the one he liked was appropriately named 'The Classic'. Built of riveted silver aluminium, it was just over thirty feet long. It could sleep up to five people and had a queen-sized bed, a shower, a galley, a fridge and a living room with sofas and a table. It had TV, a water heater, air conditioning and a heat pump. He had even seen one that had a wood stove. Prices started at about £90,000. Much less than a country cottage. And secondhand Airstreams were available at very much less.

He had spoken to the local planners and established that, if he was buying a caravan for his own use, he could park it in his garden. He didn't tell them that was where it would remain. Anyway, if Roderick wanted his house back, he might have to find somewhere to live. In the meantime, he discovered that he could plug the caravan into the electricity supply of the house. And there was also the possibility of plumbing in a diesel-powered heater if the weather was very cold. Parked though it might be, for William, it represented freedom, the possibility, however unlikely, that he could, if he wanted to, just take off. And, in the meantime, it might serve another purpose.

On the following Sunday morning, Ruth, Wendy and

William sat together having their breakfast. William's morning supplements were held in a small dish beside a glass of water, and Wendy had made coffee for Ruth and tea for herself and William. William was dressed, but Wendy and Ruth were still in dressing gowns. Muesli and granola were now on the table beside William's Ryvita.

"How did you get on yesterday with the house hunt?"

"Not good, William," replied Ruth stirring her muesli rather gloomily. "We saw some bungalows we didn't like, or rather they were in roads we didn't like. There were a couple of terraced cottages in Saxmundham, but they had no gardens and were on busy streets. We looked at some new houses being built in Snape, but they were really family houses with much more accommodation than we want and, again, tiny gardens. And the one or two houses for sale in Aldeburgh are too expensive. It's all a bit depressing. And now I am worried that we might be out-staying our welcome."

"No, you're not," said William. "In fact, I want to talk to you about that. When we've finished breakfast, could we sit down and talk?"

"Yes, of course."

Once they had cleared away the breakfast things, they moved into the living room, Wendy and Ruth as usual taking the sofa whilst William took his armchair. Florence tried first one lap and then the next before giving up and disappearing.

"We all know that this house by the marsh is a special place," said William. "And I have signed a new three-year agreement with Roderick. It might even be extended. We like it here, don't we?"

"We do," said Wendy. "I have liked it since you first

asked me to be your housekeeper. I still do. And it was wonderful of you to rescue us. But we don't want to be a burden to you."

"A burden? You're not a burden my dear Wendy. You are my delight. But I don't want to hold you here when you find your own place. And I don't want you to feel you have to stay here just to look after me."

"It is odd, William, isn't it?" said Ruth taking Wendy's arm in hers. "It is hard to imagine how our living together might work, but we have slipped into it. Wendy and I have talked about it, and questioned it. But somehow we feel at ease. And we don't feel like guests. For me, it's more like living in a family. Can that possibly be how it is? You have provided for us, and we try and care for you. We all do our own work. We share meals together. We have time apart. That's family, isn't it?"

William smiled to himself. During the last few years he had grown in ways he could not have imagined before. He still carried deeply embedded fears and anxieties, his own particular ways of being, his own routines and frailties, but he no longer felt that acute need to be loved. He liked being loved. He liked being cared for. But he could be by himself. In fact, he liked being by himself. He enjoyed the company of his closest friends, especially Ruth, Wendy and Mary, and he liked to have his family to stay from time to time and to be in touch with them on Skype. But there was something else. Solitude. Sweet solitude. Somehow or other over the years since Caroline's death, and really only quite recently, he had moved from persistent loneliness to loneliness broken by moments of a comforting solitude. It was not all the time, but it was ever more frequent, and his friendships with

Mary, Wendy and now Ruth had made that possible. Mary had made him feel at home, feel as if he was welcomed in Frampton, as if he belonged. And Wendy, dearest Wendy, had brought a tenderness and a care he had never felt before. Was it because there was no sexual relationship between them, with all that would have brought with it? Was it the difference in their ages? Perhaps it was both. But being with Wendy was a great delight to William. And Ruth had brought something else, not the same tenderness, but a rather serious and gentle kindness. There was something comforting in being with Ruth. He wasn't sure they would ever be as close as he was with Wendy, but he knew that she would become a good and loving friend. He wondered if they knew how important they were to him.

Patterns shifting, moving easily.

Wendy and Ruth had walked into the garden and were now sitting on the veranda. William went out to join them, leaning on the veranda rail and looking out at the marsh, the beach and the sea. Listening to the sea. Without turning towards them, he said, "Suppose we stay as we are. We can if we want to."

Silence.

"No one can tell us how we should live, even if they were the slightest bit interested."

"Oh, they're interested," said Wendy. "You should hear what goes on in Mary's shop. They're interested."

"Well, they might be curious. It might even be strange to some people that we should live together. But are they really interested? Doesn't it just become how it is? The three of us living together? Isn't everyone taken up with their own lives? Isn't that what they are really interested in? Paying the bills, worrying about their health, loving and mourning?"

"I think you're right," said Ruth. "The interest will pass and we will become just a part of all that happens here. And anyway, there are some who already love us. Mary, Brenda and Penelope. Wendy says that even Lady Whitely in her own way cares about us and asks the vicar to pray for us."

"Really? How wonderful. Perhaps we should ask her to tea, with the vicar. Tea with the vicar."

They laughed.

"Yes, we should," said Ruth, "but there are some practical matters that we should discuss first. For example, even if we still look for somewhere to live, who pays for what in the meantime? And sometimes, William, I feel that the three of us don't have quite enough private space. I know you have your study, but the living room is the only space for us all to sit and read, and sometimes I feel as if Wendy and I might be intruding on your space or even, sometimes, that I want to be alone with Wendy."

"I've thought about that," said William. "And I have a solution."

"You have a solution? Just like that, you have a solution?"

"Yes. I'm going to buy a caravan."

Wendy and Ruth looked at each other.

"Actually, it's not a caravan, it's a trailer. I am going to indulge a long-held fantasy."

"Don't tell me you are going to take on the nomadic life, the wandering life of a gypsy?" said Wendy.

"No, that's not it. I hate travelling! But I am going to buy a Classic Airstream trailer and I am going to park it beside the house and I am going to live in it. Well, some of the time. I will keep my study with the campaign bed, and I will keep some of my clothes in my dressing room, but, for much of the time, I will live in the trailer. So the living room will become your space, your private space. We are going to reverse roles. You two are going to live in the house and I am going to live in my fantasy trailer. It could even have a wood stove. It has a galley, a sitting room and a queen-sized bed, and I can plug it into the electricity supply of the house. I will still use my dressing room, shower and bathroom, although the trailer does have a shower. And if we like we can always meet together for lunch or supper, even breakfast."

"I am rather worried that you might mean this," said Ruth. "It will certainly set the tongues wagging."

"Well, why not? You lived in your caravan quite happily, and mine will be even more comfortable and spacious. Tucked away at the back of the house amongst the trees, no one will see it much. And when I need a quiet space or time on my own, or when you do, I will pick up my laptop and move out. If you want to have a weekend on your own, I will either go to London or move into the trailer. Perfect, don't you think? And I can have guests too. It sleeps up to five. My grandchildren will love it."

"William, you never cease to surprise me," said Wendy. "Only you would have thought of buying a Classic Airstream trailer and attaching it to your house with some kind of umbilical cord. You are the oddest person ever."

"But seriously. Don't you think it could work? At least for two or three years? For me, that's a lifetime. And you two are young enough to recover if it all goes pear-shaped. No leases, no contracts. Nothing written down, just what we say we want to do. Let's walk down to the sea."

And so they did, walking through the garden, through the marsh, across the beach, the shingle leading them to the sea. Only the sounds of the gulls again reminding them, "We live here, too."

Possibility. Madness takes many forms. But one kind is the madness of possibility, being mad enough to see what others cannot even imagine, because they have stopped dreaming. After Caroline had died, William may have been a bit mad. He had been. But now another kind of madness was in full flow, rich and juicy. There were all sorts of problems to be overcome, but they seemed small by comparison with the wonderful possibility that he had come to believe in. And now Wendy and Ruth had begun to believe in it, too. One morning at breakfast, a day or two later, as they sat quietly together, Wendy suggested that it might be helpful to share their rather odd plans with someone they could really trust, someone who loved them but would be honest with them. Mary.

"Mary knows us and loves us, and she, more than anyone else, will speak her mind. Ruth and I just think it would be helpful to ask her if she thinks we could do this. You know, William, ask her what she thinks."

"I think that's a great idea. Why don't you see if she could come to tea on Sunday? Give her a call."

"Okay."

Wendy left the table and went into the living room. She picked up the phone and dialled Mary's number at the shop. It rang for some while and Wendy was just about to put the phone down when Mary answered.

"Oh, hello Mary, it's Wendy."

"Hello Wendy."

"Mary, I want to ask a favour of you."

"What can I do for you?"

"Would you be able to come to tea on Sunday?"

"That doesn't sound very difficult."

"No, but William, Ruth and I have something we want to ask you about."

"Sunday?"

"Yes, at about three-thirty or four?"

"Four would be fine. I'll ask Winny to cover for me. It all sounds very intriguing. I can't wait!"

Just after four o'clock on the following Sunday, Mary came up the steps of the veranda carrying a plate of her shortbread covered by a tea towel, white with a blue stripe. She was wearing a frock, with a cardigan over her shoulders. The frock was patterned with flowers in blues, purples and a deep pink. It was gathered at the waist by a thin leather belt and, much to William's surprise, she was wearing high-heeled shoes. The cardigan was cashmere and the colour of lilac. William realised that he seldom noticed what Mary looked like. How dreadful. But, on this afternoon, he did and he was struck by her beauty. She was quite slim with rounded breasts and, although her hair was as usual pulled back from her face, it was now held by an elaborate and almost exotic silver clasp, revealing, as if for the first time, a shapely and delicate ear. How odd that over the years that he had been in Frampton he had never before seen Mary like this, seen her as she was.

Wendy had put together the tea tray, and she brought it into the living room, placing the cups and plates on the low table. Ruth brought Mary's plate of shortbread. William and Mary each took an armchair and, as usual, Ruth and Wendy sat on the sofa. Florence came in and chose Ruth's lap. The shortbread was passed round and each of them took a piece from the plate. Once again, William saw the chapel of the Monastery of Vatopedi on Mount Athos, where amidst the candlelight and incense, he had watched the faithful take the offered bread of the Eucharist. No one else seemed to have noticed.

"Mary," said Wendy, "as you are one of our closest friends, William, Ruth and I have something we would like to share with you and seek your guidance."

"If it's about you living together, I already know and I have for some while been feeding the curiosity of the village with lurid scenes from your private lives."

"No, Mary that's not it. Well, it is, but it isn't."

"That sounds a bit complicated, 'it is, but it isn't.' Is that what you wanted to tell me? 'It is, but it isn't'?"

"No," said William. "Just listen for a moment. We are living together and we think we will probably do so for some while. But that is not the main thing. What we wanted to tell you, is this: I'm thinking of buying a caravan."

"A caravan? Well, that would be nice."

A short pause. Mary drank some of the tea. She was thinking of something.

"But won't you need a car too? How are you going to tow the caravan if you don't have a car?"

"That's the secret, Mary. No one must know this. Promise you will keep this secret?"

"I promise," said Mary.

"I don't propose to tow it anywhere."

"So that's the secret is it? You are buying a caravan, but you're not going to tow it anywhere."

"Yes. I'm not going to tow it, I am going to park it."

"You're going to park it? That doesn't sound all that secret."

"No, but I am going to park it in my garden, in the woodland at the back of my house and then I'm going to live in it."

"So you're going to live in a caravan in your garden?"

"More or less. You see, Wendy, Ruth and I like living together, but we need a bit more room. Wendy and Ruth need to have space where they can be together without me."

"Well, why don't they buy a caravan then?"

"That, my dearest Mary, would not do at all. Two lesbians living in a caravan in my garden? What would people say?"

"Well, I don't know what they would say, but they might be curious about two lesbians living in your house whilst you live in a caravan."

"Anyway, it's not a caravan. It's a trailer."

"A trailer?"

"Yes, a very special kind of trailer. It is a Classic Airstream trailer, 'built for long-term adventures'."

Another pause. Another sip of tea.

"But you don't like travel, William, especially long distance travel."

"Please note, Mary, I did not say long distance travel, I said 'long-term adventures.' The point is in the word 'adventures.' And this adventure is going to take place in my garden."

By now all of Mary's suspicions about the odd things that people do when they live in the house by the marsh were being confirmed. And William's proposed adventure in a trailer parked in his own garden was going to be high on her list.

"But no one must know Mary, because although I am allowed to park a caravan in my garden if I am going to use it for going on holidays, I can't really do so if I am going to live in it. It's against the rules."

"But what do you think?" asked Wendy. "Do you think it could work or are we all completely crazy?"

"Well yes, you are all obviously, completely crazy, but this does not come as a surprise. It's one of the things that I like about you. And, I suppose, in some ways I must be crazy, too. Who else would run a shop, a tea room and a post office in a remote village in Suffolk. I think we are all a bit crazy."

"But what do you think though? Might it work?"

For a moment, Mary looked down at her hands on her lap, as if she was reflecting on something that she had thought about before. A stillness.

"I know people think that I am just Mary at the shop, Mary who makes Eccles cakes and shortbread," she said, her voice now quiet, "but I know something about loss and grief. Those of us who have been widowed carry our loss. It does not go away; we just live with it. And then I have a son who I have not seen for over five years. I carry that, too. So when I see people who love each other, when I see tenderness and kindness, I think it is good, something that should be encouraged and supported. I see this in you three. Odd though it may be. That is what I see. I don't see two lesbians and an old man, I see three people who are fond of each other and take care of each other. That is a precious thing. Something to cherish."

She sat forward, placing her elbows on her knees and holding her face in her hands. For a moment, she seemed lost in her own thoughts, unaware of anyone else. The clasp that was holding back her hair had slipped. She reached up and took it out. Then, as if she knew that William would like it, she took her right hand and swept her hair back behind her ear. No one said anything. They just sat together, Wendy, Ruth and William knowing they had just been blessed by a woman who ran a tea shop and a post office. Wendy leant across and took Mary's arm. They smiled at each other. William had been taken to another place. Sweet sorrow. Ruth lifted up her cup and drank some of her tea. Her mind had been made up.

When Mary had gone, William went into his study and Ruth and Wendy curled up together on the sofa with Florence.

Throughout that summer, as William and Wendy and Ruth settled into their new life together, William had been reflecting on the matter of loneliness and solitude. It was not something he thought about in any analytical way. It was more like listening to poetry. Listening. The experience of solitude was now coming to him more often. Not all the time. No, not at all. But more often. And quite frequently now, when he woke or when he was sitting and reading in bed at night-time, there was a calm quiet presence, broken only from time to time by the sound of Wendy and Ruth moving through the house. He liked that. Something about things being as they should be.

Oddly, he seemed now more aware of his own mortality, the possibility that 'ceasing to be' might come upon him at any moment. But that did not seem to bother him all that much. It bothered him a bit, but not all that much. He liked to speak to his children, phoning them more often than they phoned him. Well, they were busy with all that they had to do, and that was the way it should be, too. But, much of the time, he was content to be by himself. And, after all, he had the things he loved most – his work and a chosen family. Even the now very occasional trips to London to attend meetings of the Academy. They had become who he was. A writer and a scholar living with his chosen family. And Mary was becoming part of this, too.

He saw Wendy at breakfast time, Ruth often having already left for work or gone to London to teach. Best of all, he often had supper with them both. He liked to listen to what had happened to them during the day. And after supper he would retire to his study, leaving them to talk to each other or to sit and read. And when he was ready for bed he would walk through to his dressing room to wash and clean his teeth, returning in his pyjamas and dressing gown, before saying, "Good night you two." And they would say, "Good night William, sleep well." And he did.

And so the months passed. Summer gave way to autumn and then autumn gave way to winter and, in early December, Wendy, Ruth and Mary had lunch with William at the house by the marsh to celebrate his birthday.

Afterwards, when Wendy and Ruth decided to go for a walk, William and Mary sat quietly together.

"You know, Mary, you remind me of someone."

"Not your mother, I hope."

"No, not my mother. You remind me of another Mary."

"And who is that?"

"Mary Magdalene."

"Wasn't she a prostitute?"

"No. That is how the men of the early church decided to portray her, the penitent prostitute, but actually she was a holy woman. She washed the feet of Jesus and was the first one who came to his tomb, the first to see the risen Christ."

"Well, I haven't done much feet-washing."

They laughed.

"And why did they say she was a prostitute?"

"They were frightened of her."

"Frightened of her?"

"Yes. You see she was the disciple that Jesus loved most, his companion. Her name was probably Miriam of Magdala, but she became known as Mary Magdalene. And she wrote a gospel, or it might have been that a gospel was written about her. Towards the end of the nineteenth century, in upper Egypt, fragments of this gospel were discovered. One of the so-called Gnostic gospels. It is quite extraordinary and talks of a world of wonderment and integration. It was, of course, excluded from the canon of the official church."

"But why do I remind you of her, William?"

"Well, I think that in some ways you are a holy woman, too. When you serve us your tea, you wash our feet, and when you bring your shortbread covered in a white napkin, you bless us. It is like a Eucharist."

"You do talk the most awful nonsense, William. Now I'm going to have to tell the whole village what you said."

"You should do that. Get them going before my trailer arrives."

That afternoon, Wendy made tea for William and the two of them sat on the veranda. As it was his birthday, she had bought him an Eccles cake and gave him a card from Ruth and herself. It was of an old man, bent and walking with a stick, and inside it said, *Something to look forward to! Not just yet! Happy Birthday, with love from Ruth and Wendy.*

"Thank you, Wendy, I suppose I must regard myself as becoming old, although I don't yet feel it. I still get caught out when I am with other people and realise that they are all younger than me, that I am the oldest person there."

"Well, William, I would love you if you were one hundred and three. In fact, that would just make me love you all the more."

She leant across and kissed him on his cheek, holding her lips there for longer than a mere peck. He smiled.

"You have been such a blessing to me, Wendy. And I have learnt so much from you. And from Ruth. Are you two happy? You know, getting along okay?"

"We are," she said, taking his arm and leaning against him. "We have the usual ups and downs, but we have discovered something in each other that we couldn't find before. And, in an odd way, you have been part of that. The fact that I have a job being your housekeeper and gardener has helped. But there is something else. Before we lived with you, we always felt a bit, I don't know, exposed, even isolated. Everything depended on us. Being with you shifts the balance. We feel sort of more at home. Belonging. There is something about caring and being cared for that seems right, as if things are meant to be. Do you remember you once told me that we are meant to love? Well, once you see yourself as naturally loving, everything else changes, falls into place, doesn't it? I now understand that more than ever before."

"Me, too."

They sat for a while looking out towards the sea, a fresh wind stirring the reeds in the marsh.

Later that month, a large Land Rover drove down the
street that runs through Frampton towing a beautiful
silver caravan, or rather, a trailer – William's Classic
Airstream. The driver and his assistant arrived at the
house by the marsh and were now beginning to wonder
if their Sat Nav had taken them the wrong way. Then
William appeared and began to give directions. The
trailer had to be turned round and reversed into his
drive before he could direct it, backwards, towards its
new woodland setting. William had already arranged
for a connection plug to be fitted to the outside of the
house and the driver explained to William how to fit
the cable that would take the electricity into the trailer.
He had also brought with him a special 'no-trip' cover
made of rubber to place over the cable to protect it from
the weather. In the end, William had forgone the wood
stove. The trailer had its own electric heating and he
had also bought a German diesel-powered heater,
which he hoped would keep him warm in the coldest
months. If that did not work, he would sleep in his
study. And, in their tenderness, Wendy and Ruth had
assured him that he could always join them by the
wood stove in the evening if he promised to be
very quiet.

And so began William's adventure. Wendy and Ruth
had asked if he would prefer that they live in the trailer.
After all, they had lived in a caravan before. But William
would have none of it. It was his adventure, his fantasy

and he began to spend his evenings in his trailer, sometimes sleeping there, too, and sometimes coming back to his study. Breakfasts were shared, at least shared with Wendy, and suppers, too, although after supper William would retire to his study or his trailer so that Ruth and Wendy could have time together. William had let Roderick know that Ruth and Wendy were going to be living with him for a while and that he hoped that would be okay. Roderick had replied to say it was.

One evening, just as he was about to retire, Ruth asked him if he would sit with them for a while. Wendy stood up and began to prepare coffee for Ruth and tea for herself. William just filled his glass with water. They left the table and went into the living room. Wendy brought in the mugs of coffee and tea, placing them on mats on the low table. She curled up beside Ruth on the sofa. William sat beside them in his armchair.

"You know, William," said Ruth, "I am not sure you realise how special it is for us, for Wendy and me, to live with you. I know it works for us because we love this house and we like being by the marsh and the sea. And, of course, Wendy likes caring for you. But there is something else, something we might not have if it weren't for you. I know we have said this before, but it's about living as a family. And you are so caring of us. Taking all that trouble to make sure we have enough space. And then the way you make sure we have time on our own. You are a father to us."

"More like a grandfather."

"And actually it is not about being a father. I got that wrong. Completely wrong. It is more like having a lover, you know. Not, of course, in the usual sense, the sexual sense. But someone who cares for you, is tender and thoughtful, someone who is loving. Isn't that a lover?"

"What a wonderful thought."

"Yes, I think we shall now talk about you as being our lover."

Wendy smiled.

"I think that will be our secret," she said.

"Yes, our secret," said William.

"And," said Ruth, "we shall just say we are 'chosen family'."

"Chosen family it is then," said William.

And they laughed together.

Jane, Ben and Sally came to visit at Christmas time and, as Wendy and Ruth had gone to London to be with friends until after the New Year, William was able to fit them all into the house, although Ben wanted to sleep in the trailer and William said he would join him. He took the queen-sized bed and Ben made up one of the sofa beds at the other end of the trailer. Jane and Sally remained in the house, Jane preferring, as usual, to sleep in William's dressing room. Ben did not think his grandfather was at all mad. In fact, he thought he was 'cool'.

In the morning, Ben invited everyone to bring their breakfasts into the trailer. Which they did.

"By the way," said Jane, "I meant to tell you that Ben is applying to the University of Edinburgh to study Land and Property Management. It is something his father thinks might lead to a good job."

"And what do you think, Ben?"

"Well, I'm not sure, really. But I suppose Dad's right."

Providence heard what Ben had said and wondered if this was true.

Much to William's relief, Jane seemed to have found a way of living in Scotland. She was working part-time in a solicitor's office and had begun to take an interest in family law, something of which she felt she had experience. One of the partners was encouraging her to take some courses, possibly with a view to becoming a Family Legal Assistant. She found she was good at it, patient, straightforward, a good listener.

Knowing she was going to be on her own, William had invited Mary to join them for Christmas lunch. And so, although William, of course, would not eat the turkey the five of them sat down to a traditional roast turkey, 'with all the trimmings': bread sauce, cranberry sauce, chipolatas, Brussels sprouts, carrots, cabbage, little squares of fried bread, plenty of gravy and, of course, roast potatoes cooked in the fat of the turkey. And this was followed by Christmas pudding and mince pies with brandy butter, all of which Mary had made and brought with her. And there were Christmas crackers with paper hats and riddles.

In the afternoon, when Mary had gone home, Frederick and Ana called by Skype from São Paulo. They were having Christmas day with Ana's parents and all of them joined in to say, "Happy Christmas."

Six years had passed.

During the following year, life began to settle. Ben managed to get the A-level grades he needed for his degree course, and in September he started his studies, moving away from home for the first time and living in student accommodation on the university campus. And in the house by the marsh, Wendy, Ruth and William continued to live happily together, their routines becoming the shape of their lives. Sometimes Wendy and Ruth, or William by himself, would decide to go to London for the weekend, using the flat in Marylebone to stay in. But most often they were content to be in Frampton. Small irritations or discomforts were either talked about or just ignored and, as those who love each other do, they also spent much time in each other's company without a word being spoken, love and freedom arising.

Although he had studied the teachings of the Buddha long before, and knew about the origins of suffering, it was only now that William discovered – really felt – that inner peacefulness or equanimity which comes from the 'divine abidings' and from the spaces in between, from loving kindness, compassion and joy in and for others. In that freedom, the chosen family were becoming who they most truly were – loving beings. And perhaps there was something about the uncertainty of it all that made it so. Not knowing whether it would work. Not knowing whether Roderick would want his house back. Not knowing, this time, whether Ruth and Wendy would be content with each other. And, for William, not knowing when the 'coming to be' would become the 'ceasing to be.' In one way or another, they all had to accept what the day would bring and not fret about the morrow.

At the end of the year, the last evening of the year, when they had all been together for supper, the 'chosen family', Wendy and Ruth and William, and now also Mary, walked down to the sea in the moonlit darkness. One behind the other, they walked through the garden and across the marsh, and then they took each other's arms and walked across the beach until they came to the water's edge. The wind was now cold and they came close together for warmth.

William suggested that they should each throw a stone into the sea and make a New Year's wish. And they did.

Not all of those wishes came true.

Back in the house, Florence was curled up asleep on her favourite chair in the study, the reeds disturbed by the wind.

Seven years had passed.

PART 2

NOT ALL THEIR
WISHES CAME TRUE

CHAPTER 13

DISTURBANCE

William's study had become a place of stillness and silence. It was as if the solitary writings and the philosophical ponderings that took place there had seeped into the wooden floor, his desk, the very fabric of the room. It was, as always, neat and orderly. The campaign bed was made, the duvet folded and the pillows set straight. Every book was straightened on the desk or on its shelf; his pens and pencils in separate jars; his Kilim slippers carefully placed by the door. The only clue that he had recently been there was the pencil left in the centre of his open journal, the blue leather-bound one that Jane had given him for Christmas – his favourite present.

He was not there because he had walked down to the beach – a place which, as always, gave him solace and a sense of well-being. He was wearing an overcoat and wellington boots over his pyjamas, a scarf and a woolly hat. Today, dressed as he was, or rather undressed as he was, he'd left the house and ventured to the water's edge because he had wanted to recapture or at least reconnect with the sense of possibility he'd felt the night before when he had gathered on the shore with his chosen family, Wendy, Ruth and now Mary, too. Earlier that morning he had written in his journal:

January 1st

Beginning. The first day of the year. The first page of my journal. Now that I am seventy-seven, I am choosing to write in pencil, which fades. Like me!

Last night, Wendy, Ruth, Mary and I threw pebbles into the sea and made our wishes for the year ahead. I don't know what they wished for, but I wished that our life together would continue. I wonder if that was too much to ask for? I hope not. After all, each one of us has sought a kind of refuge here. And having found it, it would be good to have some time to enjoy it.

This morning, as I sit in bed in my study, I can hear Wendy and Ruth in the house, Wendy making breakfast. Ruth is not working today because it is a holiday, but I suppose she is so used to getting up and going to work that she is awake. Perhaps they are having tea and coffee in their dressing gowns. They probably have plans to go out for the day.

I have come to rely on Wendy rather more than I think must be good. But she knows my ways and knows how much I like the 'Order of the Day'. The daily rituals of breakfast, getting dressed and tea in the afternoon. I am blessed by my 'chosen family'. Just knowing they are there is a blessing.

I think I will walk down to the sea.

When he came back, the house was empty. Wendy and Ruth had gone. William thought it odd that they had not said goodbye, but then he saw a note on the table where Wendy had set his breakfast. He picked it up and read it. It said: 'Good morning William and Happy New Year. It's a lovely day and Ruth and I are going out. Lunch in Southwold and back for tea.' He folded the note and put it into the pocket of his coat. Then he sat down at the table and, for a moment, let the day come to him.

After breakfast, he washed and dressed, and then spent the rest of the day working on a proposal for a book he had been discussing with his publishers, Bagwoods. It was to be about T S Eliot and his wives, Vivienne and Valerie. William wanted to explore their relationships in the light of Eliot's treatment of women in his poetry. He had a lot of reading to do, but he wanted to get the proposal off before the end of the month. Everyone at Bagwoods had sounded interested and encouraging. He felt alive. Work to do.

And so the year began. And as William worked on his book, life at the house by the marsh was easy and settled. In Frampton, everything was going on in a familiar and pleasing way. His friends, Mary, Brenda and Penelope seemed well, each taken up with their own worlds. Mary was busy with her shop and her tea room, whilst Brenda and Penelope were planning a number of holidays. They had been bitten by the cruise bug and their sitting room was scattered with magazines devoted to cruise ships and holidays. Their plans for the year included a cruise in the Nordic fiords, an eastward crossing of the Atlantic and a river cruise up the Rhone from Aries to Beaune. Travel adventures. William could not imagine anything worse than being cooped up with a lot of people he neither knew nor liked, but he didn't say so. They would have a jolly time.

Spring came to the marsh and William had ordered a colony of bumblebees. Earlier in the year, he had read an article about the dramatic decline in their numbers and about a company that could provide them for your garden. For him, this was a small act of protest against a kind of mindless farming that meant the loss of hedgerows and wildflowers; of trees being cut down and the use of harmful sprays. He wanted to be on the side of the bumblebees.

And so one morning in early May, at about lunchtime, a delivery van drew up in front of William's gate. William, in his study, heard the noise of the gate opening and then the sound of someone walking across the gravel path and onto the veranda. There was a knock on the front door and William opened it to find a man standing beside two cardboard boxes, one much larger than the other.

"Shall I leave them here?"

"What are they?"

The man looked at his delivery note.

"Well, the bigger box contains a bumblebee hive, and I think the smaller one contains the bumblebees. They're buzzing."

"Oh, yes. Excellent. I had forgotten they were coming today. Would you mind leaving the larger box just over there, in the garden, by those lavender bushes? And you can leave the smaller one here on the veranda, in the shade."

"Yes, sure."

When Wendy came to make tea, William showed her the box of bumblebees. She bent down so that she could hear the bees.

"Oh my God, William! They really are bumblebees. Delivered in a box! In a van!"

Together, they opened the larger box and took out the wooden hive, which they positioned so that the bumblebees would have a clear flight path amongst the lavender bushes and the grasses that surrounded it and which provided some light shade. Then they brought the smaller box from the veranda and put it down carefully beside the hive. They lifted the roof of the hive and then opened the smaller box, reading the instruction sheet that had come with it. Wendy bent down, picked up the colony of bees in its plastic container and placed it into the hive, so that its doorway faced to the front of the hive, which had an open entrance way, like a small letter box, through which Wendy could see the doorway covered by a sliding panel. She pulled the panel back to reveal the access hole, the opening through which the bumblebees would pass to and fro. Everything was now set and the colony was left to settle in. Once they had exhausted the supply of sugar water that had been provided for their journey, they would begin to forage and to pollinate.

There was an odd sense of ritual in setting up the bumblebee hive. It was as if opening the door to the colony invoked another turn of the seasons. The possibility of the coming of summer. I felt as if I was part of something that might go on forever.

Yesterday, Wendy, Ruth and I took our supper down to the water's edge and sat together talking until the evening light had gone, enjoying being a family. It was as if we, too, might go on forever. But even though we don't talk about it, we all know this cannot really be. I know there will come a day when the two of them will want to leave and set up home together. Have their own place. That is how it should be - even though I try to push it away and pretend it is not so.

And so it was that one summer evening, in June, Ruth came back from work with something to tell Wendy. A colleague at work had spoken to her about a house that was coming up for sale in the nearby village of Friston. It wasn't yet on the market, but the owners were keen to find a cash buyer and avoid the hassle of a buying chain. She had driven past it on the way home and thought it might be just right for them. That evening, when William had gone into his study to work, they sat together on the sofa and agreed that they should at least have a look. The next day, Ruth arranged to collect the key, which was being held by a neighbour. They went to see it and, at once, knew that this is where they wanted to live. Their place. They decided not to tell William about it straight away. After all, what would be the point if they found they could not buy it? But they could. They made an offer, it was accepted and solicitors were instructed. They hoped to be able to complete before the end of August. William had to be told.

At the weekend, when they were having breakfast together, Ruth showed William a photo of the cottage taken on her iPhone. He knew at once what it meant.

"William," said Ruth, "you know that after I sold my house in Croydon we looked for a house to buy and couldn't find anything, and then you took us in?"

William was trying to hide his mounting anxiety, saying, "Yes, of course, but it was only ever meant to be until you could find something for yourself."

"Well, we've found a house in Friston which was not on the market and, because we are cash buyers, the owners have agreed terms with us. Would you come and see it with us?"

"Yes, of course."

"Shall we go after breakfast?"

"Yes, why not?"

"We would like to take Mary too. What do you think?"

"I think that's an excellent idea."

So Ruth phoned Mary, who fortunately had Winny working with her that morning, and she agreed to join them. She knew what this would mean for William.

Ruth drove them, and within twenty minutes, they found themselves in the village of Friston, pulling into the gravel driveway of a cottage, which was one of a pair overlooking the village green. Ruth unlocked the door and they went in. The cottage had one living room-come-kitchen and a small sitting room on the ground floor, and two bedrooms and a bathroom upstairs, one of which could accommodate their London friends when they came to stay. There was also a downstairs cloakroom with a shower. The cottage was snug. Pretty.

"This is just perfect for you," said William.

"Well, we think so," said Ruth. "It's been so difficult to find something we liked and could afford. As soon as we saw it and as soon as we came into the kitchen, we knew it was for us. And it has all happened without a hitch."

"Providence," said William.

"Perhaps so," said Ruth.

"I think it's very nice," said Mary. "And you have a garden, too."

"Yes, we have a garden," said Wendy, smiling with delight at Ruth.

Wendy took Mary's arm and they walked out into the garden.

"He will find your going hard, Wendy."

"I know, but he has always told us we should live our lives, not his. And it is not as if we shall leave him. I shall still look after him."

"But you won't be living with him, will you?"

"No, we won't."

"I'll keep an eye on him."

Ever since William had first come to Frampton and said how much he liked Eccles cakes, and ever since that day when she saw he had been crying, Mary had felt she might be needed by him. And now it seemed her time might be coming. She hoped so. After all, she too was alone and over the past five or so years they had become close friends. She was fond of him.

They drove back to Frampton, Wendy and Ruth talking about their plans to redecorate and to make raised beds for vegetables. Sitting in the back of the car and noting how quiet William had gone, Mary took his arm and he put his hand upon hers.

That evening after having supper together, Wendy made cups of camomile tea and brought them into the living room where William and Ruth were sitting.

"I know this must be difficult for you, William," she said. "We have been so content living together."

"But it has always been something that would come to an end," he said. "And so it should be. So it should be. Anyway, it's not as if you are going to live in Australia! And now I shall have peace and quiet." He paused and for a moment, there was silence. "Not that I have minded having you live with me. Not at all. It has been a delight."

But all three of them knew that something was coming to an end, and that William would feel left behind. And he did.

In the next weeks, surveys were undertaken, contracts were signed and the purchase completed. Wendy and Ruth were busy with their plans and spent many evenings at the cottage, measuring up and choosing paint colours. As a housewarming present, William had brought Wendy six good sized clay pots for her garden and a set of stainless steel saucepans from Liberty, which were now standing in boxes in his living room ready for moving day.

One evening, when Wendy and Ruth had gone to Friston, Mary called by. William was pleased to see her and invited her to come in.

"Would you like a drink of some kind?"

"I would love a cup of tea, if you don't mind."

"Excellent. I'll put the kettle on."

"Let me help you."

It was a warm evening and so they sat together on the veranda.

"I knew this would happen, Mary," said William, wanting to share his feelings with her. "I knew Wendy and Ruth had to find a place for themselves. But I have so enjoyed our time together. I can't help it. It does feel like a loss. Being left behind again, you know."

"It's never easy, is it?" said Mary. "Both you and I know about that. This wretched feeling of loneliness. No longer being a part of."

"And there is so little one can say about it."

"Almost nothing at all."

When William had first known Mary he had only thought of her in her shop. But then there had been times, times when they had been drawn together in reflection and conversation, when he had seen something else. This evening was one of those times. Mary was wearing her pale flowered frock, belted at the waist and a cardigan worn loosely over her shoulders. As usual her hair was pulled back behind her ears with tortoiseshell hair grips. She was wearing a pair of light sandals and her legs were summer bare.

"Let's walk down to the sea."

So they walked through the garden and across the boarded walkway to the beach. Mary took William's arm and they walked across the shingle.

"I am thinking of bringing a bench down here so that I can sit and look at the sea. What do you think?"

"I think that would be lovely. You would have to make sure it was above the tide mark, though."

William smiled at Mary's practical thought.

After Mary had gone home, William decided to go to bed early and read. He sat up in bed, his window open, listening to the sea, and writing in his journal. ❡

20th July

When Wendy and Ruth leave at the end of August, I will once again be by myself. Mad though it was, I had just got so used to their being with me. Just their being in the house made me feel good.

I cannot help but remember that we threw stones into the sea at the end of last year and made our wishes. It seems as if not all of them have come true. Not mine.

So now I have to begin again. I am finding this difficult. Perhaps the new book will take up my time?

But that was not to be, and in the first week of September, two days after Ruth and Wendy had moved out – the house feeling particularly empty – William received a phone call from his publisher, Barbara Stirling of Bagwoods.

"Good morning, Barbara. I hope you are in good spirits?"

"I am, William. Thank you for your proposal for the Eliot book."

"Yes, I am rather looking forward to getting on with it."

"Well, that is why I am calling. You see, we don't think it works for us."

William was shocked. This was not at all what he had expected. He thought they would be talking about structure, deadlines. He felt his stomach tighten.

"What do you mean it doesn't work for you?"

"Well, we have thought carefully about it and we don't think it is really suitable for us."

"But I thought we had agreed that it would be of great interest?"

"Well, we did say that. But I'm afraid there has been a change of heart. The market for this kind of book is very difficult at the moment. Libraries and universities are all cutting their budgets, and we are under the same sort of financial pressure ourselves. We have to focus on the most popular kinds of books. And I'm afraid that doesn't include Eliot. There is a feeling that everything that can be said has been said about him, including his wretched wives. It has all been said before."

And that was that. William thanked her for letting him know and rang off. Another blow. Disappointment. It triggered a memory of when, as a boy at boarding school, he had opened the birthday present from his parents. It was a pair of roller skates. Except they were the wrong kind. Everyone at school had rubber-wheeled skates. These skates had wheels made of a hard fibre. Disappointment. Almost shame. And now, as then, he could say nothing. It was done. What he might have to say about Eliot and his wives apparently didn't matter.

Suddenly his life was empty. He had been a man

living with two women and now he wasn't. He had been a writer with work to do. Now he wasn't. He felt himself begin to fall. This was not good.

William went out to the veranda. He lifted one of the benches and, struggling a bit, carried it onto the beach, where he found a place for it above the high tide line. He sat down on the bench and listened to the waves turning and then drawing back. He thought he heard someone walking across the shingle. He turned, and although he could not see anyone there, he knew who it was. He smiled.

"Is that you, Caroline?"

"Yes. I'm sorry about your book, William, and about Wendy and Ruth moving out and leaving you alone."

"Yes, I'm a bit lost."

"Well, you have Mary. She is a good friend, and you always preferred the company of women."

"Yes, I suppose that's true. Sorry."

"Why should you be sorry?"

"No reason really."

"And you still have work to do?"

"You think so?"

"Yes, I do. I think you have work to do for yourself."

"Yes, maybe that's it. Work for myself."

A light breeze was beginning to pick up from the east.

"Will you stay with me, Caroline?"

"I have no choice, William. You are still holding part of me."

"Am I?"

"Yes, you are. Which is fine by me. I like it here. But it won't go on forever. One day you will have to let go of me, too. For both our sakes."

"I will?"

"Yes, you will."

"But when? When will that be?"

But she was no longer there.

William sat for a while and then stood up and walked back to the house. Unfortunately, there was more to come. They say bad news comes in threes.

Two days later, William received an email from the secretary of the Academy in London of which he had, for some time been an Honorary Fellow. It said that the list of Fellows was being reviewed. As they wanted to invite some younger and more active Fellows and did not want the list to be too long, they were asking some of the older ones, like William, if they would consider standing down. They recognised that he was now living in the country and had not really been able to make a contribution in recent years, so they hoped he would understand. William was rather shocked. It wasn't that he wanted to go to London and be part of the work of the Academy, it was just that he rather liked being able to refer to himself as a Fellow. And, having just lost his book, now to be dropped like this was more hurtful than it might otherwise have been. Another blow. He composed a short email in reply saying that he, of course, understood and was happy to make way for younger Fellows, and then he sent it. The noise it made as it left his laptop sounded like some vital part of him disappearing into the ether. He went to bed.

10th September

I am not feeling so good. Of course, I felt a sense of loss when Wendy and Ruth moved out. But now,

now that the book has gone away and I am no longer needed at the Academy, I am wondering what is left of me. It is not that any one of these things is substantial, after all, Wendy stills looks after me, and neither the book nor the Academy are that important. It is just that coming together as they have done I now I feel utterly abandoned.

Ten years ago when my life was 'busy,' I thought that to let go of responsibilities and burdens would be liberating. But it isn't. I have never liked being left behind, and now I am frightened.

I suppose I hadn't given the possibility of this happening enough thought, and perhaps I should have seen it coming. But I didn't. To choose to let go of something is one thing. But to be told that you are no longer needed, to be left behind, is something else. And the sensation is physical. A kind of fear. I remember how it felt at school not to be selected for the football team. To be left out. Waiting for the list to be pinned on the noticeboard and feeling the anxiety in my stomach. Wondering if my name would be there. Sometimes it was. But when it wasn't I felt a terrible rejection. Not good enough to be included.

And this is how I feel now: not good enough to be included. Left out. I can feel the fear rising. My demon. In the last year or so, I thought it might have gone forever. But it has not.

CHAPTER 14

CRISIS

When Wendy arrived the following morning at nine, William was still in bed. She knocked on his door.

"You okay in there?"

"Just a bit slow this morning."

"Breakfast is on its way."

"Okay."

William came out of his study wearing his dark blue dressing gown over his pyjamas. Bare feet. He was not feeling good, but didn't want to talk about it. He waved at Wendy and disappeared into his dressing room, eventually reappearing dressed as usual in his loose linen trousers and jacket over a white collarless shirt. He walked through to the kitchen and sat at the table. Wendy brought him his porridge. He straightened his knife and the spoon beside the jar of marmalade, and took his napkin from its silver ring.

Wendy could tell that something had happened.

"You're very quiet this morning."

How was he going to tell her how he felt? It was pitiful really that he should have let these blows knock him down. It was just that these things had become who he was. And now he wasn't. He remembered that when Caroline died he had been shocked that one moment she was alive and then she wasn't. In the snap of a finger, she wasn't. And now this. In the snap of a finger he wasn't who he had been.

"Just a bit thoughtful, Wendy. One or two things have gone wrong. Nothing fatal."

"Sorry about that. What would you like for lunch?"

"Oh, I don't know."

"We have one of those roasted vegetable tartlets from Waitrose. Would you like that? You could have it with salad."

"Yes, that would be fine."

"And I have put a white wash in the washing machine, if you could put it in the dryer later."

"Yes, okay."

"So, I'll see you this afternoon then."

"Yes, that's good. See you this afternoon."

After Wendy had left, William sat at the table holding his mug of tea in both hands. Unable to move. He had not slept well. His sleep had been broken and short. He felt tired, very tired. Then, as he sat there, something shocking happened. It was as if, in that moment the whole of his past life caught up with him and was now dragging him down. Sitting there in his dressing gown and holding his mug of tea, he felt its weight upon him. It was as if a dank and clinging blanket came down and fixed itself all about him. Slowly, it spread over his entire body. He was suffocating and could hardly breathe. His chest tightened. His jaw was set. He took a handkerchief from the pocket of his dressing gown and mopped his forehead. He was frightened. He closed his eyes and then took one or two very deep breaths. He sat still. After a while, it eased. He stood up and poured himself a glass of cold water, which he drank. He poured another and drank that, too. Gradually the anxiety subsided and he began to breathe more easily.

He walked through to his study and opened his journal. His hand was shaking. He waited, and then began to write.

I think I may have just suffered a panic attack. I have never felt anything quite like it before. It was frightening. And now, for some odd reason, I have in my head the words, "Who loves ya baby?" I seem to remember it was a catchphrase used years ago by a TV character called Kojak. He used to suck a lollipop and say it: "Who loves ya baby?" I can't remember why he said it or what it was meant to mean. But in this moment, sitting here in my study, it's in my head. Going round and round.

So, is that what all this is about? Wanting to be loved? Is that what happened to that Small Boy? Is that why I tried so hard to be in the first team? To be selected. To be loved. Is that what this is about?

Being rejected, being left out? Sounds a bit dramatic, doesn't it?

Again, he sat still, then he remembered something.

Late in the afternoon, one day in mid-August, I went to inspect my bumblebee hive. For several days, there had been no bees passing in or out, and when I lifted up the roof, I discovered what I had expected. The new Queens had left to find wintering places for hibernation. The old Queen and her workers were dead. They had done their work, and were no longer needed.

Now I, too, am no longer needed.

William put down his pencil and closed the journal. He had hoped the writing would calm him, but now the anxiety was returning. He went to his bed and lay down. He took off his glasses and closed his eyes. Again, the panic receded, but he remained lying down and, after a while, he fell asleep.

When he awoke, he looked at his watch. It was almost midday. He sat up and could hear the sound of the sea. He put his glasses back on and stood up, needing some fresh air. Picking up his Panama hat, he walked out of the house, and onto the beach, along the water's edge, watching the seagulls swooping low over the waves and then rising up and round in a curve. Then he came back to his bench and sat down, feeling the warmth of the sun. After sitting there for a while, he walked back into the house.

Over the next few days, William did not leave his house, but stayed inside, hoping that the routine of his days would bring him comfort. Which it did. Order. Slowly, his body began to find its own pace. In the morning at around three, it woke him to go to the bathroom for a pee. He did not put on the light. He went back to bed and slept on and off until he became wakeful at six, when he would sometimes read. He was often disturbed by a night of dreams. Trying to get somewhere, but never doing so. Another visit to the bathroom. Old man's bladder. He then returned to bed and lay quietly on his back, calming his agitated mind by using a mantra given to him by a Tibetan monk: "*Om, Ah, Hung, Sri,*" a Buddhist mantra of purification. He repeated it, slowly.

At seven-thirty, he sat up and, with a glass of water, took two of his supplements, Gaba and L-Theanine. These were meant to calm the ancient, reptilian depths of his body and mind.

Since he no longer shaved, taking a shower, drying himself and cleaning his teeth took very little time. Ten minutes. Then he would dress. Most of the year, he would not wear socks and this summer was unusually warm. Barefoot, he walked from his dressing room to the kitchen, feeling the silence, feeling the wooden floor beneath his feet.

Each day, the same morning routine: breakfast, supplements, his mug of tea, the mug white with the swirling pattern on the base. He sat at the table and let silence and stillness be his prayer of thanks, for the day, for the food and drink, for his well-being. He liked the repeated Orthodox prayer of the Hesychasts, "Lord have Mercy," and the one he had made for himself, calling on the Holy Mother, the Great Mother: "Holy Mother full of grace, comfort me and bring me peace." It was not that he thought that these prayers were to someone, a person, a Lord, a Mother. But they called forth from within him a necessary sense of his own insignificance, his own smallness. A dot on a dot on a dot. It comforted him. And in his present mood of fearfulness, it brought him some kind of ease, a glimpse of an inner peacefulness he now sought. Abide there. This was the beginning of his day. Every day. And as it was into a chasm that he had fallen, was still falling, it enabled him to hold on. Without it, he would have been lost.

In the evening, there was a similar ritual for his supper, a light supper, soup or eggs. And this prepared him for an early bedtime. But it was the vast landscape of the day that was most difficult. His only survival was to place within it markers of time. Because lunch was his main meal, its preparation and eating broke the day into two parts: a morning, which despite all that had happened, he still regarded as his main work time, a time for him to read or write in his journal, and an afternoon when he would often sleep, returning to his work in the late afternoon and then again in the evening after supper.

And then there were his children, Jane and Frederick. He needed to speak to them. First Jane. He rang her.

"Hello, Dad. Where have you been. I was beginning to wonder whether you had gone away somewhere."

"Most unlikely. In my present mood."

"What 'present mood'?"

"Well, I've given up. Given up my life. You know I spoke to you about the Eliot book?"

"Yes."

"And you said you wouldn't read it?"

"Yes"

"Well it turned out that nobody wanted to read it. I didn't really want to write it and probably no one wanted to read it."

"Dad, just because I didn't want to read it doesn't mean that there aren't lots of people out there who do."

"No. You were right. It's been done before and no one is any longer interested in Eliot's sex life."

"So, what happened?"

"My publishers decided not to publish it."

"Oh dear."

"And then the Academy decided to end my Honorary Fellowship."

"That's a shame."

"Well, it's touched an old wound, and now I feel lost and abandoned, and I find myself on the edge of a very deep and dark looking chasm. A void."

"Dad, that's not so good. I've been there or somewhere like it. It's not good. What are you doing?"

"What did you do?"

"I sulked. I panicked. I drank most of a bottle of Rioja, which gave me a wretched headache. Then I remembered I had two children to look after."

"At least you could feel angry. And you had Ben and Sally who depended on you. At least you were still a person with things to do. My void is just that. A void. Empty. And I am shocked by it. I know it's out of all proportion, but that is how I feel. Shocked."

"Poor old Dad. What are you going to do?"

"I don't know, Jane. At the moment, I don't know."

They talked for a while about Ben and Sally, how they were getting on with their studies. Then they said goodbye and Jane said she would call in a day or two. William had intended to speak to Frederick, too. But now his energy had gone and he couldn't speak to anyone.

He went to bed.

The following morning at nine-thirty, just as William was finishing his breakfast, his phone rang. It was his son, Frederick, calling him from his office in São Paulo. Jane, being the older of the two, would no doubt have rung him.

"What's all this about dark chasms and the edge of the void? Jane has been on the phone telling me you are suffering shock and feeling abandoned. What on earth is going on?"

"Oh, yes. Sorry about all that. I have lost part of who I thought I was."

"But why the dark chasm?"

"Well, it happened quite suddenly."

"And?"

"Well, firstly Wendy and Ruth found a house of their own and moved out, then my publishers decided not to publish my book on Eliot, then the Academy in London decided to end my Fellowship.

He paused.

"You might think that at my age I would be relieved. But actually, Freddy, I'm not. I feel left out, dismissed."

"Yes, I see that. If your life is your work and then you give it up, who are you?"

"That's it. Who am I?"

"Well, you're my father for a start-off, and you're Jonathan's grandfather."

"Thank you, Freddy."

"By the way, I have some good news. We have another baby on the way. A girl. And she will be called Maria Caroline."

"That's wonderful news. Your mother would have been very pleased."

"Yes, I hope so."

They spent the rest of the call catching up on Frederick's work and what was happening to Jonathan, now coming up to age three. The age William had been when he had first been wounded, seventy-five years ago!

"Are you and Ana planning a trip to London at all?"

"Not until next year sometime."

"I look forward to it, perhaps you could come and stay in my trailer. Jonathan might like that."

"That's a plan. A definite plan."

"Give my love to Ana."

"And she sends hers to you, Dad. Let's keep in touch a bit more. Let's have a Skype call more often, so we can see each other, and you can say hello to Jonathan."

"Okay."

William put down the phone and finished clearing away his breakfast, slowly putting everything in its place before walking into his study.

I have sunk low. Pathetic really. Who did I think I was? Somebody that mattered? Somebody who was honoured? Someone who was published? Is that who I had become? Pathetic. And suppose I

had been those things. Was that all I was? An actor.
A performance.

I see now that this was bound to happen someday.
And now it has.

But Freddy and Ana are expecting Maria Caroline!
A glimmer of hope ...

Sometimes the words came to him easily, sometimes not at all. They were the worst times. Nothing. Nothing to say. That was frightening. But when it happened the only thing to do was to stay there and continue the practice. Continue the task of finding words and writing them down. Even if he no longer had his book, or papers for the Academy, he had to write. If only to prove he was there. Old texts unfinished and revisited, short pieces, sometimes about nothing at all really. Just the practice of writing. In order to prevent himself falling, he felt compelled to write.

Apart from Wendy coming and going, for some weeks William remained alone. Even Mary, sensing his need to be by himself, did not visit. It was a silent and lonely retreat. Having withdrawn into himself, he had fallen into a dull absence. And now he felt overwhelmed by a lack of purpose. A kind of pointlessness. A lethargy. He was not accustomed to it. Was it his age? Was it some growing fear of death?

Was this what happened in your late seventies?

It was midnight and William was awake. He had gone to bed later than usual, at about five minutes to eleven. He had read for a short while and then fallen into a deep sleep. Half an hour later, or a little more, he was awake. His short sleep had been broken by a dream. A troubled dream. He was seventeen years old and in his A-level English Literature class at school. He was with the English mistress whose name he could not remember, only that he desperately wanted to impress her, be given her approval. But his life was a mess and he was having difficulty holding it together. He had no one to share it with. He had forgotten which books he was meant to have read. He hoped at least that if he had the list of books that would be a start. But he couldn't find a piece of paper upon which the list could be written, upon which he could write it. He was panicking. He woke up. It was not good. He turned on the light, picked up a pencil and wrote the dream into his journal.

Then he got out of bed and put into the music player on his desk the Leonard Cohen album that Freddy had sent to him. He began to listen to the dark, sorrowful and golden voice singing 'Leaving the Table':

> *I don't need a reason*
> *For what I became*
> *I've got these excuses*
> *They're tired and lame*
> *I don't need a pardon*
> *There's no one to blame*
> *I'm leaving the table*
> *I'm out of the game*

'There's no one to blame.' It was the last album Cohen had made before he died, and it was called *You Want it Darker*. Was there something in the darkness which he was missing? He opened his journal.

Darkness

There's no one to blame. We each make our own world, and I made mine. Who made the mask I wore on stage? I did. Who designed the costume I chose to wear? I did. Who wanted the applause? Me. And if I made that world, perhaps I can make another. And perhaps Providence is giving me a clue in Cohen's wonderful world of darkness.

Providence has set me thinking. Or rather feeling. Just suppose, just suppose that every error and falsehood lies not in darkness, but in the light. In the bright light. Maybe the problem is not too much darkness, but too much light. Suppose that truth and sweetness lie not in the light, but in the darkness, the only ground of transformation. The magic of winter. Might this be possible?

And actually, I am beginning to tire of the brightness, the bright and ever-strident glare of expectation, always looking for something, always trying to have more, to be more. Isn't that the problem of our culture? Too much brightness, too much expectation. But suppose we succumb to the darkness. Acceptance. Transformation.

And this something I now know. Being anxious is not an idea. It is not even really a feeling. It is a physical sensation arising in the gut, low down in the pit of the belly. And from that ancient place, the sensation rises, then we feel it and then we name it. 'Anxiety'. Now it has a name. But it starts as a physical sensation over which we have no control. It is just there, low down.

We try to push it away as if it should not be there. But suppose it has a purpose. Suppose it arises because there is something to be frightened of. Perhaps its purpose is to show us what this is so that we face up to it. Suppose I am frightened because there is something I must face up to, but don't yet have the courage. Perhaps that is what I need, not self-pity, but courage!

I must talk to Mary.

Something was stirring in William. Something new. He could not quite see it. It was no more than the very slightest glimmer. And yet it was a feeling of something coming to be. Quite what it would turn out to be, he was not sure. But there it was, at the edge of his knowing. And he knew there was no way back. He had to take courage and begin the exploration. "Old men ought to be explorers." Is that what Eliot had meant? He began, and, day after day, alone and in the quietness of his study, he placed one foot in front of the other, letting go of who he had been and finding who he now was. Putting together the pieces. Leaning upon his ordered life to give him a necessary comfort, a sense of himself.

He picked up his phone and called Mary. She had been expecting a call.

"Hello, William. Are you okay?"

"Not really. I have suffered one or two blows."

"What do you mean?"

"Any chance we could have tea together?"

"Yes, of course."

"This afternoon?"

"Yes. I'll bring Eccles cakes."

So that afternoon, Mary came to the house by the marsh, and had tea with William. They sat on the veranda and William told Mary all about what had been happening to him.

"Why didn't you call me sooner?"

"I just couldn't. I couldn't talk to anyone."

"Well, that won't do. What kind of friendship do we have if we can't talk to each other?"

"Yes, I'm sorry. It caught me by surprise. I wasn't expecting it. Truth is, Mary, I was frightened."

Mary took William's hand and held it in hers. They sat until the light began to go. Mary understood loss and loneliness and knew that there wasn't much to be done.

"You know, William, I may not know much about your life of writing and books, but there is a lot to be said for the company of a loving friend."

"Is that us? Are we becoming, loving friends?"

"Maybe. I hope so."

Wendy had invited William to have tea with her and Ruth at their cottage and, at four o'clock, she arrived to pick him up. They drove along the country roads and were soon pulling into her driveway. As soon as he got out of the car, William could see the work that Wendy had been doing in her garden. Raised vegetable beds.

"This all looks good, Wendy."

"Well, it's prepared for the spring. Like me! Come on in and I'll put on the kettle."

"It is very kind of you to ask me to tea."

"That's okay, I happened to be home today so it was no bother. And anyway, Ruth and I have been worrying about you. In fact, Ruth told me this morning that I had to make sure that I looked after you. She said that she had dreamt about you last night, and that you were very distressed, wandering about and not knowing which way to go."

"Dear Ruth. How kind of her to even have been thinking about me."

"You know, William, Ruth and I have been talking quite a lot about you recently. You have always been so generous to us. Befriending us. Taking us in when my caravan was destroyed. Letting us stay with you in the house by the marsh, buying your trailer to give us space to be by ourselves. Letting us use your flat in Marylebone. You have been a wonderful friend to us. And you have never asked us for anything."

"Except your love and companionship. And the truth is, I miss it."

And William began to tell Wendy about what had been happening to him.

"I have lost myself a bit. It's as if all of those things

– people, work, books that I was to write – were what defined me. And once that fell away, there was nothing left. A shell."

A car pulled into the driveway.

"I think that's Ruth," said Wendy. "She said she would try and get home in good time."

The door opened and Ruth walked in. She had been working at the Ipswich Hospital out-patients clinic, as an occupational therapist, and she still had on her white coat. She put down her bag, took off her coat and gave William a hug.

"I am so glad you have come to see us," she said. "We have been getting quite worried about you. I have even started dreaming about you, seeing you wandering around looking lost."

"Yes, Wendy told me. I am sorry to have been disturbing your dreams."

"Isn't that the oddest thing? Do you know, when Wendy and I were apart and I didn't really know where she was, I dreamt about her living in a caravan. And when I found her, she was. How strange is that?"

"You must have a sixth sense."

"I must have a sixth something. And now I need a cup of tea."

Wendy put the kettle back on the hob and took out from the cupboard a box of Rooibos tea bags. She put one in a cup and poured on the boiling water. She brought the cup through and placed it on the table in front of Ruth.

"Thank you, darling."

"Born to serve."

"Born to be wonderful."

Wendy put an arm round Ruth and they embraced.

"So here we are together again," said Ruth and reached across the table to take William's hand. He smiled.

They talked about their time together at the house by the marsh, and about what had been happening since the move to Friston. Although Ruth and Wendy were, of course, happy to have found a house of their own, they admitted that something had been lost by their being apart. They missed Frampton, the marsh, the beach and the sea.

William told them in some detail about what had been happening to him. Wendy and Ruth, now curled up on the sofa together, listened without saying anything. They knew that William just wanted to tell them how he had been. And when he ran out of things to say, they let the stillness and the quiet take over the spaces between them.

"You know, Mary and I are beginning to come closer together. When I was really down I wasn't in touch with her, but now I am, and I find her a great comfort. There is something about her, a depth, that you might not see at first, but it's there. And we have much to share."

"I have always liked Mary," said Ruth. "She sees the absurdities of life. And I am not at all surprised that the two of you should feel a comfort together. Two of our favourite people!"

After a while, Wendy spoke.

"You could stay with us tonight if you would like. Stay and go back tomorrow, that would be fine by us. We could have supper together. Maybe watch a film. I'm sure we can find you a toothbrush. We always keep ourselves well stocked for unexpected visitors!"

"Yes, do stay," said Ruth. "It will be just like the house by the marsh, except this time we will be your refuge."

And so William stayed the night in the Friston cottage, sharing supper and watching a Fred Astaire and Ginger Rogers movie on Netflix. He slept well in the double bed in the spare room and, in the morning, got up in time to have breakfast before Ruth had to go to work. They sat together at the table, whilst Wendy made cups of tea and coffee and her own special muesli and fruit. William felt comforted, at home.

"Thank you, Ruth. Thank you for having me to stay, being my refuge. It has meant a lot to me. I feel wonderfully refreshed. Perhaps it's the tea, or perhaps it was just sleeping in your very comfortable double bed!"

"It is always lovely to be with you, William. We miss you."

Once Ruth had gone to work, Wendy drove William back to the house by the marsh, where he went into his study.

I think the worst may have gone. Somehow, being with Wendy and Ruth last night and feeling their love for me has shifted something in me.

William stopped writing and looked at what he had written. Was that it? Was that what he felt? And what now? Putting down his pencil, he got up and walked into the kitchen, putting the kettle on the hob. He made some tea and brought it back into his study. Silence. He sat down again and picked up his pencil.

I am struck by how little remains when you let go. When you leave behind the character you have been playing. Leave it all behind. It's almost as if it is necessary to become nothing at the end of life? Is this what this falling away is for? Is this what renunciation is? Renunciation?

I remember reading somewhere that in the Indian tradition, it was always understood that to step aside was a proper thing for an elderly man like me to do - first to pass over to his children all those workaday responsibilities and obligations and then to retire. And after that, when the time came, at last to renounce altogether the material life of possessions and family. Renunciation. I am not quite ready for this, but I may be on my way. Perhaps it is my time to step aside, step into a more reflective place, put down the burden and let go?

I must call Mary again. I have a question to ask her.

William called Mary, but she was not there. He left a message on her answerphone, asking if she would come for tea with him the next day.

It was one of those unbearably beautiful late September days of sunshine and warmth. The trees aglow with deep yellows and reds. William was sitting on his veranda when he heard his gate open. He looked up to see Mary walking towards him. He stood up and greeted her, kissing her on both cheeks. She sat beside him.

"I got your message."

'Thank you for coming."

"Well, I need company, too. I sometimes find this time of year a bit difficult. Coming towards winter."

"Mary, I have a question I must ask you."

"Okay."

"Do you still speak to Albert?"

"It's odd that you should ask that. Something has changed. Quite recently. As you know, in the past I have felt Albert close by me. Spoken to him and heard his voice."

"Just as I have with Caroline."

"Yes, just like that. But about a month ago, I realised he was not there. It was not that he had let go of me, but more as if I had let go of him. I remember waking one morning and realising it had happened. It was like a clearing. Strange, isn't it? But once it had happened, I realised that it had to be so. I had to let him go. For his sake, not just mine."

William took Mary's arm, came closer to her, which seemed to be what she wanted, too.

"I have to tell you something. I think it is about to happen to me. I think I am about to let Caroline go. I don't really know why I think this, but I do and I am a bit frightened. And I thought you might help me."

She took his hand in hers.

"You know, William, for some while after Albert died I could not find my way out of the loss and the loneliness. I struggled and I struggled. But it didn't work. In fact, it seemed to make it worse. And then, not so very long ago, I decided I couldn't struggle any more, and I gave up. I surrendered. And that is when I came to see that I had to let him go. So I did. The odd thing is that ever since then I have begun to feel some kind of peace. How odd is that?"

Surrender, was that it? They sat for a while.

When Mary stood up to go, William held her and kissed her on her lips. She seemed pleased.

Before he went to bed, William again walked out onto the veranda and sat overlooking the reeds. He knew she would be there. And she was. His beloved Caroline. She had overheard his conversation with Mary.

"So, my dear William, is this when we say goodbye?"

Tears came to his eyes and he felt a strange yearning sensation in the middle of his chest.

"I am not sure about this," he said. "Are you?"

"I think so. But it is easier for me. Your world is so full of attachment. In mine it is almost not there at all."

"Are you happy, Caroline?"

"It's not about being happy, William. It's about being part of the whole."

"It sounds wonderful."

"It is."

"So how do we do this?"

"You just close your eyes and say 'goodbye'."

William closed his eyes, summoning his courage. And then he said it. "Goodbye, dearest Caroline."

"Goodbye, dearest William."

He began to sob, and he turned to look for her. But as the wind passed through the reed bed, he knew she had gone.

It had been nearly eight years.

Wendy and Ruth invited friends from London to be with them for Christmas. Frederick was in São Paulo and Jane and her family were going to try and get together with her ex-husband at his parent's house in Perth. Brenda and Penelope were, of course, cruising somewhere or other. So, Mary and William decided they would have Christmas lunch together. Just the two of them. William would provide the turkey, although, of course, he would only eat the vegetables, the gravy and, the bread sauce. No flesh. And he would choose the wine. Mary would bring all the rest, including an apple crumble instead of Christmas pudding, which neither of them liked.

"If we are to have Christmas lunch together, Mary, they're will be a lot to do on Christmas morning. I was just thinking that it might be a good idea for you to stay overnight at my house on Christmas Eve, so that we can be together from breakfast time on Christmas Day. We could even go to the church service on Christmas Eve. If you think this would work, I'll get Wendy to prepare the spare room. It has its own bathroom. We will be snug."

"That sounds lovely, William. I should enjoy us being together like that."

William liked the word 'us'. He smiled.

So that is what happened. On Christmas Eve, they went to the candlelit Communion service in the village church, St. Peter's. Mary stayed the night and, on the evening of Christmas Day, she decided to stay the night again. Only this time she and William curled up together in the double bed in the spare room. It was the first time that either of them had slept with another person for many years. And they liked it very much. The soft touch of Mary and the warmth of her body beside him opened up a part of him that had been shut away. Mary stayed the next night too. They had enjoyed their Christmas together very much.

And a few days later, on New Year's Eve, when Wendy and Ruth came over to the house by the marsh, the four of them walked down to the edge of the sea, arm in arm, and threw stones into the waves, making their wishes.

Something has shifted. This year has been more difficult than I could have imagined. Painful in every way. Letting go and being let go of. I didn't see it coming! So painful I thought I would never recover.

But I have finished in a good place, released in some strange way and now with the possibility of companionship. I have longed for that. Mary surprises me all the time. And I think I may have surprised her!

Happy New Year!

CHAPTER 15

RECOVERY

The day before Christmas, William had received a phone call from his grandson, Ben, asking him if he could come and stay in the New Year. He had something he wanted to discuss. William was delighted and they arranged for Ben to come on 4th January. David, the taxi man, would meet him at Saxmundham station. The day arrived and David's car pulled into the driveway. Ben stepped out, picked up his rucksack from the boot and ran up the steps to the veranda. They greeted each other with hugs.

"Now you can either have the trailer or the spare room, whichever one you would like."

"It has to be the trailer, Grandpa."

"Okay, I thought you might say that. It's all ready for you, but you will have to switch on the heater, and I suggest you use the shower in my dressing room in the morning."

William gave Ben the key to the Airstream, and he went off to unpack his rucksack. There was something in Ben that William recognised, perhaps in a way remembered, an openness and a vitality. When he came back, he had put on a thick blue sweater.

"Can we go down to the sea?"

"Yes, of course, let's go."

William took his coat from the hook by the door and they walked together across the marsh and to the beach. Ben ran ahead, down to the water's edge, and threw his arms wide, shouting at the seagulls. William laughed, pleased to see his grandson's obvious delight.

"This is such a special place, Grandpa. I often think about it, and whenever I am here I feel a sense of freedom and possibility."

William realised that was what he too had always felt and how, in the year that had passed, he had lost it. It was a stiff reminder of how low he had been, and that this would not do. He was being lifted by his grandson's energy.

They sat on the bench by the shingle.

"Great idea bringing this bench here, Grandpa."

That enthusiasm again.

William could tell that Ben had something to tell him, but he thought it best to wait until he was ready.

"Are you hungry?"

"Ravenous."

"Right, let's go and see what we can find."

As they walked back to the house, William noticed that his grandson was now taller than he was. Ben growing and William shrinking. That seemed right. They walked back into the house, Ben following his grandfather's example and taking off his shoes and leaving them by the front door.

"Wendy has left us this macaroni cheese. Fancy that?"

"Sounds great."

"Make yourself comfortable."

William took the macaroni cheese, covered the top with tinfoil and put it in the oven.

"It'll be about half an hour. Look, I've got some crisps here. And we could have a glass of wine. Do you like red wine?"

"I do."

"Good."

Taking their glasses with them, they walked into the living room and sat down, William in his armchair and Ben in the other one. Florence walked in and jumped up onto Ben's lap.

"Push her off if you don't want her, Ben."

"No, she's fine. I like cats. One at a time."

"Just like me." They laughed.

"Cheers, Ben."

"Cheers, Grandpa."

William looked at Ben, a young man, lanky with long hair and unshaven stubble, and he was trying to remember how he had been at this age. Not so much at ease. Ben was looking around the room, reminding himself of the books and photographs of his family. And he could see this old man sitting opposite him. His grandfather. Someone he was only just getting to know, but someone he loved. Although he had only been an occasional visitor to the house by the marsh, it meant something to him. Something like a refuge. And although he had not spent all that much time with his grandfather, he saw him, too, as a refuge. He had somehow always known William would be there for him, if need be. Like now.

"So, Ben, how are you?"

"I'm pretty much okay, Grandpa."

"But? I hear a but."

"But I need to make a change."

"That sounds good."

"Good? You think making a change is good?"

"Nearly always."

"I knew you would get it, Grandpa."

"Get what?"

"I knew you would understand why I might want to change what I'm doing. Everybody else is telling me I must be stupid. That I should complete my degree first and then think about what I want to do. But I knew you would understand. Mum said you were always making changes in your life."

"Well, I did make some."

They laughed. And William remembered how constrained he had been when, at Ben's age, he was trying to work out what it was he was going to do with his life. Although his parents had wanted the best for him, their experience was narrow and he had to work it out for himself. Just as Ben was now trying to do. He wanted to help Ben find himself, his true self. He wanted his grandson to have a wider space in which to grow.

"Tell me a bit more, Ben."

"Well, as you know I started off taking a degree in Land and Property Management. And, to begin with, I liked it. Good teachers, and I liked the courses on property law and economics. But then I began to get involved with some students studying Environment and Society, and ever since I have been looking at the work on climate change. It's pretty scary!"

"Yes, I believe it is."

"I just feel that of all the things the world needs right now, it's not another estate agent."

"Okay. I see."

"I want to study something more important, something more relevant to the problems we are going to have to face."

"What would that mean? Can you move to another course or do you have to start again?"

"I have been talking to the professor who heads up the courses on Environment and Society and he thinks I could transfer after Christmas. Take my first year as a credit. I'd have to work really hard to catch up the lost term. But I would want to do that anyway. Trouble is, being at university costs money and I don't want to put Mum or Dad under financial pressure."

"Of course not, but the money part must come second. Never forget that, Ben. It must always come second. The first thing for you to do is to be as clear as possible about this possible change."

"I am clear."

This was the moment to open the door that Ben feared might be closed.

"Then you should do it."

"Do you really think so?"

"Yes, of course I do."

Ben sat back in his chair, his long legs spreading out in comfort. He let out a long breath, pushing it through his lips.

"I really hoped you'd say that, Grandpa. I needed someone to understand what I am trying to do. I thought it might be you."

"Well, it can't make any sense to continue to study

something you're not interested in and, as far as I can tell, you are entirely right about climate change. And as for the money, you'll just have to sort it out. What do your Mum and Dad say?"

"Well, they are both a bit shocked, but I think they would want me to be true to what I believe in."

"Yes, I think so, too. We'd better tackle that macaroni cheese."

Over lunch, Ben was full of his new plans and William was happy to listen. Something was changing in Ben. He was growing up. Becoming who he was going to be: passionate, energetic and thoughtful. Just the kind of grandson that William would have hoped for.

"I was wondering if we could go to Aldeburgh, Grandpa? Take a walk along the beach."

"Yes, let's do that. I'll have to ask David to take us. Unless Wendy could. I'll ring her."

Wendy was happy to come over and take them to Aldeburgh. She had some shopping to do whilst they walked. Then they could go back to her cottage and have tea with her and Ruth.

It was a good afternoon, Ben walking with his grandfather, and asking him about what he had felt at his age. Nineteen. What had happened to him and how he had begun his work, the changes he had made in his career. Had he had any regrets? And what was he interested in now? And William asked Ben about the work he was doing, looking at the consequences of climate change, social and economic, as well as environmental. He asked Ben to tell him about climate change, and what was happening; the warming that was now evident even on the east coast of Suffolk.

"It's scary," said Ben, and then went on to give an account of what might be expected; the impossibility of keeping within the plus 1.5 or, indeed, the plus 2 limit that had always been regarded as the risk threshold.

"I'd like to know more about this, Ben. Can you keep me in the loop?"

"Yes, of course I can," said Ben, delighted that his grandfather was interested in what he was planning to do.

Wendy was waiting for them as they came back along the path from Thorpeness, and soon they were sitting round the table in her kitchen in Friston. Ruth had just come home from work and both she and Wendy wanted to hear Ben's news, taking an interest in what he had to say and, like his grandfather, urging him to do what he felt was right for him.

"Would you like an early supper? Scrambled eggs on Marmite toast?" asked Wendy.

"That would be great," said Ben, looking to his grandfather for agreement. So they had supper with Wendy and Ruth, and then they were driven back to the house by the marsh.

"I think I might just sit and read for a bit," said William. "Would that be okay?"

"I'd like that," said Ben. "I don't often get this kind of peace and quiet. I like it."

"Good."

And so the two of them sat beside the wood stove and read, William making his way through a thick volume called *Homo Deus*, written by a Jewish scholar from the Hebrew University in Jerusalem, a book about 'the dreams and nightmares' of the twenty-first century, and

Ben was studying some of his course papers, catching up on the term he had missed. At half-past nine, William said goodnight, and retired to his study and Ben went to his trailer.

"See you in the morning."

"Yes, see you on the morning."

As he lay in his bed the thoughts of the evening rose and fell, and William felt as if some part of him might now be lived in the life of Ben. That Ben, the young warrior, might have a courage he had never found, but now he could share.

William was up and dressed by the time Ben came through to take his shower. And Wendy was there making the porridge and tea.

"Tea or coffee, Ben?"

"Tea is fine."

William smiled with approval.

Whilst they were having their breakfast, Ben talked about the Airstream trailer and suggested to William that whilst it was safe tucked behind his house, what it really needed was an adventure. William laughed.

"You had better see what you can do, Ben."

Providence heard that.

By the time Ben was ready to leave Frampton, a new bond had been made between him and his grandfather, and he promised to come back and stay again once everything was sorted out with his change of course.

"Yes come, and bring your friends. They might like the trailer, too."

"Wicked!"

After Ben had left in the taxi, William rang Jane.

"How did it go?"

"It was fine. You have a very wonderful son."

"Well, some of the time. I suppose you told him to do what he thought best. Be true to himself."

"Yes, I did. What else can he do? He's not yet twenty!"

"I suppose so, but I thought he was settled and now he isn't."

"Isn't he? I thought he sounded very settled. Settled on making a change in his life. I think that's what happens when you are growing up."

"Well, I hope Sally just gets her A-levels, goes to university and stays there until she graduates."

"How is Sally?"

"She is fine and thinks her brother is 'all over the place.'"

"Does she still want to study medicine?"

"Yes."

"That's a long slog."

"Yes, but she is very organised and determined."

"Well, I look forward to seeing her. Perhaps she would like my advice, too."

"I rather doubt it, Dad. One like you in my family is enough."

"I'll try and take that as a compliment."

"Oh, and by the way, I have a new friend. His name is Alan."

"Sounds good, what's he like?"

"He's very nice. He's an accountant."

"Sounds promising."

"Shut up, Dad. He's fine."

Enlivened by Ben's visit, William called Mary and invited her to supper to tell her all about Ben and his new plans. She could sleep over if she wanted to. She did.

"I have a batch of roasted vegetable tarts, which I've made for my freezer. Shall I bring one?"

"That would be great."

Later that day, the phone rang. It was Roderick calling from Italy.

"Good morning, Roderick, this is a nice surprise. How is Italy today?"

"It is fine. The sun is out and Edward and I are going to have a late lunch at our favourite restaurant in the village. Lots of pasta, or sometimes *ribolita*, which is made of toasted stale bread and beans in a sort of stew, and red wine."

"Well, I have to tell you that today the wind is in the east and there is no sun at all. It's very grey!"

"You have just reminded me why we came to Italy!"

They laughed.

"William, I have something to tell you. You see, now that Edward and I have decided to stay here in Italy, we no longer need the house by the marsh. In fact, we would rather find a flat in London, which we can use when we come back to visit friends from time to time."

William felt his stomach tighten.

"So I'm sorry to say that we have decided to sell, and

I have asked the agent in Saxmundham to give us a valuation. He will be in touch to make an inspection. I'm sorry about this."

William did not know what to say.

"No, of course. You must do what you need to. It is, after all, your house, not mine."

They talked for a while about life in Tiberina and then the call ended. For a while, William was shocked that this was happening to him, that his life in the house by the marsh could end so abruptly. He walked into the kitchen and poured himself a glass of water. Then he walked down to the sea and sat on his bench. It had been so sudden. And then his own words came back to him, "It is after all your house not mine." There it was staring at him. It had to become his house. He walked back into the house and called Roderick. There was no reply. Of course, they had gone out to lunch. William sent an email.

Roderick

I hope you enjoyed your lunch!

I have been thinking what you said this morning and wondered whether you would agree to sell to me? I would like to buy this house, and could do so straight away. I wonder if this might work for you?

What do you think?

William

That afternoon, the phone rang again and it was Roderick.

"Did you get my email?"

"Yes."

"And what do you think?"

"Well, both Edward and I feel it would be just right, although we would have to agree a price, of course."

William tried to hide his delight. This, more than anything else, was what he wanted.

"Okay. Well, let's see what your agent comes up with. By the way, I would like to buy the house with its furniture and contents. All in. Would that work?"

"Well, that's an idea. I doubt the furniture would fit into a flat in London anyway. Let me speak to Edward. In the meantime, the agents will be in touch to make the inspection."

"Okay. I'll wait to hear from them."

Two days later, William received a phone call from the estate agent to make an appointment to come and see the house and, shortly after his visit, Roderick sent William an email with a price for both the house and its contents. William thought it a bit too much and made a counter offer. It was accepted on the basis of a rapid exchange and completion, which was entirely to William's liking. The house by the marsh was to be his.

That evening, William and Mary enjoyed their supper together and Mary stayed the night. William told her about his phone call with Roderick and the possibility that the house by the marsh would soon be his.

"And so it should be, William. That is wonderful news."

They went to bed early, but could not linger in the morning because Mary had to open her shop at eight-thirty. When Wendy arrived just before nine, she noted how light-hearted William seemed.

"Well, there are two very good reasons, my dear Wendy. Firstly, Mary came to supper last night and stayed for breakfast. We have such a good time together."

Wendy smiled.

"But I also have some other rather wonderful news."

"Tell on!"

And he told Wendy all about his discussions with Roderick and that he would shortly be not the tenant but the owner of the house by the marsh.

"I am so pleased for you, William. Perhaps wishes do sometimes come true?"

"Perhaps they do."

After Wendy had gone, William went to his study to write in his journal.

I can hardly write these words lest in so doing I break the spell. Just when I was giving up all hope, Providence has been good to me. For it now seems possible that the house by the marsh is to be my house. To be able to live here forever. It is as if my life has only just begun.

This is where I shall now remain.

Contracts were prepared and exchanged and, six weeks later, the sale of the house and its contents was completed. William called Mary to let her know, telling her how good he felt about this providential change in his life, and hoping that she and he would now have plenty of time to get to know each other. To really get to know each other. At the other end of the line, Mary smiled and nodded. And Mary had news, too. Well, gossip really. There was a rumour that Lady Whitely might be leaving High Winds to be nearer to her son in Dorset.

I had not thought this possible. But here I am, sitting at my desk in what will soon be my study in my house by the marsh. And when I have gone, it will be there for my children, and perhaps theirs too. I cannot think why this matters to me, all things being impermanent, but it does. Whether my time here is short or long, it is my time, my here.

Never before in my life have I felt so much at one with where I am. Throughout my life I have always wondered whether I could trust good fortune or whether something would happen to take it from me. Now here I am, and here I will stay. This is where I want to be, and what I want to do is all here. By the marsh, by the beach, by the sea.

I am thinking of those lines from Eliot's Little Gidding:

We shall never cease from exploration
And the end of all our exploring
Will be to arrive where we started
And know the place for the first time.

Is that it? Shall I know this place for the first time?
I know I shall be at peace dwelling here. And
although I know that finding that peace is my
task, my task alone, I cannot deny that Mary has
become my guide.

At nine o'clock that evening, tired by the day and by
the swirl of emotion he had felt, William decided to go
to bed.

He opened the window so that he could hear the sea
and climbed into his bed. He had meant to read for a
while, but now he knew he was too tired to do so. He
switched off the lamp and lay there on his back, his
hands resting upon the duvet, upon his chest. He closed
his eyes and listened to the wind as it swept through
marsh and tossed the waves onto the shingle. If these
would one day be the last things he ever heard, he would
be content. He fell asleep.

The next day, William woke early. Six o'clock. He had
slept right through the night. No waking. No having to
have a pee. A good sleep. Here he was. A smile settled on
his face. He got up, walked through to his dressing room

and put on a dressing gown. He opened the front door, slipped on a pair of his brown Birkenstocks, and walked onto the veranda. The sun was just rising. He walked through his garden, through the reeds, on to the beach and down to the sea. It was calm, and he watched as the rays of the sun began to cover the water. He sat down on the bench set in the shingle. Already awake, the seagulls were circling the sky. Squawking.

"Okay, I know you're there. I know I am in your kingdom, but this is now where I live, too."

Somehow, becoming the owner of the house by the marsh had given William a sense of belonging, really belonging. A kind of restfulness. After all that had happened the year before, he felt at last as if he might be able to find his way again. His quest for peacefulness. He walked back into the house.

There are many lessons to learn from this beautiful place, but the one I should most like to understand is the lesson of peacefulness. I have failed so far, although at times I have been close. Restless and overly concerned with what I thought other people required of me - seeking their approval - I have always allowed myself to be distracted by the things I thought I ought to do. And perhaps it is only now - now that I have let so much of my past go, now that I know I shall remain here forever - that I can find my way. And I have a sense that this discovery will be not so much by intellectual enquiry, but by simple and solitary practice. Perhaps the place of despair, the dark place in which I found myself,

*will be the ground of some kind of shift in my being,
a step towards inner peacefulness. This peacefulness
will arise out of the darkness. I have yearned for it
but in my despair I could not quite touch it. I now
know it can only be found by being at peace.*

*Is this what Caroline meant when she talked to me
about writing for myself? Is this how it is to be?*

I have work to do.

William spent the rest of that morning in his study.
He was reading a book by a social biologist, Humberto
Maturana, and a psychologist, Gerda Verden-Zöeller,
in which they claimed that humans were innately
loving – *Homo sapiens-amans.* That our ancient being
was loving. And there was a passage in which the
authors talked of our present ways as the ways of *Homo
sapiens aggressans.*

*There is a passage in 'The Origin of Humanness in
the Biology of Love' in which Maturana and
Verden-Zöeller describe our present culture as
being shaped not by love, but by aggression - Homo
sapiens aggressans. I suppose then it should not
be surprising to find that much of the literature
and discussion of peace is about war. After all,
those most concerned in the work of reconciliation
and conflict resolution find that they are enmeshed
in violence. But it does seem odd to me that
peacefulness is only discussed as an alternative to
violence, not as a way of being that stands alone,*

or rather as a part of us that needs to be cherished if we are to be well, if we are to be who we truly are. I suppose this can hardly be surprising since the language of 'aggressans' regards those who seek peace as worthy but naive. "It is all very well," they say, "but in the real world..."

He stopped writing and read more of Maturana. And as he did so he was beginning to see another possibility, another reality. As he continued writing, he could feel his energy returning.

But Maturana asks us to question what that 'real world' is. And I do, too. For if I look carefully, really carefully at my experience up until this moment, I can see, throughout my life, that love has always been there. Not only in my private life, but in my life at work as well. Not just loving family, but colleagues who were loving and thoughtful, who went the extra mile without being asked to do so. There were plenty of times where we cared for each other.

He suddenly thought of Caroline, and of the long years they had spent together. All the hurts and the irritations, but also a kind of constant loving that they had become used to. Was that what they had? A constant loving. Is that what he mourned?

And Maturana speaks of love coming up through the cracks. What is that line of Leonard Cohen? Oh, yes: "There is a crack, a crack, in everything. That's how the light gets in." Mad, wonderful poet!

William looked out of his window. The winter sun was catching the tops of the reeds. He stood up, walked into his kitchen and took from the fridge the jug of filtered water. He poured himself a glass and drank it. Cold. Wet. He went back to his desk and read what he had just written. Something was beginning to stir, not so much in his mind but in the depths of his being.

Suppose for the moment that Maturana and his colleague are right. Suppose that at the root of our innate being there are qualities of love, compassion and a care of each other. Suppose that Love with a capital 'L' is of the essence, and that the desire for peacefulness is innate in us. If this is true, it changes everything. If this is true, hatred and violence are an aberration or, at least, no more than a consequence - a consequence of adopting, or being forced into, forms of perception and practice that are rooted in a most particular and aberrant mode of being, the conflictual and selfish mode of being that has only relatively recently been who we are. Well, seven thousand or so years - not much in the whole scope of our evolution!

So, if we are, by our much more ancient nature, loving and nurturing, inclined to community and family, inclined to care, then peacefulness is simply an essential part of who we are and who we strive to be. In which case, in so far as there is a lack of concord, the task is not to study violence, but to study peacefulness. The questions we should ask, that I should ask, are these: What are the qualities of peacefulness? How is it cultivated?

Was that it? The cultivation of peacefulness, inner peacefulness? Was that to be his work? Is this what Caroline had meant? Providence smiled.

On 14th March, William received a phone call from Frederick.

"Hi, Dad. Good news. Maria Caroline was born yesterday evening. She's beautiful and has dark hair like her mother. All went well."

"Well done, you two, and welcome to Maria Caroline. Bring her to see me when you can."

"We will."

"Give my love to Ana and to Jonathan, too."

"I will."

Another wondrous beginning.

A week before Easter, whilst William was sitting in his

study looking for some papers he had copied from the web on the continuing decline of bumblebees, there was a swooshing noise on his computer announcing the arrival of an email. He went to his inbox and there it was. An email from his grandson, Ben:

Hi Grandpa

Would it be possible for me to come and stay at Easter in the Airstream with my friend, Rosemary?

Ben x

William clicked onto the email and replied:

Hi Ben

Yes, please come, and bring Rosemary.

Thine with love

Grandpa x

Within a few moments, another email arrived:

Thanks Grandpa. I will let you know when we are arriving.

B x

William was delighted.

Ben and Rosemary arrived at Saxmundham station just before midday, and William had arranged for David, the taxi man, to meet them and bring them to the house by the marsh. They put their rucksacks in the boot and got into the car, Ben taking the front seat and Rosemary sitting in the back. Soon they were passing along the country road to Frampton, fields on either side and patches of woodland. By the time they arrived at the house by the marsh, William had already opened the gate to his drive, and so David parked his car beside the steps up to the veranda. He opened the boot and Ben pulled out the two rucksacks. William came out and paid David, picking up Rosemary's rucksack and leaving Ben to carry his own.

"Hi Grandpa, this is Rosemary. Rosemary this is William."

"Hello Rosemary, it is lovely to have you to stay. As requested I have prepared the trailer for you. Is that okay? I've put the wi-fi details on the table in the galley."

"Thank you, William. Ben has been telling me all about this house and, of course, the trailer. It is everything he said it would be."

"Let's walk down to the sea and introduce you to the seagulls."

Ben and Rosemary went arm in arm and William followed them, across the marsh and onto the beach. They were lucky with the day, one of those cold and sunny days of spring, with only a light wind coming from the north. They walked down to the water's edge and stood looking out across the North Sea. On the horizon, a container ship from Felixstowe was heading northeast to Rotterdam. Slipping out of sight.

"What are you studying at university, Rosemary?" asked William.

"English Literature."

"And are you enjoying it?"

"I am actually. I love books, and the opportunity to study some of my favourite writers – mostly contemporary writers – is just bliss."

"Ben's grandma, Caroline, loved books. And so does his mother, Jane."

"Yes, I know. She and I share books. You write, don't you?"

"Well, I scribble. I used to publish, but these days I only write in my journal. In pencil. It's just the writing that matters. The actual task of writing. I'm obsessed with it."

"You mean the writing is enough? Just the writing?"

"Yes, exactly that. I have discovered that the art form is the writing, not the publishing."

"I told you he was weird!" said Ben.

"In fact," continued William, "it might be that reading is an art form, too. Don't you think?"

"I've never thought about it like that," replied Rosemary, now enjoying William's odd thoughts. He was very inclusive. He drew you in. She liked that. "But perhaps you're right, which means I am a practising artist."

"Exactly!"

William liked the way Rosemary engaged in the banter between them. They walked back up the beach, this time,

Rosemary and Ben walking arm in arm with William, one on each arm. It just seemed the right thing to do.

"Now lunch," said William as they walked. "I thought we could have a vegetable lasagne and fresh broccoli tops."

"No flesh, no seafood, no onions, no mushrooms and no spices," laughed Rosemary. "Ben has told me all about your bizarre eating habits."

"Yes, sorry about that."

"Well, I'm a vegetarian too, but I do eat mushrooms."

"Actually, I think there may be some in the lasagne."

They had now reached the house and William walked in ahead of Rosemary and Ben. He took the lasagne that Wendy had left in the fridge for them and put it into the oven to heat through. Then he washed the broccoli tops and placed them in the steamer ready to go on the gas hob.

"We shall be ready in about thirty-five minutes. What about a glass of wine?"

"Water for me," said Rosemary.

"And me," said Ben.

Remembering their glass of wine together, William looked at him and smiled.

"Water it is."

And William poured three large glasses of water from the filter jug in the fridge.

"Now, you two settle in. I have a couple of things to do in my study."

Easter

Ben has come to visit with a delightful friend, Rosemary. She loves books and reading, which is rather wonderful. She seems studious and is rather quiet. Shy perhaps? Seeing them together, arm in arm, even arm in arm with me, gives me hope, although I cannot imagine what their lives will be like.

We talked about writing.

After a while, Ben called out.

"Grandpa, lunch is ready."

William walked through to find that Ben and Rosemary had set the table and put the lasagne and the broccoli tops in dishes ready to be served. They sat down together round the kitchen table and Ben took a large spoon and served their lunch.

"This is rather good, Grandpa."

"Well, Mary's shop has quite a range of pre-prepared foods in its freezer, and all I have to do is heat them up. I like this one, and, as Ben knows, there is a very good macaroni cheese. Now, do you two have any plans for your weekend?"

"We just want to be here and enjoy the peace and quiet."

"I thought we might have tea with Mary in her tea room this afternoon."

"Sounds good."

"And I shall probably rest after lunch."

"Okay. I'll take Rosemary for a walk along the beach."

Just as they were finishing eating, Ben said, "Did you know that Mum and her friend Alan are living together?"

"No, she hasn't told me that. In fact, I haven't heard from her for a while."

"Well, Alan still has his house, but he stays much of the time with Mum."

"I only met him once, when you all came to stay for the weekend last year. He seemed nice enough."

"He's okay. And he is very kind to mum. They seem happy together, so that's good."

"My mother and father were divorced three years ago,'" said Rosemary. "When I was in my last year at school."

"I'm sorry about that, Rosemary."

"I manage!"

William stood up and began to clear away the dishes, putting them into the dishwasher.

"We'll finish that up, Grandpa. Go and have your rest. We'll see you later."

"Thank you, I will."

And William left Ben and Rosemary and went into his study, closing his door behind him and adding a paragraph to his journal.

It's a strange feeling being here with Ben and Rosemary on their own. It's another generation walking into the house by the marsh, feeling at home. Of course, they are still very young, but they seem so grown up, having to cope with broken families, and then their studies. I know they are both very taken up with concerns about climate change – which I hope Ben will tell me something about later – and they seem serious and responsible. No wine. Just water! And Rosemary is a vegetarian. Hurrah!

That evening, when William was sitting in his armchair reading, Ben and Rosemary came and sat on the sofa beside him.

"Grandpa, Rosemary and I have something we would like to discuss with you."

William put down his book.

"It's about your Airstream. You know you and I joked about taking it on an adventure? Well, we have found one."

William's eyes widened. "You have my attention."

"Rosemary and I have been working for some time to raise awareness of the impact of climate change. A big part of this is that the solutions have to be shared, internationally. Brexit is a tragedy for us. At a time when greater collaboration is needed, we have politicians working to separate us. We can't have that. And in the end, it isn't politicians that matter. We matter. And we will take our own responsibility for building friendships."

William remained quiet whilst Ben kept going, enjoying his evident passion for his cause. It reminded him of moments of his own life when enthusiasm for an idea had overtaken him, a mixture of excitement and wonderful uncertainty. And now here was his grandson doing the same.

"We've decided to take this proposal for collaboration across Europe seriously, and to go and meet up with those who think like us. Working online, and with two of our friends, Izzy and Frank, we have developed a really extensive network of other young people who feel as we do and who want to demonstrate their commitment, regardless of whether men and women in suits take any notice. Rosemary and I have been building this network for some months, and Izzy and Frank, who know all about social media and publicity, have been developing online links and connections. The power to make connection is huge, Grandpa. And now we want to embody it in person by making a journey around Europe."

William could see where the conversation was going, and he was being swept along by it.

"And what you need," said William, "is a command bus – or rather a trailer, a Classic Airstream trailer 'built for adventure.'"

"That's it, Grandpa. You've got it. That is it!"

There was a silence. William looked at Ben and Rosemary, their lively eyes, their vitality, the hope of this band of warriors. There was only one way for him to respond.

"It's a great adventure. And one entirely suited to the Classic Airstream, queen of all trailers. Yes, of course, you must take her with you and make her the centre of your great task."

Delighted by their outrageous courage, his face was covered by a smile.

"You mean, just like that?" said Ben. "You don't want to know how it will be done, or what insurance cover we will have or who is going to pay for it all? All that kind of thing."

"Not really, Ben. I know you and your friends will do all that stuff. And anyway, going on an adventure is full of risk. But we have to set forth, otherwise we are defeated before we start. You can tell me about all those things in due course. But for the moment, yes, take the trailer. You will need a sturdy vehicle to tow it."

"Well, we have a bit of luck there," said Ben. "As chance would have it, although nothing is by chance …"

William smiled hearing that his grandson was saying such a thing.

"… as chance would have it, Izzy's uncle sells Mitsubishi cars and they have a 4x4 hybrid, an Outlander PHEV, and he wants to lend it to us. He wants to use our adventure to advertise the car, appeal to a younger audience, show that Mitsubishi have green credentials, extend his customer base. That sort of thing."

"Or perhaps he is just caught up with the audacity of the whole adventure, as I am," said William. "Your passion and energy are infectious to those of us who are, shall we say, more into decline."

"You're never going to be in decline, Grandpa. You have to live forever!"

"And then, in the real world …" said William. And they all laughed.

For the rest of that evening, William sat and listened. It felt good. Faced with a growing political culture of separation and nationalism, Ben and his friends were determined not to be defined by it. They were going to shape their own lives according to nobler values. And now he could be part of it, vicariously. His trailer, his fantasy trailer, would be a part of it. They talked about protest and he talked with them about avoiding anger. Or only using it as a drive for their own energy.

"The enemy encourages our anger," he said. "They want us to be angry. Once we are angry, they have us where they want us. They will have defined us as 'angry' and as 'trouble makers'. And then they know where we are, raising our placards and shouting at them. But when we refuse their anger, when we mock them, or better still when we ignore them and move forwards as if they were not even there, they lose control, they lose their power over us."

"Wow, that is so interesting Grandpa," said Ben, always impressed by a new idea.

"When we simply ignore their rules and prejudices and reach out to each other, they are mightily flummoxed. Mightily flummoxed."

"I like that. They shall be mightily flummoxed!"

"The power lies not in fearfulness, but in your love for each other."

As he saw Ben scribbling a note of his words in his notebook, William smiled. And he looked across at Rosemary, always quiet, and she smiled, too.

Ben explained that the trip was being planned for July and August, and so they would come for the trailer sometime in June. They promised to write a blog of their travels and make sure he was plugged into it.

"They shall be mightily flummoxed," laughed Ben. "Mightily flummoxed."

The next day, they had breakfast and then David arrived to take them back to Saxmundham station for their train to London. They had stirred the house into life. And then, when they left, it settled back once more to William's slower pulse.

One Saturday morning in June, Ben, Rosemary, Frank and Izzy arrived in the Mitsubishi hybrid, which they reversed into William's garden and attached to the Airstream Trailer. Slowly, they edged the trailer out until it was parked beside the house. William had found all the literature about the trailer, its operation and maintenance filed in a drawer in his study. He had put it into an A4 folder to give to Ben.

The warriors came into the house where Wendy had provided lunch for them – flans and pies, salad and mayonnaise potatoes, bread and cheeses. They sat around the kitchen table with their iPads showing William where they were going: crossing into France and then driving up through Germany to Poland, Hungary and Romania before coming back through Austria and northern Italy to France again and then home. They had a schedule of events being arranged by a network of student organisations, with rallies and festivals. They had made a large campaign flag of hands reaching out towards each other set on a light blue background, the colour of a summer sky. They gave William the details of their website so that he could follow their blog.

When William was alone with Ben, the others having run down to the sea, he passed him an envelope of Euros.

"I thought it might be a good idea for you to have an emergency fund in case something goes wrong with the trailer. Just keep it aside. Just in case."

"You're a star, Grandpa, and really you should be coming with us."

"No, I don't think so. But I shall follow your progress and I will want to know all about it when you return. I am so very proud of you, Ben."

Ben came to his grandfather and hugged him, holding him close and not letting go.

"You have been such an important support for me, Grandpa. Just when I was being told to 'get real' and 'get a job,' you said follow what you believe in. It was wonderful. And, in case Mum asks, I will get a job when I have to!"

They laughed and walked down to be with the others on the beach, where Rosemary was hunting for carnelian.

As promised, throughout the summer, William received a stream of blogs and video clips.

I have just been looking at my Airstream trailer in the middle of a large crowd of young people, a flag showing outstretched hands upon a sky blue background flying from its doorway. There are links to news stories and to other footage and pictures being shared on social media. Ben gave me a note on how I can follow what is going on, and it has now become part of my daily routine. They all seem to be having a good time, their faces a mixture of earnest protest and laughter. There is much singing, and placards in many different languages, all of which proclaim the refusal of these young warriors to have their lives shaped by politicians and corporations who want to separate them. There has been some angry shouting, but mostly there is an evident sense of well-being and friendship. Ben features prominently, often with a loud-hailer held to his mouth and one arm raised in protest or encouragement.

The latest video was taken in a town square somewhere in provincial France where a great crowd of young people sat in complete silence, their arms around each other, the flags of all the European countries flying amongst them, with a constant flash of pictures being taken and sent on their phones. The armed police looked confused, or perhaps just bored. And there, to one side, was the trailer, with its sky-blue flag! I feel a great sense of pride that both my grandson and my trailer are part of all of this.

He forwarded the video to his son Frederick, and then called his daughter.

"I have just been watching Ben and his friends in France, sitting in silence in support of friendship. It was very moving. You have a rather marvellous son. And I have a marvellous grandson."

"Yes, I saw that. I thought it wonderful, too. But his father is getting cross and agitated about it. Says you should have never lent him the trailer. That all this protest nonsense will not look good on his job application form."

"Ah. The job application form. I wouldn't worry. I think you may find that when the time comes, there will be plenty of people who want to give Ben a job. Anyway, how are you? Has Sally been offered a place at medical school yet?"

"We should know in a week or two. I do hope so. She has quite set her heart on it."

"And you and Alan? Are you okay?"

"Yes, we're fine."

"Good. Let me know when Sally gets her news."

"We will."

When Frederick called on Skype a couple of days later, he was full of admiration for what Ben was doing and took his mobile number so that he could text him with encouragement. All was well in São Paulo.

Ten days later, Sally was on Skype.

"I got in Grandpa! I don't know how, but I got in."

"Well done, darling. How wonderful. I expect they liked you and thought you are clever."

"Maybe!"

In a way, just as William had helped Ben, so too, Ben rescued his grandfather. All that had happened since his first visit in January, his visit with Rosemary and then the wonderful European adventure, had helped William recover himself. That and, of course, buying the house by the marsh and now having the loving friendship and intimacy with Mary. As summer was coming to an end, he felt something shifting within him.

An afternoon in late August

I am sitting on the bench by the sea, watching the seagulls swoop down to the water and then rise back up again. This is my place, and as I look back towards my house, I feel a deep contentment. Something I have never felt before. Not like this. Mary is coming to supper and we shall go for a walk before bedtime.

At the end of this year, I shall begin the last year of my seventies. Absurd really that I should still be feeling so much, that so much still matters.

Ben's adventure was wonderful and now the Airstream is back behind the house. They gave me their sky-blue flag, which is now flying from the veranda!

I have a new energy, not for the world out there – I can leave that to Ben! – but for something much deeper within.

This year, I welcome the autumn. The waters of reflection. The turn of the year.

CHAPTER 16

BEGINNING AGAIN

Over the summer, Ruth and Wendy had begun to attend the local Quaker Meeting in Leiston. A friend of theirs was a regular attender and had suggested they might like to try it out, might like its stillness and silence. So, they had given it a try and had enjoyed it. Now they would often go and, knowing that William had been brought up as a Quaker, they asked him if he would like to come, too, and then have lunch with them. Although when he was a boy, his father would take him to meeting for worship every Sunday morning, it was a long time since William had been, but now that he was beginning to explore his own inner peacefulness, he liked the idea, especially the bit about lunch. So he agreed to go and soon it became something he often did. And then he asked Mary to come, too. She loved the stillness, slipping easily into the gathered silence.

One Sunday, the meeting started with a long period of silence, but then an elderly woman, too frail to stand, read a passage from *Quaker Faith and Practice*. It was part of the Quaker peace testimony, something that had been written in 1693 by one of the first Quakers, William Penn. In the passage she read, there was a line that spoke directly to William: "Let us then try what love will do." For the rest of the meeting, the words stayed with him and on the way back to Friston for lunch, he asked the others what they had thought of the words in the passage.

"I thought they were lovely," said Ruth. "And I also liked the last line, 'Force may subdue, but love gains: and he that forgives first, wins the laurel.'"

"Yes, that too," said William.

I have been thinking about those words of William Penn: 'Let us then try what love will do.' Trying what love will do. Is that what inner peace requires, making a space for love to dwell? Is it by finding love that we find peace? By abiding in love?

How do we do that?"

In a book I was reading the other day, the Buddhist scholar, Stephen Batchelor, said that although we are alone and responsible for ourselves, we can only practice love, compassion and generosity with each other. Our being is always with others. That sounds right to me. Being with. So perhaps our abiding in love must be abiding with others in love.

*If abiding means actually being with, I suppose
my loving community is Wendy and Ruth and
now Mary.*

Having Sunday lunch with Ruth and Wendy, and
with Mary too, now became another part of William's
routine. His order. Either they would all go to the meeting
together or, if they did not, Wendy and Ruth would pick
them up from the house by the marsh at about twelve
o'clock. William and Mary would be waiting for them,
sitting on his veranda looking out across the marsh to the
sea. After lunch, Wendy, Ruth and Mary would talk
together, sometimes going for a walk, and William would
often fall asleep. He was getting to like Sundays.

Six-thirty on the first day of September. A warm
morning. It was already light and promising, and
William was refreshed by his sleep. He decided not to
lie in bed, but to have a shower and get dressed. As
usual, a collarless white shirt and then a natural
coloured linen jacket and matching loose linen trousers.
No socks. In the warm weather, barefoot as always. He
wanted to wait to have breakfast with Wendy but, for
now, he made himself a cup of black tea. He wanted
to work.

Ever since Caroline died, I have felt times of deep sorrow and loneliness. I know that everyone says you're supposed to cope with these feelings for yourself. Take responsibility for yourself. Be strong! But it is a lonely task, and I also know how good it is to be loved. How much it helps to feel love close by. And, sometimes, especially most recently when I have been with Mary, it has helped me to catch a glimpse of that inner peacefulness I yearn for.

So there is work to be done. All that has gone before, important though it has always seemed at the time, may have been no more than a distraction. I must set out again. Begin. Take the first step.

He opened the front door and sat on a bench on the veranda. The sun had risen but was still low, just above the horizon, sending its beams slantwise across the marsh. The seagulls were already in the sky. He really had no idea what would happen next, but as it was his own adventure; he would have to begin alone. And he would begin with practice, in stillness and quietude. He listened to the sea and the sound of the wind in the reed bed. He walked back into his study.

Working alone, I am beginning to experience a sweet sadness at the centre of all that is. I seem to remember this is what the hermits of all time have known. Somewhere in the deep darkness of sorrow lies a peace that cannot be found in the bright light of happiness. Happiness is insatiable and requires feeding. Sorrow is humble and requires only acceptance. After all, it is in the darkness of winter that the seed is transformed. It's a kind of magic. Spring brings promise and summer abundance. Autumn brings endings that are really new beginnings. But winter is the realm of transformation. All that is begins with darkness. Without sorrow there is no yearning for the one. The One. This year, I have accepted the sorrow of autumn and now, at last, I am looking forward to the coming of winter. More Leonard Cohen than Julie Andrews!

He had been at work for a couple of hours when Wendy arrived. She knocked on the open door and came in, taking off her shoes and calling out to him to let him know she was there. She went into the kitchen and put the kettle on the hob to boil water for tea. William walked through from his study and greeted her with a hug. The love they felt for each other was deeply embedded and without condition. Even though they no longer lived together, he felt safe with her. Without having to talk about it, she understood how much he needed the balance and order she brought to him. Breakfast was but one of the rituals with which he had constructed his life and managed his old wound, anxiety. He liked his meals at the same time every day. He liked the plate to be centred on the mat and the knives, spoons and forks to be straight. Obsessive? Of course. But harmful? Most unlikely. The porridge had been mixed with Manuka honey. The tea was black and bitter. The marmalade was Wilkins. There was Ryvita. Wendy knew all of these things.

"Do you have plans for today, William?"

"Only to spend the day as I now spend all my days, quietly and alone."

"Will Mary be coming today?"

"I don't think so."

And so another day began.

When Wendy had cleared away the breakfast, she put a load of white washing into the washing machine and checked the larder cupboard, making a note of one or two things that needed to be replenished. Green pesto, basmati rice and rice cakes. She wrote these onto a list and took it with her. Both Wendy and William still liked lists.

Left alone, William went into his dressing room and turned on the shower in his bathroom. Standing beneath the shower was a good place to start, letting the hot water cascade over him. He took the towel from the heated towel rail. It was large, soft and, as always, he dried himself in the same order from his head to his toes. Deodorant, no aluminum. He cleaned his teeth, using toothpaste with a special whitener. Then he combed his hair with a wide-toothed comb and set it with a gel to prevent the wisps from going astray. He dressed.

William looked at himself in the mirror. Was this the person with whom he would be spending his day? It seemed as if it would. Not entirely hopeless, even if he was older than he thought or felt himself to be. "Inside this ageing carcass," he thought to himself, "is a man much younger than my birth certificate claims."

Before going into his study to write his morning journal, William stood for a while on the veranda, as always looking across his garden to the reed beds of the marsh, and then to the shingle beach and the sea. On a morning such as this, when there was hardly any wind, everything was still. From the reed bed came the piping sound of a tit or a warbler. Another day.

Afternoon. Having made himself a lunch of cheese on toast, William was sitting in his armchair in the living room looking again at, Stephen Batchelor's book, *Alone With Others.* Here was a paradox. We are all alone and yet we are alone with others. It is part of what it is to be human. To live inside a body separate from everyone and everything else, and yet to live in communion, at least with those close by, and of course, even if we do not know it, with all that is. He began to make some notes.

Moving between these two realms of being is part of who we are. Some may favour the one and some the other, but the paradox remains.

In Batchelor's book, there was a reference to the writings of Heidegger and his notion of 'being-with others', which sounded really interesting, but it was not long before his eyes closed and he slept. And in this sleep he dreamt.

He was walking through a marsh, the reeds tall, up to his shoulders and his feet wet. He somehow knew he had to cross the marsh to dry ground, but wherever he turned there was no way out. Just as he thought he had at last found the pathway, he found himself walking on the sea, walking on the waves. In his dream, he wanted to sink and find comfort in the quietness beneath the waves. At last, he was sitting on the sea bed, looking up at the light above him. Finally, he felt calm and at peace. Then something landed on top of him making a strange noise, and he woke up to find Florence sitting on his lap, looking at him and purring. He sat up and pushed her off, and she walked away with as much dignity as she could, then settled upon the sofa and began to clean herself with her pink tongue.

William went back into his study and switched on his computer. He googled 'Heidegger' and selected a link to *The Guardian* where there was a series of blogs written by the English philosopher, Simon Critchley. They were fascinating, and he was clearly meant to be reading them, for they described the very condition he was experiencing, the apparent tension between being alone and being with. According to Heidegger, both were part of a whole, what he called 'being alone with'. Furthermore, and this really intrigued William, Heidegger had apparently also spoken of that nagging condition that had always lain deep within him, 'anxiety'. But instead of presenting this as mere fearfulness, Heidegger presented it as a necessary part of the manner in which we, as humans, differentiate ourselves from the vast sweep of Nature, enabling us to make sense of and reflect upon a world of which are a part.

For the rest of the afternoon, William read and re-read the blogs, making notes in his journal.

Heidegger

Deep anxiety, and what it means to be alone or to be with. Is that where reality lies? And death, too? The horizon of death? Heidegger apparently said that, 'to philosophise is to learn how to die.' That's a thought. And there are two particular insights that speak to me. The first is that it is through anxiety that we find freedom from the world of things. Discernment. And the second is that however much we might feel alone, being is always being-with.

Perhaps these are not two but one. Perhaps there is no 'between' in the space between being alone and being with, only being 'in the midst of.' Alone with.

It seems to me that as I get older and my days pass, the boundary between being and not being begins to slip.

With this understanding of 'being alone with,' William was discovering a new possibility. It explained so much that he had come to know, but had not before been able to understand. Both the loneliness and the yearning to be loved. And the possibility that feeling anxious might be necessary to our being, even a doorway to freedom, was liberating. There was no longer any need to fear it. If he added to this all that he had learnt from Humberto

Maturana about our being naturally loving, then at last he felt he might find his way to a kind of peacefulness. Perhaps, within his own world, he would be at peace. Day by day, he led his ordered life and worked quietly in his study.

Then there was Mary. In her he had found that other part of 'being with' – a loving companion. Honest, direct and seemingly uncomplicated, although he knew she had her own wounds, too. Loss and loneliness. Separation from her son. As they came closer, he was becoming more and more content, and was learning to know, and even to have compassion for, his frailties and his discomforts – accepting his loneliness, accepting his old woundedness, and marvelling at the love that was being brought to him. All of this seemed much more real than the world he had once lived in.

Until now, I thought I had a pretty good grasp on 'reality'. But ever since I began to enter this wondrous realm between being and not being, I am not at all sure. I know there is a reality that is made for us by other people, mostly people who would like us to buy something or, at least, not to get in the way of their becoming rich or powerful, or both. I've been there. But now I seem to be losing touch with it. Letting it go. Of course, I know all that stuff about the world not really being as we say it is, the illusions of the material world of 'things' and 'events'. And I have read the Buddha's teaching of impermanence and attachment. I've read a lot of books about that. But this is something else. It's a physical sensation, a sensation of not being entirely where I am. It is as if a part of me is always somewhere else, just out of sight.

And now, Mary …

And so William went to have tea with Mary, walking up the street to her shop. Outside was a table on which Mary had placed fresh vegetables and fruit, together with two vases of cut flowers. He took one of the vases and brought it into the shop. Mary was sitting beside the till looking at a magazine of holiday cruises.

"Good afternoon, William. Have you ever been on a cruise?"

"No, of course I haven't."

"So, not for you then?"

"No, not for me, ever! Never was and never will be."

William placed the vase of flowers by the till.

"I should like to buy these flowers, Mary. How much are they?"

"The whole vase?"

"Yes, the whole vase."

"Well, I think the whole vase would have to be twelve pounds."

William took a twenty pound note from his wallet and gave it to Mary. She rang the till and gave him his change.

"Do you want them wrapped?"

"No, thank you."

"Are you going to take them home like that, dripping with water?"

"No."

"No?"

"No, Mary, I am not going to take these flowers anywhere. They are not for me, they are for you. I need you to make me some tea with a plate of your shortbread. The flowers are to go on the table, as I hope you will have tea with me."

This was just the kind of thing that reinforced Mary's belief that living in the house by the marsh turned people a bit mad. First, there had been Roderick and Edward, who never quite fitted in. Then there had been William, Wendy and Ruth. That had caused a stir. Then William again, living there on his own, sitting in his study and walking down to that bench by the sea. All of them had been, or were, a bit mad. There was something about that house that caused people to behave oddly. Even her own private moments with William were something she could not really explain to herself.

"There are times, William, when I think I should have never have come to Frampton. But then I think that, if I hadn't, I would never have met people as odd and lovely as you are. Well, you and Wendy and Ruth."

"So where shall I sit?"

"I suppose you will sit where you always sit, either by the window at the front where you can see what's going on, or by the window at the back where you can look into the garden and see my underwear hanging on the washing line."

"I think I'll take the table by the window at the front. I'm not sure I can manage your underwear this afternoon."

They laughed, and as William went to sit at his table, Mary disappeared into the back of her shop to make the tea. Although only William knew this, Mary did indeed wear beautiful underwear. Lingerie.

Mary's tables were a perfect example of a world between being and not being. At one level, they were quite ordinary. Round tables with white table cloths, and a small sprig of flowers in a vase in the centre. The cups and saucers and the milk jug were always plain white, and the plate of shortbread would, of course, come on a white plate covered with a white napkin with a blue embroidered border. The milk jug would be covered with a lace napkin. The teapot would be either white or blue, but the dish for the tea strainer would always be white. Small silver spoons, and bone-handled tea knives. But if this appeared to be an ordinary table set for tea, it was really quite something else. It was a holy place. A place of communion. The offering of the tea and the shortbread were the bread and the wine, and Mary was the priest, or rather the priestess. Once again, the memory returned and William thought of the monastery of Vatopedi on Mount Athos where the Eucharist was served in the Katholikon dedicated to the Theotokos, the Holy Mother. Another Mary. There the monks were comforted as they knelt and received the small pieces of bread in their mouths. Here, at Mary's table, her congregation was also comforted as they sipped their tea and bit into the buttery shortbread. Hers was an act of love.

William, who had been looking out of the window to see what, if anything, was happening in Frampton – nothing as far as he could see – turned to see Mary coming towards him with the tea tray; she was followed by her helper, Winny, carrying a vase into which the bunch of flowers had been put. He had to smile to himself, because he saw again that Mary was beautiful.

Placing the tray on an adjoining table, Mary put two tea cups on the white table cloth, side by side. The plate of shortbread with its white linen napkin was placed in the centre of the table. Everything so carefully done. Beside the place at which she would sit, and by which the cups and saucers now stood, Mary put a blue teapot set on a plain raffia mat, with the jug of milk beside it covered with a lace napkin. Winny removed the small vase with the flower sprig and replaced it with the vase of cut flowers that William had bought. She then retreated, and Mary sat down with her back to the shop.

"Shall I be mother?"

"Yes, please. No milk for me."

"William, you may think me very stupid, but over the years I have known you, you've come to have tea in my tea shop many times. I think you can be sure that I know that you do not take milk in your tea."

"Just making sure!"

They sat together and had their tea. Mary was able to tell William that Lady Whitely was definitely leaving High Winds, and that the house was now on the market. Lady Whitely, for so long a part of Frampton, would soon be leaving.

"I must write to her to say goodbye," said William. "In her own way, she welcomed me here when I first came. And she was very good to Wendy, letting her park her caravan in her field."

"Yes," said Mary, "I just felt a bit sorry for her. It was as if she had been left behind. But that could happen to you and me, I suppose."

"And what of Brenda and Penelope, I haven't seen them for a while?"

"As you know, they are travelling about quite a lot, visiting friends and taking their holiday cruises. But they were in the shop yesterday, buying a few things and posting some letters."

"I must give them a ring and catch up."

"They would like that."

Just as they were finishing their tea, Mary leant across the table and touched William's arm.

"William," she said, "I have something I need to talk to you about, something private. Can I come and see you this evening after I have closed the shop?"

"Yes, of course. Shall we have supper?"

"Okay, scrambled eggs, or something like that."

"I'll open a bottle of wine."

"Good, see you at about six."

They finished their tea and Mary cleared away. William paid and, leaving the flowers behind on the table, walked back to his house. Being with Mary, having tea and hearing the village gossip had been good. But now he was wondering what it was that she wanted to talk about. Something private.

Just after six o'clock, Mary knocked on William's door and he opened it and invited her in, kissing her. She slipped off her shoes. They went into the kitchen and Mary prepared the scramble eggs, whilst William opened the wine, pouring a glass for Mary and one for himself. They toasted each other and clinked their glasses.

"To us, Mary."

"To us, William."

William liked that.

They sat together at the table and for a while talked about what had happened that day. Who had been into the shop. Who might buy Lady Whitely's house. Then Mary became thoughtful and William realised she had something important to say.

"So, what is this private matter you wanted to talk about?"

"Well, it's to do with the shop. I shall be seventy next year and I am finding the work a bit of a burden. Not just having to be there from early morning until late afternoon every day of the week, but the unrelenting responsibility of keeping the stock topped up, the paying of bills, taxes, all that sort of thing. I've had enough and I want to stop."

"Yes, of course."

"Trouble is, I am not sure how to do it."

William sat quietly, reflecting on what Mary had told him.

"I was wondering, William, if you think I should retire? That's the first thing. Then, will I regret it if I do?"

"It's not easy, is it? You give your life to something, something that in a way defines who you are. And then, quite suddenly, it stops. And there is loss."

"Is that what happened to you?"

"Yes, in a way it was. Although I didn't have a shop."

"No, of course not, but you had become your work, hadn't you?"

"Yes, I had. And letting it all go was more painful than I could have imagined."

They sat quietly.

"But," said William, "painful though it was, it was the right thing to do. And anyway, some of it was done to me, not the other way round. It just happened. At least you are making the decision for yourself."

Mary stood up and cleared the plates from the table, whilst William topped up their glasses and carried them into the living room, putting another log into the wood stove. He sat in his armchair and soon Mary came and sat on the sofa. Florence, who was sitting on the other armchair, opened one eye and then closed it.

"You know, William, this is partly your fault."

William looked surprised.

"You see, our friendship has become very important to me, and I have watched you this year as you have begun, at last, to find some of that peacefulness you talk about. I would like to find that, too."

He reached out and took her hand. She drew him to her.

"I wonder if you would mind holding me for a while," she said. "I am a bit frightened."

William came and sat beside her, putting his arm around her so that she could lean her head on his chest. Gently, he rubbed her arm with his hand.

"You know, Mary," he said, "fear is an odd thing, but I have now learnt that it has a purpose. We should attend to it because it helps us see what we are frightened of so that we can summon the courage to face it. In a way, I think that is what I have been trying to do. And it has helped me."

"I never quite understand what you are saying, my dear William, but I can see that I should face up to getting older, to my tiredness, and to the fear of loneliness, of being left behind."

"You are not going to be left behind, Mary. Not by me, anyway."

"I hope not."

"And you will always be you. Shop or no shop."

Mary laughed, comforted at last.

Over the next few weeks, they talked a lot more about what would be involved in Mary retiring. Providence was listening.

In December, people began to make plans for Christmas. Mary was going to Dublin to be with her son and his family. Jane had been in touch to see whether William would like to come up to Scotland. And Wendy and Ruth had invited him to be with them in Friston. But William decided to spend Christmas by himself. He wanted to be alone, to be with his work. On Christmas Day, he had phone calls with his children and grandchildren, and Wendy had left him a special nut roast that she had made.

"I'm rather proud about this," she had said. "No flesh."

On Christmas morning, William cooked brussels sprouts and roast potatoes. Before she had gone away, Mary had brought him some of her mince pies, some bread sauce and an apple crumble. All was well.

On New Year's Eve, he put on his coat and his wellington boots and, wrapping a scarf round his neck, walked down to the water's edge, looking out across the North Sea and remembering those times before when his chosen family had cast their stones into the waves and made their wishes. As he bent down to pick up a pebble from the beach, he heard someone walking across the beach behind him. He stood up and turned around. There they were, Ruth and Wendy.

"We couldn't stay away. We knew you would be here, and so we came to join you and make our wishes again."

"That's a wonderful idea," said William.

They picked their pebbles, good sized ones, round and smooth, and Ruth checked her watch.

"Two minutes to twelve."

They waited and on the count of midnight threw their stones into the sea, each one of them making their own wish.

"Happy New Year," said Wendy and linked her arms with both Ruth and William. The three of them joined together. Only Mary was missing.

Nine years had passed since William had become a widower, and at the end of this next year, he would be eighty.

CHAPTER 17

LEFT BEHIND

Providence does not always do her work in ways that we expect, and when she heard Mary speak of her retirement, she did not waste any time in beginning events that would change life in Frampton forever. In the meantime, and unaware of what was to come, Mary continued to confide in William, now often coming to have supper with him when the shop had closed, and staying with him so that they could talk together in the evening. She was still unsure what to do.

That winter, the marsh had been wetter than ever before and sometimes smelt stronger, a damp smell of vegetation and mud. And now there were other disturbances, heavy and unexpected rainfall and then periods of no rain at all. Ben was keeping William informed about the latest evidence of climate change and, each month, he checked the website that Ben had found for him with the data for Suffolk. It was scary. The rainfall in January and February had been above average, both in amount and intensity. And the days were warm. Unusually warm. William had mosquito screens made to go over the windows of his study and the two bedrooms at the back of the house.

And then, in early March, William was attacked by a most unpleasant virus that he later learnt was 'everywhere'. And although Mary seemed unaffected, he thought he must have picked it up one day whilst waiting at the till in her shop, where he had been aware of a good deal of snuffling and coughing. Anyway, where it came from was not important, but it had taken residence in his not-so-young body.

It set him back. For the first time for as long as he could remember, he was ill. On the first night it struck, he shivered in bed and had to get up to find another blanket, sleeping in his dressing gown for added warmth. By the morning, as the fever took hold, he was boiling hot – and coughing. When Wendy came, he warned her to keep her distance. But she made him tea and prepared his breakfast. He got up washed and changed his pyjamas that were wet from sweating.

"Come into the kitchen and have breakfast. It's warm in here and I've put extra honey in your porridge. I'll change your bed and then I'll go down to Mary's shop and get you some Lemsip and some of that Broncho Stop cough linctus. And I'm going to check your temperature."

"Thank you, Wendy. I feel a bit sorry for myself today."

"Well, that's okay. I feel sorry for you, too."

Wendy washed her hands and then took the thermometer out of the drawer in the kitchen, washed it under the tap and pressed the button to set it before placing it in William's mouth. It showed a reading of 38.7 degrees celsius.

"Back to bed for you, William. As soon as you have finished your breakfast, back to bed. I'm making a hot water bottle."

Wendy went through to William's study and stripped his bed, putting on a clean sheet and pillowcases and a fresh duvet cover. She set the central heating to continuous so that his room would remain warm, and took an extra blanket from a drawer under the bed, laying it over the duvet.

William finished his breakfast and, still wearing his dressing gown, went back to bed, taking with him his hot water bottle wrapped in a woollen cover. The clean sheets and duvet and the hot water bottle were a comfort and, at first, he sat up against the pillows thinking he might read. But, too tired for that, he took off his glasses and closed his eyes. He was a little frightened. He felt the fever in him. He felt the strain that it was putting on his old body. The congestion on his chest and in his lungs, the racking of his body with the coughing. His body was suffering. He felt the weakness. Frightening.

The fever lasted five days and, each morning, William's chest rattled with congestion. He coughed and coughed, bringing up a thick dark-yellow mucus. He kept by his bed a large box of Kleenex, throwing the used tissues into a wastepaper bin. By mid-morning, he would feel better, but later the virus would return and he continued the battle. It was another week before he felt his strength returning and over three weeks after that before he was well. It had been a long struggle.

And then to add to his suffering, the effect of the fever and of the Lemsip on his digestion, caused a haemorrhoid to burst, with dramatic bleeding. So now, on top of the coughing, he had to spread on the Anusol cream and pad up! He felt miserable.

He picked up the phone and rang his daughter.

"I have not been well."

"What kind of not well?"

"I picked up a virus."

"And?"

"And I ran a temperature for about five days. Lots of coughing and congestion on my chest. Whole body racked by the coughing."

"Poor old you."

"The emphasis being on the 'old'."

"Yes, not so good at your age."

"No, not so good."

He decided not to mention the indignity of the Always pad.

"And you, how are you?"

"I'm good, Dad, really. As I think Ben told you, Alan and I are living together most of the time. It's funny getting used to someone again. And I am conscious of what this means for Ben and Sally, especially Sally. But we've talked it through and she seems okay. Fortunately, she likes Alan."

Some comfort, but not much. The talking had irritated his cough and he took another dose of Broncho Stop. He felt old.

As spring left winter behind, there was something in the air that seemed to invite change and renewal. Or was it just that Providence was hard at work? One morning, some time after he had recovered from the virus, Wendy and Ruth rang William to ask if they could come and see him. Not knowing what it would be about he had, of course, said yes, and they had arranged to meet him at his house the next day. They arrived at eleven o'clock and William invited them in, sitting together in the living room. Ruth began. It was about Mary and her shop.

"Have you ever thought, William, that Mary might be coming towards retirement, that she might not want to go on running her shop and her tea room?"

William did not wish to share the private discussions that Mary had been having with him since before Christmas.

"I suppose you must be right," he said, "but I had just assumed she would be there forever."

"I know, but when she came to see us a week or two ago, she was talking about how tiring she finds it. She's not quite sure what she wants to do, but she's beginning to wonder if she could find someone to help her run it. I don't think she wants to give up entirely, and anyway, she lives there. But even with Winny helping her a bit more than before, she is finding managing everything by herself is more than she can do."

"And?"

"Well, she wanted to know whether Wendy and I would be interested in becoming partners with her. I don't think she is entirely clear what that would mean. But that is what she asked us."

William's head was buzzing with questions, details and worries, difficulties and obstacles.

"Is this something you would like to do, or is this something you are thinking about because you think Mary wants you to do it?"

Again, it was Ruth who replied.

"Well, given how fond we are of Mary, it is difficult to separate the two. But then – and this is why we have come to see you – something else has happened. We were at a party in London at the weekend and met a couple who run a bread and pastries shop in Hackney. They were telling us that they wanted to leave London and come and live in Suffolk. Not retirement, they said, but a slower life. Because Mary had spoken to us about wanting to find a partner, we mentioned her shop to them and they were really interested. Now they have been in touch to say that they would like to come and visit Frampton and meet Mary. They want to come on Saturday."

"Have you told Mary about this?"

"Not yet. We wanted to talk to you first."

"What are these people like?"

"They seemed very nice. Their names are Andrew and Amy Browning, and I suppose they are in their early fifties. But you can't really tell what people are like just by meeting them at a party."

"No, of course not. I suppose one of the problems is that, even if they were interested in the shop, Mary would probably want to continue to be involved for a while. And, as you say, it's where she lives. So any kind of transition would have to be gradual. How flexible are Andrew and Amy likely to be?"

"I think they would be flexible. They told us that whilst their shop in Hackney covers its costs, they have other income. Amy writes for a food magazine and Andrew does some kind of web design work. From what they said, it seems that the shop is something they just like to do, a project they work on together. But anyway, we want to know whether you think this is just a daft idea, or whether we should talk to Mary about it."

"I don't think it's daft, although I can see there is a lot to be thought through. Not least, what is best for Mary. But only she can decide if she wants to meet them."

They talked on for a while and then Wendy and Ruth left. They had decided they would speak to Mary that afternoon.

That evening, Mary came to have supper with William and afterwards they sat together by the wood stove. William in his arm chair and Mary on the sofa. Florence walked through from the study and then disappeared through her catflap. William knew why Mary had come. She was thoughtful and quiet.

"Do you want to talk about your plans for the shop, Mary?"

"I do, William. Have Wendy and Ruth spoken to you?"

"They have."

"I thought they would, but I hope you didn't tell them about our discussions."

"Of course not."

"They want me to meet these friends of theirs, Andrew and Amy Browning."

"I'm not sure they're friends. I think they just met them at a party."

"Yes, I think that's right. But anyway, I've said I'll meet them, although I'm quite nervous about it. I'm still finding it difficult to know what I want. I have got so used to the shop. It's who I am. Mary's shop."

There was a pause.

"Oh well, I suppose I should meet them. At some point, I will have to find someone to take over from me, and perhaps we might be able to work something out. And anyway, talking to them might help me decide what I want."

"Well, you won't know until you meet them. And you don't have to take all the steps in one go. Maybe you can begin something that will take place gradually."

There was a pause.

"My son has asked me if I would go and live closer to him in Dublin."

"Oh," said William, fearing what might be coming next.

"But I don't think I want to do that."

William was relieved.

"Only you can decide that, Mary, but you have family here, too. Don't we both have family here? Wendy, Ruth, you and me? Aren't we a kind of family? We are fond of each other. We take care of each other. Isn't that family?"

"Yes, it is," said Mary, leaning over and taking his hand in hers. "And I don't want to be without you."

"That's good."

"So what do you think I should say to Andrew and Amy?"

"Well, Wendy and Ruth only told me a bit about them. It's not clear what they might have in mind, but no doubt they'll tell you. You'll need to discuss how it would happen and, of course, how long you would be able to stay living there."

"Oh, William, come and sit beside me. I can hardly bear to think about it. You will help me go through this, won't you? I would really find that helpful. You always seem to be able to see possibilities, instead of just obstacles."

"Yes, of course, I'll do what I can."

And they sat together, William with his arm around Mary.

But it soon became clear that neither Mary nor William could resist what was coming. When Andrew and Amy Browning met Mary that weekend, they were charming and listened to Mary's proposal that the transition should be gradual, allowing her to remain where she was for two years. But the truth was, they neither knew nor cared much about what might happen to her. They were keen to take charge of the shop, running it the way they ran their shop in London. And this did not include working alongside Mary. Although they would bide their time, they had plans.

And there was something else. They had been talking with a friend of theirs, Graham Seville, a banker who was thinking about his own retirement and looking for 'things to do.' He was interested in the shop and suggested that if they went ahead, he might be their financial partner, buying the property and providing working capital. Graham talked with Andrew and Amy about the possibility of developing the homemade foods that Mary had always provided, with a new, 'branded' delivery service, for people visiting in the area and wanting locally-sourced food. He saw potential in developing the kitchen, buying a van, and delivering in the wider local area. And then, when he looked up Frampton on Google, Graham Seville discovered that High Winds was for sale. This also intrigued him. During the week, he drove up with Andrew, looked at the shop and made an appointment to look at High Winds, too. In the softening of the market that had followed Brexit, the price of High Winds had come down, and having seen it, he thought he might have spotted a bargain. Back in London, he asked a friend of his, who was a property developer, to explore the possibility of the development of High Winds, dividing the house up into three or four holiday homes and building new houses on the field in which Wendy's caravan had been parked. He liked what he was told. He made an offer. It was accepted.

Change was on the prowl. New people. New blood. New energy. Providence had been hard at work.

That summer, Frampton was full of new arrivals. Having taken advice from a local estate agent in Saxmundham, Mary had agreed a price for her shop on the basis that she would remain there for two years, and Andrew and Amy had begun to work with her, renting a cottage in the village. Meanwhile, planning consent was given for the conversion of High Winds and apparently, there were to be wonderful bathrooms, boarded floors, massive American-style fridge-freezers, washing machines and dryers and of course, wi-fi. Graham Seville was enjoying himself.

And he turned out to be a super-keen gardener. Ever since Lady Whitely had left High Winds, the gardens had been abandoned and were now looking overgrown and unkempt. Wanting to pursue his passion, and mindful of the beneficial effect this would have on his investment, Graham Seville began a restoration. His comings and goings soon became the topic of much discussion in Mary's shop. Lorries carrying large trees and shrubs were observed turning into his driveway, and word had got out that he was looking for at least one, if not two, experienced gardeners. Wendy thought about it, but decided against it. In the end, gardeners were found in Saxmundham. Trees and shrubs were planted, patios and pathways were constructed. And, of course, a water feature was installed, which spouted from the mouth of a large fish into the old lily pond.

It was now July. There had been another cloudburst, the rainwater running down the village street towards the marsh. Often now, calm days would be followed by storms, and the height of the tide had moved up the shingled beach. William had repositioned his bench. Then there would be no rain at all and the water level in the marsh dropped away, much lower than before, the reeds becoming dry and brittle. The marsh harriers swept over the reed beds searching for food.

Despite the terms of the agreement she had signed, Mary was finding it difficult to be part of all that was happening to her shop, or rather what had been her shop. Backed by Graham Seville, Andrew and Amy were full of ideas for changing the stock and improving the kitchen. Mary's holy offerings of tea and shortbread soon gave way to much more exotic slices of frangipane and Danish pastries, which customers seemed to like – although not William. They had plans to make the shop and its tea room more widely known, developing what they called an "online presence". And now, they were making their intentions clear. They wanted to give up the tenancy of the cottage they were living in and move into the shop. Whilst they were prepared to compensate Mary for agreeing to this, she would have to go.

Hearing about all this, Wendy and Ruth had told Mary that they were sorry they had made the introductions to Andrew and Amy in the first place, and were embarrassed about what was happening, but were powerless to stop it. Loving them as she did, Mary said it was not their fault. Something like this was bound to have happened sooner or later.

The changes that were being made by Andrew and Amy were drawing in new customers, not just for tea, but now in the evenings too, rivalling restaurants in Aldeburgh and Saxmundham. And the initial responses to the possibility of a delivery service of home-cooked food, were looking very promising. A lot of the people who came for weekends or short holidays wanted home-cooked food, but did not want to have to cook it themselves. And the recent fall of the value of the pound against other currencies in Europe and elsewhere was encouraging them to holiday at home. Another Frampton was coming into being.

For both William and Mary, all that was happening was disturbing. They had become used to the utter remoteness of their lives. And yet they knew that without the visitors, the shop, the post office and the tea room, the very heart of the village, would not remain. Without such new energy, life in the village would dwindle away – like them. Accepting the inevitable with her own special grace, Mary agreed to find somewhere else to live. And William, no longer wanting to go to London, had decided to sell his flat in Marylebone. Despite the market being quiet, it was sold within a few weeks. Another part of his life had gone, but this time he was pleased. Now he would spend most of his time in his house and seldom leave the village.

One afternoon after lunch, Mary came to see William for advice and comfort. She brought shortbread and they went to bed. As they were sitting there together, propped up against the pillows, with the duvet drawn up about them, Mary rested her head on William's shoulder.

"I thought the handover of the shop was going to be much easier than this. I thought I was going to be relieved to let it go. But I'm not. I'm actually feeling as if it is being taken away from me. My shop. Another awful loss!"

"Liberation is often very depressing," said William.

They drew close to each other.

"I like being here with you, William. Like this. Isn't it strange? We never talk about it, and no one else knows."

"Except Wendy."

"Yes, except Wendy, but she's family!"

"All these brave things we are meant to do for ourselves. Take responsibility. Face up. 'You have to look after yourself.' 'Only you can look after you.' All those dreadful self-help books written by smug people. It all sounds sensible, but it's harsh too."

"Yes, I feel exactly the same. However much we all have to take responsibility for our lives, there's a lot to be said for being in bed under the duvet with someone of whom you are fond."

They laughed out loud.

"By the way," said Mary, "the couple who own the cottage next to Brenda and Penelope want to sell it and they have asked me if I would be interested. Apparently, Brenda had said something about me wanting to make a move. They live in Ipswich and only use it at weekends, and, even then, not very often. They have given me the key and I have been to see it. It's quite small. But cosy. Needs a new kitchen."

"Why don't we go and have a look at it together?"

"When?"

"Now? We haven't got anything better to do."

And again they collapsed into laughter. The absurdity. Their own wonderful absurdity.

They got up, dressed and walked up the street to the cottage, William putting on his Panama hat. Mary opened the front door. It led straight into a sitting room, behind which was a kitchen, a utility room, a cloakroom and another room that had been built on at the back, which was being used as a study, but which could be a bedroom. A staircase led out of the sitting room and up to two bedrooms and a bathroom. The owners had put a wood stove in the sitting room and, although the kitchen did need a bit of an uplift, the upstairs bathroom had quite recently been improved and there was a shower in the downstairs cloakroom. A small garden at the back of the house faced west and ran into the garden of the house behind it, which was set at a right angle facing the drive, which also led to a garage that went with the cottage. William walked outside to get a look at the roof and the external walls. All seemed in good order.

"Well, it's cosy, Mary. That Velux window over the kitchen makes it very light. Easy to manage. Close to your friends. Room for your family to stay, at a squeeze, especially if you use the study as a bedroom."

"And it fits my budget."

"That's good. Does it have a name?"

"No, but I thought I would call it Mary's Cottage."

"Why not? That is what it will be."

"So you think I should try and buy it?"

"I do."

"You always seem so certain, William."

"Well, I think it is possible that life may be much simpler than we suppose."

"I would hardly call my life simple."

"That's true, Mary. But perhaps it will be."

"Perhaps."

They walked back down the street and Mary went into her shop – or what used to be her shop – whilst William went back to the house by the marsh. Wendy had arrived with shopping from Waitrose, which she was putting away in the larder cupboard. She nodded her head towards the plate of shortbread that Mary had left, covered by its linen cloth, with a blue edge.

"I see Mary has been to see you," she said. "That must have been nice."

"It was, Wendy. It was."

They smiled at each other and William took a small piece of the shortbread and ate it.

"Mary and I have just been to see a cottage that she might buy. It's just right for her."

"Oh, that is good news. Ruth and I have been feeling so bad about what has happened."

"There's no need. In a way, you have enabled Mary to move on. It's all been a bit painful, but it was inevitable. Providence!"

Mary made an offer for the cottage, and it was accepted.

3rd August

So Mary is going to leave her shop and move house. That's a big thing. At least she has found somewhere in the village close by. It will be called Mary's Cottage, which seems just right to me. Honest and direct, like Mary. I would miss her if she were not here. And I think she would miss me.

I am finding it difficult to come to terms with all that is happening to Frampton. All the things that bring new people to the village, the new houses, the development of what was Mary's shop into something much more lively and, I suppose, appealing. It is leaving me behind. And Mary, too. And that is as it is bound to be. I am now nearly eighty and Mary has turned seventy. This is no longer our world.

In a way, none of it really affects me that much. It just isn't part of my life. All that first drew me to the house by the marsh is still here, its stillness and its silence. A few more people walk along the beach and through the woodland, but they leave me alone. And Mary and I spend more time together. In a way, we are happy to be left alone.

Now that Mary has retired, and only helps out occasionally at the shop, and now that she has settled into her cottage, we are spending more time together. Doing not much. Although sometimes she takes me with her in her car to Aldeburgh or

*Southwold and, the other day, she took me to where
she used to live, Bury St. Edmunds. In fact, we have
ventured across the county to visit Lavenham,
with its wonderful church and its timbered
guildhall. We had lunch at The Swan, all beamed
ceilings and stone floors. That was a good day.*

*We always have something to talk about - our
families, memories and loneliness.*

Because their friendship had developed over a long
time, nearly ten years now, it had an easy feel. And for
reasons they had never quite understood, they felt
comfortable whether they were walking arm in arm or
sitting up together in bed. Sometimes, more often now,
Mary would stay the night with William and share his
breakfast. Wendy never remarked upon it when she
found them together in the morning. She was fond of
both of them and so it seemed quite natural that this
should be happening. She had told Ruth, but Ruth was
even more matter of fact about such things. She
shrugged and smiled. She was pleased that two of her
dearest friends, two of her family, were finding
comfort together.

William and Mary talked to each other a lot about
what their lives had now become, left behind by the tide
of events. As if it had taken a different course, now
leaving their part of the shore untouched. Driftwood.
And for William, in their easy tenderness, Mary was
becoming more and more beautiful. For years, he had
not really been aware of her body, which was slim, or the
colour of her eyes, which were dark brown, or the shape

of her hands, which were fine. But now he was. And she delighted him. Mary had always thought William was attractive, if a bit wayward. But now she had settled into the familiarity of his company, she liked to feel his evident enjoyment of her body. She cared about him and he cared about her. It was true, they had been left behind, but perhaps Providence had intended that, that after all the excitement of people coming and going they should find peacefulness and contentment. A late flowering.

The other day I discovered that there is a rose that flowers into autumn. It has an 'upright habit and excellent disease resistance'. That is how I should like to be! The flower of the rose is especially beautiful. In the summer it has a full blossom and makes a display. But sometimes, in late autumn, as I am, it will flower again, this time offering only one or two buds which may still be there when the first of the frosts appear. Then it is especially wondrous. Its name is Compassion. Compassion is the sister of Wisdom.

I remember once going to an exhibition of the last work of Patrick Heron at the National Gallery, paintings done at the end of his life, when he was an old man. They were of gardens, full of clear colour and vitality. Huge in size. Wonderful, wonderful paintings. A late flowering.

I have begun to wonder what the future is. Not how it might be, but what it is. Even when it shortens, it lies there before us, waiting for us. Those opening lines in Eliot's **Four Quartets:**

> *Time present and time past*
> *Are both perhaps present in time future,*
> *And time future contained in time past.*
> *If all time is eternally present*
> *All time is unredeemable.*

I like the word 'perhaps'. Perhaps. I am never sure what Eliot means, but there is something in his words, in his voice, that catches how I feel.

I used to be someone, but perhaps now I am just here. And Mary is with me.

A couple of days later, Mary was in her cottage when she received a call from William.

"Hi, Mary, it's me. Do you fancy going to a film? There is something on in Aldeburgh that I would like to see. It's a special showing of *The Lavender Hill Mob*. Do you remember it? It's an early 1950's classic in black and white, all about smuggling gold bars in the shape of Eiffel Towers."

"Oh, yes. Of course, I remember. It would be fun to see it again. When is it?"

"Tomorrow at five in the afternoon."

"Okay, let's do that and you can have supper with me afterwards."

"That would be very nice."

"I'll pick you up at about four-thirty."

"Okay. Do you think Brenda and Penelope would like to come too?"

"I'm sure they would. Ask them."

"Okay."

Brenda and Penelope said they would love to come to the film and then have supper after, and that they could provide a pudding.

It was a very successful outing. All four of them enjoyed the nostalgia of the film. A time when the world seemed more straightforward – although it probably wasn't. And it was very funny. By the time they were back in Mary's cottage, they were full of laughter.

Mary had prepared pesto pasta and Parmesan with broccoli, William and Penelope both being vegetarian. And Brenda and Penelope had brought an apple tart with custard. William had brought a bottle of red wine and Mary had bought a bottle of local apple juice. They sat around Mary's table and discussed the film before Mary asked what everyone thought about the changes at the shop. As usual, Brenda had many opinions.

"Well, of course, we liked it as it was when it was just your shop, Mary, but I have to say that Andrew and Amy are being very brave in introducing new ideas. We don't need their delivery service, but we have bought their ready-cooked meals to put in our freezer. It makes it so easy then to take one out for lunch. I miss your shortbread, but they have introduced quite a range of pastries. It is a bit of a speciality of theirs. Isn't it what they used to do in

London? They're very good. We haven't been there for supper, but someone we were speaking to in Aldeburgh said they had, and had been very pleased. A limited menu, but beautifully cooked and presented."

"And," said Penelope, "we have noticed more people going to the shop and going for an evening meal. Apparently, they are attracting people from as far away as Ipswich and even Colchester."

This was not altogether what Mary had hoped for and the conversation drifted for a while. And then, for some reason, the conversation turned to former husbands and wives.

"You know, Penelope," said William, "You have never said anything very much about your late husband. I have often wondered what he was like."

"That won't take long to describe," said Brenda with a tone of indignation in her voice. She had never liked Penelope's husband, thinking him utterly dull.

"Well," said Penelope, "Brenda is right. He was rather a dull man. Very private in his ways and unambitious. Never really wanted more than he had."

"That's not such a bad thing," said Mary.

"No, it's not. He was brought up in Bedford. His father worked for the county council and so, when his time came, Reggie did, too. His name was Reginald, but everyone called him Reggie. He went to work for the County Council when he left school and he stayed there. He was a clerk really, what in those days we called a clerk. We lived in Bedford for all of our married life. I did some part-time voluntary work with the local hospital. It was an unexciting life. And we never had children. We would have liked to, but it didn't happen for us. So when

Reggie died, Brenda came to my rescue and took me in. And here I am."

Penelope telling the story of her dull life had quietened the room. It hadn't amounted to much.

"Brenda, of course, led me astray," she continued. "Her friends were always more colourful than mine. And it wasn't until I went to live with her that I realised she was gay. We certainly never talked about it at home. I had always thought she had simply not found the right man to live with and that she just had girlfriends. I don't think my parents thought about it at all. It wasn't until I lived with her that I realised that some of her girlfriends were lovers. I wasn't shocked by it. I just hadn't known about it."

"Well, I've loved having you live with me," said Brenda. "You are very good company, with clean habits. And they weren't all my lovers. You make me sound promiscuous."

They laughed.

Quite suddenly, William felt tired and decided he should go home. He thanked the others for the supper and took his leave, walking slowly back down the village street to the house by the marsh. The lights were still on in what he still thought of as Mary's shop. Quite a good number of people having supper. Laughter. Conversation. Cars parked in the street. He walked on and came to his gate, opening it and closing it behind him.

"I don't suppose," he thought to himself, "I don't suppose the frangipane is served with a white cloth. I don't suppose they celebrate Eucharist when they take the Danish pastries."

It was a warm night and he walked through his

garden and the marsh, and onto the beach. The sea was very still. He sat on the bench, set high on the shingle, and watched the waves touching the edge of the beach, just the slightest sigh as the small waves drew back from the shore. On the horizon, were the lights of a ferry making its way towards Felixstowe. A lone seagull was sitting in the water. A herring gull. William stood up and walked back up the beach to his house, up the steps to the veranda and put the brass key into the welcoming lock, which turned with ease. He pushed open the door, slipped off his shoes and walked in, not turning on a light until he was in his study, where he turned on his bedside lamp.

The sea is very still tonight.

Something this evening has taken me into that place of emptiness and loneliness, which is part of who I have become. The emptiness and the loneliness of the widower. That part of us that is empty and alone. Has to be. In her marriage Penelope learnt to accept less than she would have liked. Something was always closed to her. But isn't that how most of us live? Even in my dear friend, Mary, I sense a part that cannot quite open, for fear - for fear of what? For fear of being overwhelmed? For fear of being hurt? Perhaps we all keep ourselves a bit closed. Just in case.

He walked through the dark living room and into his dressing room, where he turned on the light on his chest of drawers, then the light above the basin in his shower room. He undressed, washed his face and hands, cleaned his teeth and put on his pyjama trousers and a T-shirt. He turned off the lights and walked back into his study, climbing onto the campaign bed and pulling the duvet about him. Quite often now at night-time he had begun to wonder what would happen if he were taken ill. Perhaps he should install a panic button of some kind.

He picked up the book Jane had sent him. It was a crime story written by Ian Rankin, *Rather Be the Devil*. He opened the book at Chapter 1: "Rebus placed his knife and fork on the empty plate, then leaned back in his chair, studying the other diners in the restaurant." William knew at once that he was going to enjoy his read and settled into the story. Half an hour later, his eyes beginning to droop, he put down the book, marking the place with a bookmark, turned off his lamp and went to sleep. Comfort and fear in one bed.

9th September

We had another heavy rain last night. Almost a month's rainfall I should think. I lay in bed and listened to it in the early hours of the morning. No lightning or thunder, just an incessant heavy rain with a strong southwesterly wind. Looking at the debris in the garden this morning, the winds must have been forty miles an hour, perhaps even gusts of fifty.

Often now I lie in bed wondering if it is worth getting up. But Wendy comes just before nine and I like at least to be out of bed when she arrives. She brings me joy. One of the great delights of my life has been the reunion of Wendy and Ruth. When I first met Wendy she was a refugee, lost to her lover. Then Ruth found her and came back to her. That time we had together in this house was very special, the three of us living together. Chosen family. And now they seem settled, steady and contented.

The plans of Andrew and Amy Browning and their friend, Graham Seville, seem to have no end.

But mine do.

CHAPTER 18

EMPTINESS

And so the days passed, and William and Mary spent more time together, sometimes the whole day, and sometimes only at teatime or supper. But even when they were apart, they were now never far away from each other – being alone with. And since they had been left behind by all that was happening in Frampton, their worlds were shared more privately. Both sought rest in the same places, the dappled shadows and the broken sunlight. The brightness of noontide was more than either of them could now bear. They preferred the early morning and the late afternoon, when the sun was lower in the sky, and the shadows were long.

Although William would seldom get dressed until eleven, he still liked to have his breakfast at nine. And after breakfast, he would often put on his wellington boots and, clad in a woollen hat and scarf, with a coat over his dressing gown, walk down to the beach and sit on the bench by the sea. Seagulls squawking. Black-headed gulls, black-backed gulls, common gulls and herring gulls. The terns had now left for their migration. He would sit there looking out across the North Sea, almost as if he were waiting for something. Then, after a while, he would return to his study.

As Mary was becoming much more a part of his life, Wendy only came to the house by the marsh in the morning, preparing breakfast, feeding Florence and doing any laundry that needed to be done. She would check the larder and prepare William's lunch, leaving the vegetables ready to cook and taking the macaroni cheese, the vegetable lasagne or the vegetable tart out of the freezer. If there was nothing that needed to be done in the garden, the rest of the day was left to him. And to Mary.

Sometimes Mary would come for lunch, and most often she would make tea in the afternoon, and then she and William would sit and talk, or just sit. Neither of them wanted to eat much for supper, but sometimes Mary would make them soup or baked beans on sourdough toast, or William would make scrambled eggs. All of this was comforting and familiar. If Mary stayed for the evening, they would sit together in the living room and read, or William would be in his study writing, keeping the door open so that he could hear Mary moving about the house. When they were together, they went to bed early, usually at nine o'clock. But if Mary went home to spend the night in her cottage, William would stay up a bit later, writing in his journal.

Both Mary and I are coming to a place that lies between. As our lives become pared down, with less and less contact with people and events, we are moving towards an 'other' realm that lies both within us and beyond us, too. A place that is both close by and as far away as any one can imagine and then a bit further. Without any deliberate intention, our world is filled with long periods of silence and stillness. Not the formality of a meditation practice. Not at all. It is simply a way of being that is close to continuous prayerfulness, living within rhythm and pattern. Timeless. Eternal. A place in which we lose ourselves because we give no resistance. Surrender.

We never discuss what it is that we are doing or why. We never ask if this is what we want, or whether it might ever end. It just is. It is unspoken, it is how we have become. But we check to see if each other is okay, and sometimes we share some part of our wondering.

One afternoon in early October, another day that had been unnaturally warm, William and Mary were sitting side by side on the bench by the sea and as she would so often do, Mary put her arm through William's arm and came close to him.

"I cannot remember an autumn that was as warm

as this one. What is happening?"

"I don't know, but Ben sent me a link the other day which was all about global warming. Apparently, every month this year has set a new record. The warmest April, the warmest May, the warmest June and July. Ben says that there is now no chance of us being able to stay within the limit of warming that we were once told we would have to keep within to avoid the risk of uncontrollable climate change. No chance at all."

"Will you and I be here when it happens?"

"I don't know. We may have gone by then. But it may not be much longer."

"Our going or the fatal warming?"

"Both, I suppose!"

Mary stood up and walked to the water's edge. She walked a little way along the shore and bent down to see if she could find beads of deep amber-coloured carnelian amongst the smallest stones at the edge of the narrow band of sand exposed by the ebbing tide. The trick was not to look too hard, but to let the eye drift over the surface; let the translucence present itself … And there it was, about the size of a small pea, sitting on top of the shingle, left behind by a wave. Rounded. A shine. A bead of carnelian. Mary picked it up and brought it back to William, holding it in the upturned palm of her hand.

"For you."

William took it and held it between his thumb and forefinger, lifting it so that the last rays of sun shone through.

"Hallelujah!" cried William.

Mary laughed. She liked that William was a little mad.

They walked back to the house arm in arm. Florence met them at the door, rubbing her face against the doorpost. William went into his study and Mary picked up her book and curled up on the sofa. Florence came and sat beside her.

I was talking to Mary today about an article Ben sent me regarding the possibility of uncontrollable global warming. And Mary asked me if we will still be here when it happens. I don't really know about these things, but when I look at what would be required to stop it, I feel the calamity will come. I know it is hard to say so, but I think it will come. I think we are already too far along the path to be able to stop it coming. It is too deeply entangled in who we have become, entwined in our chosen ways of being, our addiction to having more.

There was a time when there was a drag on the tide of money and consumption. There was a time when the sacral days and the prayerful presence of the monasteries held back its onward rush and flow. Even in my own life I remember that at the end of each week there was the quiet day of Sunday, the Sabbath, a pause and a rest. But then the tide swept it away, so that now there is nothing to prevent the rising water.

Nothing in Nature is without limit, and I suspect that all that we have put together with the illusion of omnipotence will one day break under its own weight. The system is more fragile than it appears, and it will not take much more for it to break and fall apart.

And when the falling apart comes about, everything will change. First, there will be a time of confusion as the river walls collapse and the waters flood under the weight of our greed. Then, as the tide turns and begins to ebb, we will feel lost. Nothing that we now know will help us. This will be a frightening time. But perhaps, as we begin to find a new way, as one day we will have to do, we will seek a different kind of sustenance. Perhaps, for solace, we will recover the holy days and the prayerful communities. Perhaps all that has been repressed will re-emerge and begin to find expression. The recovery of Divine Wisdom.

Just before nine-thirty, Mary came to the door and said, "Shall we go to bed?"

"Yes, I'm tired. Let's go."

As they lay together, William said, "By the way, thank you for the carnelian."

"You are welcome, William. Good night."

November. William was in his dressing room when Wendy arrived. He had showered and was now putting on his clothes. He walked through to the kitchen as Wendy was finishing the porridge, adding the Manuka honey. He sat at the table and poured his tea. Since the early hours of the morning, he had been agitated by something. Another letting go. And it had to happen now.

"You're up early!" said Wendy, surprised to find William showered and dressed. "Are you okay?"

"Yes, I'm fine. But I need your help."

"What kind of help?"

"I want to get rid of the clutter."

"Clutter? What clutter?"

William drew a large circle in the air with his arm, outstretched to include the whole of his house.

"All of this. I have too many books. I have too many papers, I have too many clothes. I have books I have not read for years and never will. I have papers I never look at. I have clothes I never wear. I want to get rid of them, get rid of all the clutter."

Wendy heard a troubled urgency in his voice, as if this needed to be done right away, as if he thought he was short of time.

"That's okay, William, I can help you do that."

"Good. Perhaps my family would like my books, and if not, we can take them to that shop in Aldeburgh, the St. Elizabeth Hospice shop. And the papers can just be put in the recycling bin."

"Okay."

"And my clothes. I want to give them away."

"And when you have done all of this, my dear William, what then?"

"Then I will live without them."

"Okay," said Wendy, "I'll help you, but is there anything about this that you are not telling me, William?

You're not dying are you?"

"No more than usual."

They laughed, but Wendy was relieved that there wasn't something hidden behind William's plans. For some weeks she had noticed a difference in him. Somehow, it seemed now as if he was not always there.

Over the next few days, William and Wendy made a list of books he wanted to be rid of, and sent it to Jane and Frederick, with an instruction to Jane to share it with Ben and Sally. Jane replied with a longish list of the ones she and her family would like, and Frederick asked for just a few of the books, mostly art and gardening books that had belonged to his mother. These were carefully set aside whilst Wendy went to the post office to buy packing boxes.

Getting rid of the papers in William's study was a bit more straightforward, since most were only of interest to him, or rather had been. These were bundled into black sacks and taken by Wendy to the recycling Centre in Leiston.

Wendy encouraged William to keep a few more of his clothes than he would have liked, but three or four large black sacks of clothes were taken to the hospice shop in Aldeburgh, who seemed delighted to have them. The last of William's suits were taken and all of his ties except one, the blue one with horses heads on it, which he kept out of sentiment and for memory. It had been given to him by Caroline when they were first married. It had been a Christmas present.

By the end of the week, there were empty shelves and cupboards and drawers. William gave a sigh of relief. He had lightened his load. It felt good, and he began to suggest other stuff to be rid of. He had too many pictures, many of them just standing leaning against the walls. And he had a couple of shelves of DVDs and CDs, although Wendy told him that hardly anyone bought these any more.

"Well, they will have to go. Richard, the postman, might like some of them. He's keen on music. And Mary likes to watch films. I will speak to her about it."

A week or so later, after parcels of books had been sent, William's phone rang. It was Jane.

"The books have arrived. Thank you, Dad. I hope this is what you want."

"It is. Are there any of my DVDs or CDs you would like?"

"Probably."

"I'll make a list and send it to you."

"What's this all about. Is there something you haven't said to me?"

"Not as far as I know, Jane. I am old and tired, but not unwell. I just have a strong desire to lighten my load. To be carrying less. And anyway, I want you to have these books. You love books. What news?"

Jane told William all the latest about her family, including her deepening relationship with Alan, which she seemed pleased about. Both Ben and Sally were immersed in their studies and their work.

"Oh, and by the way, Dad, we can't do Christmas this year because Ben and Sally have their own plans, and I want to be with Alan, but I have been talking to Wendy about your birthday."

"My birthday?"

"Yes, Dad, your eightieth birthday. Don't pretend you don't know."

"Well, I don't want anything special."

"I know, Dad. But we are arranging a party for you. It may have to be just after your birthday, at the beginning of the Christmas holidays. I shall come with Ben and Sally, but I shall leave Alan behind."

"Well, you and Sally could have the spare room and Ben could have my dressing room. Unless he wants to stay in the trailer."

"Won't that be rather cold?"

"My dear Jane, you may not have noticed it, but our weather is becoming unusually warm."

"Yes, I suppose you're right."

"You should ask Ben. He knows all about it."

How odd it is to want to be empty. To actually want to be empty. All those years ago I read about emptiness - the Buddha was keen on it! But now I feel it. At one and the same time both empty and full. It is good.

And so, in December, William had two birthday parties. The first one was organised by Wendy and Mary and took place in his house in early December. Tea, shortbread and Eccles cakes. Wendy and Ruth, Mary and Brenda and Penelope, all sitting round the wood stove in the living room and wishing him, "Happy birthday!" And then in the week before Christmas, Jane arrived with Ben and Sally, staying a couple of nights before returning to Edinburgh. Of course, Ben the Warrior chose to stay in the Airstream.

On the morning of his birthday, Wendy had arranged for William to be in his study and at his computer. At ten o'clock, a Skype call came through from Brazil. It was Frederick, Ana, holding Maria, and Jonathan singing, "Happy birthday to you."

"Thank you. Thank you."

It was ten years since Caroline had died.

William and Mary had Christmas together.

26th December

Mary and I spent Christmas Day together. Just the two of us, although we both spoke to our families on the phone. We were content.

So little happens now. And I am taken with the rhythm of the day and the night. The turning of the year. We have passed the shortest day, and now the light will begin to return.

I must order my bumblebee colony for May time. Is that a plan? I suppose we can't quite ever stop planning, although it makes little difference to what happens.

After the Christmas break, Wendy and William made a list of DVDs and CDs and sent it to Jane and Frederick, giving a copy to Richard and Mary. Soon two more shelves would be emptied.

Emptiness

I have studied the Buddha's teachings on emptiness and no-thing-ness. And I have sat in meditation, letting all thoughts drop away, or lie in a pile beside me. But now something else is emerging, something which is at one and the same time both empty and whole.

The weather was fine today, and this afternoon I walked down to my bench by the sea, where I sat for some while letting my eyes rest upon the waves, letting my ears receive the sounds of the seagulls and letting my nose and my mouth smell and taste the wet saltiness of the air. My breathing faded to the faintest of breaths and I became steady. I felt both empty and utterly connected to all that was.

As the sun was setting behind me, its long rays caught the tops of the waves with an orange light and cast my shadow eastwards upon the beach and water. Somehow, in that moment, I knew that my most inward being was at the same time a part of all that was, and that all was well.

Perhaps this is as close as it gets.

The year turned and another year began. During the cold and dark of January, William withdrew into himself and into the house by the marsh. His days continued to be marked by the routines he had set and learnt to follow, but more and more he was not always living in the present time. Wendy and Mary cared for him, but they both knew that he was often somewhere else, no longer always with them.

When William came through into the kitchen at nine each morning, he would be in his dressing gown and pyjamas, and Wendy, and sometimes Mary, too, would sit with him whilst he had his breakfast. Most often in silence. Sometimes he washed and dressed after breakfast, and sometimes he did not dress until later in the morning. It was always in the same clothes. And whether he was dressed or not, William spent most of the morning writing his journal in his study or sitting in his armchair by the wood stove and reading. He had a pile of books and he was making his way through them, one after the other. There were books of poetry, and there were novels that Jane had given him. No-one emailed him any more. Most of the people who had once known him had long since forgotten about him.

At tea time, Mary would make tea and sometimes she would stay the night, even if William chose to sleep in his study. William was not unwell, nor was his mind confused. He had simply slipped. He had untethered himself. No plans or expectations.

In February, Mary and William were having supper and afterwards they sat together in his living room to drink the last of their wine. Mary looked across to William and watched him drifting. He turned to her.

"You know, Mary, there is something special about this small part of the world. I'm not quite sure what it is, but I sometimes think it's both what is here and what is not. The things I find here and the things I escape from."

He took a sip of his wine.

"And there is something else, too. I sometimes find myself inhabiting two worlds, the 'now' world of events and people and another quieter place that has yet to be. I find I am slipping between the two. Here and not here."

"Can you be in two places at once?"

"Well, that is the mystery."

They sat quietly, letting their thoughts wander.

"I sometimes wonder whether peacefulness is found at the boundary between being and not being. Might that be possible?"

"Too deep for me," said Mary, and took the empty glasses into the kitchen.

But this was where William had come to, a place between being and not being. Some part of him was here and some part was beginning to dwell in another place. He was drifting between the two. Still holding on to this world, but drawn to somewhere else. Or perhaps the two were one. Or would become one.

The house by the marsh had always been a refuge. For William when he had to leave London; for Wendy and Ruth after their caravan had been destroyed; for Ben, when he was unsure about what he should do; and for Mary when she was struggling with leaving her shop.

Now it was there for William as he made this journey between worlds. Slipping between.

The next morning, as they sat together having breakfast, William asked Mary a question.

"You know we were talking last night about the two places we slip between?"

"Yes."

"Well, I was wondering whether they were really close by."

"What do you mean?"

"I was wondering whether they seem close together because they're not really separate places at all, simply our outer and inner being."

Mary was putting a spoon in the jar of Wilkins marmalade. She took out some of the sweet jelly and placed it on her plate. She lay it on the Ryvita, upon which she had already lain a thin layer of Bertolli olive oil spread. She took a bite.

"This is very good marmalade, William."

"I'm glad you like it. It's made just over the border, in Essex, in the small town of Tiptree."

"I can't imagine they grow oranges in Tiptree."

"No, but they do make marmalade."

"Is this our outer life? Marmalade, Ryvita, Bertolli olive oil spread, eaten here at the table?"

"I believe it is."

"And at the same time, do we live some kind of

unspoken inner life that in some way is more real than Ryvita and marmalade?"

"I believe so."

"So, are they here side by side? Or layer within layer?"

"They could be."

10th February

Mary sometimes says the most wonderful things.

This morning I am sitting in my study and reflecting on all that has happened since Caroline died. It seems quite a long time ago, almost ten years. Poor Caroline. Unfair. How wretched I was. Badly wounded. Left behind. Vulnerable. I wanted so much to love and be loved. Enter Jennifer! But she was just a fantasy. It wasn't her I wanted. I was trying to bring Caroline back to life. A nonsense of course. Madness.

But then Providence brought me here to the house by the marsh. I couldn't believe how beautiful it was. From the very beginning, it was a refuge, it brought me home. And then Wendy, and then Wendy and Ruth. Chosen family. Wondrous. Another madness, I suppose. But I settled in. Amongst friends. I wanted it to last forever.

So I was not prepared when Wendy and Ruth decided to leave. I should have been, but I wasn't. I suppose I had known it would happen, but was trying not to admit to it. I know it's selfish to say so, but it was a blow for me. Another loss. Then the book went away, and the Academy decided they no longer needed me. A dark time. It left me feeling abandoned. Pathetic really.

How strange it is that that dark place should have been the beginning of such wonderful discovery. This house becoming mine, Ben bringing life and adventure, and Mary, dear Mary, my sweet companion, bringing love and tenderness. Rescued!

But now, as my fears have faded and I have found a place to be, something else is happening. I am slipping between two worlds. One that I have lived in for over eighty years and one towards which I am moving. Another place. Something else, somewhere else. I need to prepare myself. We all die alone. Can I be at peace?

Mary never ceases to amaze me. At one moment, she pretends that all this stuff about slipping between is beyond her understanding, but then, this morning, she said something that shows that she is, indeed, my guide. My Wise Woman.

In March, Frederick and his family came to London for some meetings he had to attend, and they took the opportunity to drive up to Frampton to stay a couple of nights with William. Wendy had prepared the spare room for Frederick and Ana and his dressing room for Jonathan and Maria, Wendy having borrowed from a neighbour in Friston, a high chair and a cot with a mattress and cover, and a couple of Mothercare blankets. By the time they arrived, Jonathan was tired by the journey and fractious. Maria was asleep and blissfully unaware.

"Hi, Dad."

"Hi, Freddy. Let me help you with the cases."

"I can manage."

"Hi, Ana. So this is Maria. Welcome Maria."

William eased his forefinger into Maria's tiny fist and, in her sleep, she held it tightly.

"She is beautiful, Ana."

"Well, I think so!"

"How was the journey?"

"Actually, apart from a rather unhappy four-year-old, it was fine."

"Hello, Jonathan, shall we go down to the sea?"

"Okay."

"Let me just help Mummy take her case into her room."

"Okay."

William took one of the bags and led Ana into the spare room, showing her the dressing room with the bed prepared for Jonathan and the cot for Maria.

"Will they be okay together?"

"I don't know. I might have the cot in with us. I'll see what Freddy says."

"Right. I'll leave you to it. Come on, Jonathan, let's see if the sea is still there."

"Of course it is, Papa."

"Well, we better just check."

"You are silly."

"I hope so!"

And William and Jonathan set off through the marsh and across the shingle beach to the water's edge, whilst Ana and Freddy moved the cot into their room and unpacked the bags.

As soon as he had crossed the marsh, delighted at last to be out of the car, Jonathan ran towards the sea. At the edge, he stopped for a moment and then picked up a handful of stones and threw them as far as he could into the waves. Splish, splash, splish. William came to stand beside him, bent to pick up a single round pebble and then threw it far into the sea where it landed with a much more satisfactory splosh. Jonathan was impressed, and tried to do the same.

By the time they returned from the beach, Frederick was making lunch, whilst Ana was feeding Maria, or rather Maria was insisting on feeding herself, with food everywhere. Frederick and Ana had brought smoked salmon with them, and hummus and a goat's cheese, which they thought William would like. They had also brought pasta for Jonathan, who was hungry after the journey. Plates had been set upon the table with sourdough bread and rice cakes, butter and William's Bertolli olive oil spread. Jonathan had opened a bottle of William's Rioja, and poured glasses for William, Ana and himself. Jonathan tucked into his pasta.

William asked Frederick about his work and Ana

about her parents. Her father was on quite a lot of medication for his weak heart and her mother needed help in looking after him. Jonathan had started at a pre-school, a short walk from where they lived. Listening to them, William felt the distance between his life and theirs. São Paulo is a long way from Frampton.

After lunch, Ana took Maria away for a sleep, and stayed in the house to have a rest, whilst Frederick, William and Jonathan went for a walk. Down to the sea, northwards along the beach and back through the woodlands behind William's house. For a while, Jonathan ran ahead of them, stopping and looking back to make sure they were following him. But then his legs were tired and Frederick carried him on his shoulders until he was ready for more running. William felt good being with his son and his grandson.

"This is such a lovely place," said Frederick. "There is something liberating about being beside the sea."

William smiled, inwardly delighted that his son felt the same as he did. Perhaps, one day, he would return. Perhaps.

By the time they arrived home and had tea, everyone was feeling comfortably tired and William went to his study to read and have a rest on his bed, enjoying the noises of his family moving about the house.

It is so good to have Freddy and his family in the house by the marsh. He and Ana are loving towards each other, attentive. Comfortable with each other. It's physical. They have become a true family. And yet, when I look at them I am filled with a deep sadness. Sad that Caroline did not live to see this?

Yes. Sad that it can never be an everyday experience for me, always distant? Yes. Sad that Jonathan and Maria will grow up without really knowing me. Perhaps Jonathan will remember the beach and the sea? Throwing stones. I hope so.

After breakfast on Sunday, all the bags were packed and put into the car and then Frederick and his family set off back to London. William stood and waved until they disappeared up the street, listening for the sound of the car as it made its way to Saxmundham and the A12. He turned and walked back along the veranda and into the house, closing the front door behind him. Suddenly he was frightened. Frightened that might have been the last time he would see his son, to hold him close.

CHAPTER 19

Endings

What happened next is not altogether clear. As the days and weeks passed, William and Mary continued their lives together. Everyone in the village now took them for granted. William and Mary. It was almost as if they were married. But that was not something they ever spoke of. In the meantime, Ben who was beginning to think about what he would do when he left university, came to stay, bringing Rosemary with him. He had been in touch with the Suffolk Wildlife Trust and they had offered him some work for the summer. It was agreed that if he took up their offer he could live in the Airstream and that Rosemary would visit him. Sally was now well into her studies at the medical school, and expressing an interest in General Practice. And Jane and Alan had announced they were going to get married. Frederick and his family remained in Brazil. Brenda and Penelope were indulging their love of cruising and, in Frampton, Andrew and Amy Browning continued to develop the shop and its restaurant, whilst Grahame Seville's various projects seemed to prosper. The holiday houses at High Winds were all sold and occupied, and the new houses were now being built. The world was turning.

William felt tired.

1st May

Seven o'clock in the morning. It's a cold day, and I am in bed, sitting up against my pillows, wrapped in my duvet and my white blanket. I have opened the window to let in the morning air - cold and slightly damp, smelling of the marsh. Wendy will come at a quarter to nine.

It is such a comfort to have let go of any expectations or plans for a future. How did I manage to do all that before? Why was I so taken up with it all? To what end?

And that word, 'end.' There it is.

But now, for the present … There it is, something else, other words, 'the present'. I suppose it's all we have. Just the present. Like sitting in bed and writing my journal before Wendy comes or Mary opens the door to say, "Good morning." Sometimes the present seems hardly to be here at all.

But there is something else that I catch a glimpse of. I think it may be acceptance. And it seems to require nothing of me, nothing except everything. To sink entirely into something that is already there, waiting for me. Has always been waiting there, had I but known it.

Do I know it best when I close my eyes? Am I waiting? Sometimes I feel as if I am. But even waiting presumes a future, waiting for something that is to come. This isn't really waiting, it's some kind of other way of being. Disembodied being.

I watch my body do what it has to do. I try to take care of it, encouraging it to live for a while longer, modestly, or rather simply. That is a better word. Simply. I watch my body as it begins to tire and wear away. Poor old body. Skin and bone and hair. I feed it and I wash it. I try to take care of it.

I have been remembering these word from Eliot's East Coker.

> *"I said to my soul, be still, and wait*
>   *without hope*
> *For hope would be hope for the wrong*
>   *thing; wait without love*
> *For love would be love of the wrong thing;*
>   *there is yet faith*
> *But the faith and the love and the hope are*
>   *all in the waiting*
> *Wait without thought, for you are not yet*

ready for thought;
So the darkness shall be the light, and the
stillness the dancing."

That night, William had a dream. He was walking across a water meadow, and over his pyjamas he was wearing a long coat mottled in grey, lavender and brown. He had on shoes and socks and his favourite Panama hat. He was walking along a rutted path towards a river bank from which he could see a wooden jetty with a boat moored alongside. The tide was ebbing. He knew that if he were to get into the boat and let go the mooring he would never be able to return. But it seemed as if everything was calling him to set sail.

He made his way down to the jetty and, at that moment, a small bird settled on the prow of the boat. It was dull, with a brown back and grey chest, but it had a yellow ring around each of its eyes. And on the river bank, on the other side of the river, there was a large hare, its ears pricked up as if it was listening. He stepped into the boat and hoisted the gaff sail. There seemed to be very little wind, but as soon as he had let go of the mooring and pulled in the main sheet, a light breeze picked up from behind him and he was off.

With the wind behind him and the tide beneath him, it was easy to sail the boat down river. And as he did so the hare ran along the other bank ahead of him and the bird fluttered around him, sometimes taking a rest on the top of the mast. In the boat he found a canvas bag. Opening it, he found banana sandwiches and a flask of tea.

"Excellent," he thought. "Excellent."

After a while, the wind dropped away. Now drifting on the tide, he saw on the other side of the river another jetty. The hare ran up to it and sat, as if waiting, and the bird settled on the prow of the boat as if she was giving directions.

William took down the sail and steered towards the jetty. As the boat bumped up against it, he took ropes and secured them fore and aft to two large metal rings. Everything was very still and everything was very quiet. He felt both a sense of arrival and a sense of unease, wondering what would happen if he left the comfortable boat and went into the land beyond the jetty.

"I think," he said to the bird, "I think I will just take a rest for while." And with that, he lay down on the floor of the boat and fell asleep.

When he awoke, he found both the hare and the bird sitting on the jetty, looking at him as if they had already been waiting for too long. He sat up, rubbed his eyes and yawned. Then he stood up and put on his hat. There on the floor of the boat was a hazel stick with a curled ram's horn handle. He picked it up, stepped out of the boat, his long coat unbuttoned and open. After walking a few paces along the jetty he looked back to see if the boat was properly tied to the mooring. But it was not there. No boat, no jetty, and no river. There was no way back.

Led by the hare and the bird, he found himself walking through beautiful countryside. Soon he was passing through gently rolling fields of corn, with well-kept hedges and small woods. The sky was a clear but gentle blue and everywhere he looked he could see bees and butterflies in the meadows of wild flowers. He could not tell how long he walked – perhaps a few hours – but, after a while, he saw in the distance what appeared to be an abandoned cottage, overrun by bramble and ivy and set within a garden surrounded by oak, horse chestnut and beech trees.

Somehow or other, he knew that this was where he was going to. He felt a strange vigour running through his body and his steps lightened. He looked up into the sky, where the swallows were circling and saw both the sun and the moon. Indeed, he could see the stars and other planets sparkling in what was now a deep blue – neither day nor night, neither moonlight nor sunlight, but a clear and shining brilliance everywhere.

Walking towards the abandoned cottage, he let his coat fall to the ground and he placed his stick against a hedgerow tree. He took off his hat and flung it into the air, where it whirled around and disappeared. He took off his shoes and his socks and left them by the path. And as he walked, the sun began to settle behind the cottage garden.

Soon he was there and, although the garden was overgrown, it was every garden he could remember – with valerian, cosmos, hydrangeas, cat mint, roses and a large buddleia, its blossom covered with butterflies and bees. There was an ancient apple tree and a drift of silver birch. He opened the garden gate and went in.

"So this is it," he thought. "This is the ending."

Underneath the apple tree was a garden bench facing to the west. He sat down upon it and felt the day begin to close. Just before it set, the rays of the sun took on a new intensity and, at once, he was surrounded by a bright and wondrous light, the colour of eternity. Rising from the bench, he stood in the light and, as he did so, he felt every part of his body breaking into the tiniest pieces and dropping away from him. Soon it was gone, all of it was gone, and with tears flowing from nowhere, he let himself dissolve into the light. As he did so he heard, as if in a whisper, the voices of all of those whom he had loved and who loved him.

It was over. And as he became at one, and the sun sank below the horizon, the light gave way to a deep and wonderful darkness. All was quiet. Light into darkness. Disentanglement. There was no more to do.

When Wendy came to the house the following morning, she found William lying on the floor of his study. Just as his mother had done fifty years before, he had suffered a sudden heart attack. He was holding his journal in his hand, the pencil having fallen to the floor beside him.

No Time Like the Present.

When those words came to me just now, 'no time like the present,' I had to laugh. It is four o'clock in the morning and I cannot sleep. I am more tired than I have ever been, but I cannot sleep. I feel a bit of discomfort in my chest. Probably indigestion.

I wonder if there is no time in the present at all. No time at all. Just an ever-present eternity.

I wish Mary was here. Hey ho!

Just over a year later, Ben and Rosemary came to live in the house by the marsh. The family had decided to keep the house, at least for a while, and Ben, who was taking up a job with the Suffolk Wildlife Trust, needed somewhere to live. He had always loved the place – and his grandfather. And Jane and Frederick were pleased he would be living there. So was Florence. He and Rosemary soon made friends with Wendy and Ruth and, of course, Mary. And sometimes, when they sat on William's bench by the sea, they thought they heard someone close by, but perhaps it was just the wind passing through the reed bed.

.

Printed in Great Britain
by Amazon